W0050198

EBURY PRESS

SIVAKAMI'S VOW: BOOK IV
SHATTERED DREAM

Ramaswamy Krishnamurthy (1899–1954), better known by his pen name Kalki, was an editor, writer, journalist, poet, critic and activist for Indian independence. Kalki's expansive body of work includes editorials, short stories, film and music reviews, and historical and social novels. His stories have been made into films, such as *Thyaga Bhoomi* (Land of Sacrifice, 1939), the M.S. Subbulakshmi-starrer *Meera* (1945), *Kalvanin Kadhali* (The Thief's Lover, 1955), *Parthiban Kanavu* (Parthiban's Dream, 1960) and, most recently, the Mani Ratnam-directed *Ponniyin Selvan* (Ponni's Beloved, 2022). One of the most renowned names in Tamil literature, Kalki was awarded the Sahitya Akademi Award for his novel *Alai Osai* (The Sound of Waves).

Nandini Vijayaraghavan, born and raised in Chennai, is the director and head of research at the Singapore office of Korea Development Bank as of 2023. Her translation of Kalki's *Parthiban Kanavu* (*Pratibhan's Dream*, 2021) was shortlisted for the Valley of Words Awards in 2022. Nandini's columns on finance and economy have appeared in *BusinessLine*, *The Hindu*, *Economic & Political Weekly* and *Financial Express*. She co-authored *The Singapore Blue Chips* (2017) with Umesh Desai, and her first India-centric business book, *Unfinished Business*, was published in 2023 by Penguin Random House India. Nandini blogs at www.litintrans.com.

In this series:

SIVAKAMI'S VOW

BOOK IV
SHATTERED DREAM

KALKI

Translated from the Tamil by
NANDINI VIJAYARAGHAVAN

EBURY
PRESS

An imprint of Penguin Random House

EBURY PRESS

USA | Canada | UK | Ireland | Australia
New Zealand | India | South Africa | China | Singapore

Ebury Press is part of the Penguin Random House group of companies
whose addresses can be found at global.penguinrandomhouse.com

Published by Penguin Random House India Pvt. Ltd
4th Floor, Capital Tower 1, MG Road,
Gurugram 122 002, Haryana, India

Penguin
Random House
India

First published in Ebury Press by Penguin Random House India 2023

ISBN 9780143460053

Typeset in Adobe Caslon Pro by MAP Systems, Bengaluru, India
Printed at Repro India Limited

www.penguin.co.in

MIX
Paper from
responsible sources
FSC® C047271

This is a legitimate digitally printed version of the book and therefore might not
have certain extra finishing on the cover.

Contents

Characters

Pallava Dynasty

Mahendra Varma Pallavar	Emperor of the Pallava kingdom
Bhuvana Mahadevi	Queen consort of Mahendra Varma Pallavar
Narasimha Varma Pallavar aka Mamallar	Mahendra Varma Pallavar's only son and the crown prince of the Pallava kingdom

Chalukya Dynasty

Satyasraya Pulikesi	Emperor of the Chalukya kingdom
Vishnuvardhanan	Pulikesi's younger brother and the king of Vengi

Other Royalty

Jayanta Varma Pandian	King of the Pandya kingdom
Durvineethan	King of Ganga Nadu
Manavanman	Prince of Sri Lanka

Monks

Thirunavukkarasar	A Saivite monk
Naganandi adigal	A bikshu

Civilians

Aayanar	A renowned sculptor of the Pallava kingdom
Sivakami	Aayanar's daughter and a talented danseuse
Paranjyothi	A rustic youth from Thirusengattankudi in Chola Nadu
Kalipahayar	Commander of the Pallava army
Shatrugnan	Head of the espionage force of the Pallava kingdom
Gundodharan	A Pallava spy
Kannabiran	Mahendra Varma Pallavar's charioteer
Kamali	Kannabiran's wife and Sivakami's friend
Ashwabalar	Kannabiran's father
Rudrachariar	An exponent of music and Mahendra Pallavar's music teacher
Namasivaya vaidhyar	A renowned physician and Paranjyothi's uncle

Foreword

Kalki Krishnamurthy bore *Sivakamiyin Sabadham* in his head and heart for nearly twelve years. Originally scripted as a film, it did not reach the screen but got broadcast as a radio play several years later. As destiny would have it, the short play grew into an expansive novel that was serialized in his own magazine, *Kalki*, from October 1944 for a period of two and a half years. The lengthy incubation and the ripening of the author's skills and thought process give the novel a special sheen. Kalki had, in these years, actively campaigned for the recognition of Bharatanatyam as a performing art and had been inspired by great artists like Balasaraswathi and Rukmini Devi. He also travelled to Ajantha and Badami to study the relics and absorb their spirit and wove an authentic tapestry that forms the background of his novel. History, heritage, poetry and the fine arts unique to the Tamil region come together in this work, not just as strands but as aerial roots that hold up the magnificent banyan. Art as a threatening weapon, the heights, depths, strengths and weaknesses of outstanding artists, the futility of war, the frailties and burdens that a monarch suffers—all contribute to the whirlwind of emotions that the novel evokes. Not surprising that critics consider this to be the best among Kalki's novels, though popular opinion places *Ponniyin Selvan* first, and the author himself felt that 'if any, it would be *Alai Osai* that would stand the test of time'.

Sivakamiyin Sabadham had a direct impact on the Tamil populace. Many households engaged Bharatanatyam gurus to teach their daughters. Mamallapuram became a must-see heritage site. The beauty and depth of the *tevarams* and *prabandams* became manifest to thousands of readers who began journeying into them. Author and Tamil scholar Dr Prema Nandakumar has acknowledged that her interest was fired on reading Kalki's novels and the breathtaking placement of the verses amidst the story.

The challenge for the translator of such an elevated work of art is limitless. Will the reader of the English edition shed the same tear, feel the same fire, seek the same heritage as the Tamil reader? Nandini Vijayaraghavan, thankfully, has not let these questions disturb her attempt or her flow of language. This volume makes for compelling reading and has a smooth flow.

Having read the Tamil version multiple times, the story was not new to me. That the English version sustains the eager anticipation and evokes the same goosebumps is the translator's success.

Seetha Ravi
(Author and fomer editor, *Kalki*)
Chennai

The Story Thus Far

Paranjyothi, a brave, rustic youth from Chola Nadu, travels by foot to Kanchi, Pallava Nadu's capital, to educate himself. He befriends Naganandi bikshu on the way. On reaching the Kanchi fort, the duo learns that the arangetram of danseuse Sivakami, the renowned sculptor-cum-painter Aayanar's daughter, was interrupted that evening. The Pallava emperor, Mahendra Pallavar (aka Mahendrar), had ordered the fort gates to be sealed. Speculation of the Chalukya emperor, Pulikesi, invading Kanchi is rife. Naganandi and Paranjyothi part ways.

An elephant runs amok and attacks Aayanar and Sivakami, who are returning to their forest residence. Paranjyothi, who fortuitously arrives there, wields his spear at the pachyderm, which chases him. Aayanar and Sivakami are rescued. Paranjyothi escapes unhurt but is imprisoned. Naganandi helps Paranjyothi escape from prison and introduces him to Aayanar, who agrees to educate the youth. Meanwhile, Sivakami clandestinely meets her lover, the crown prince Narasimha Pallavar (aka Mamallar), Mahendrar's only son.

Naganandi persuades Aayanar to send Paranjyothi to Nagarjuna mountain to learn the secret of the indelible dyes used in the Ajantha cave paintings. Aayanar, who is keen to unravel the mystery, procures a steed and travel permit for Paranjyothi. Naganandi gives Paranjyothi an epistle to carry.

En route to Nagarjuna mountain, Paranjyothi befriends Vajrabahu, a warrior. Vajrabahu drugs Paranjyothi to sleep and replaces Naganandi's message with one penned by him. Paranjyothi continues his journey and stops at a monastery, as instructed by Naganandi. The senior bikshu of that monastery sends Paranjyothi with horsemen who are supposedly heading to Nagarjuna mountain. The horsemen forcibly take Paranjyothi to the Chalukya encampment, where he runs into Vajrabahu. Pulikesi is unable to comprehend the message Paranjyothi is carrying. He solicits Vajrabahu's assistance, who states that the message may be for Vishnuvardhanan, Pulikesi's brother and Vengi's king.

Pulikesi commands horsemen to accompany Paranjyothi to Vengi and kill him if Vishnuvardhanan is unable to decipher the message. Vajrabahu helps Paranjyothi escape. The duo kills the horsemen and rides to the Pallava encampment. Vajrabahu promises to help Paranjyothi, who is eager to join the Pallava army. On reaching the camp, Vajrabahu asks Paranjyothi to wait outside till he secures Mahendrar's permission. The Pallava army suddenly turns jubilant. Paranjyothi learns that Mahendrar has reached the encampment.

Paranjyothi's rise in the Pallava army is meteoric. Mahendrar appoints him commander of the Kanchi fort. By making Mamallar promise to remain confined within the fort, Mahendrar separates him from Sivakami. Naganandi accuses Mamallar of being a coward and a womanizer. Dejected by the separation, Sivakami believes Naganandi's allegations. She ignores Mamallar's missive asking her to remain at her forest residence. Naganandi, Aayanar, Sivakami and her aunt leave for Nagapattinam, where the bikshu promises to arrange for Sivakami to perform before an august audience.

En route they meet Gundodharan, a Pallava spy masquerading as Aayanar's apprentice. Gundodharan disabuses Sivakami of her misconceptions about Mamallar. He delivers a message to Naganandi which states that King Durvineethan of Ganga Nadu, as instructed by the bikshu, is invading Kanchi. Naganandi, who gave no such instruction, realizes treachery is afoot. He asks Aayanar and his family to stay in a viharam in Ashokapuram and rushes to meet Durvineethan. Gundodharan disappears too.

A few days later, Aayanar and Sivakami observe the Pallava warriors chasing the Ganga Nadu soldiers. Mamallar and Paranjyothi pass by the viharam while pursuing Durvineethan. Mamallar sees Sivakami but does not speak to her.

Gundodharan returns to Ashokapuram and shadows Naganandi. He is unable to stop the bikshu from breaching a dam amidst a cyclone. Gundodharan pushes Naganandi into the dam, though, and hastens to Ashokapuram. The flood waters reach Ashokapuram ahead of Gundodharan, who manages to procure a boat. Mamallar returns to Ashokapuram to rescue Sivakami. He and Gundodharan row Aayanar's family to a village named Mandapapattu. At Mandapapattu, Mamallar promises Sivakami that she will be his queen-consort when he ascends the throne.

Meanwhile, Mahendrar and the spymaster, Shatrugnan, search for Mamallar. So does Paranjyothi, who traces Mamallar to Mandapapattu. They comply with

Mahendrar's missive instructing them to return to Kanchi. Mahendrar and Shatrugnan reach Mandapapattu and meet Gundodharan, who informs them of Naganandi's attempts to kill Mamallar.

Mahendrar and Shatrugnan visit the guest house where Aayanar and Sivakami are staying. Mahendrar deduces that Naganandi is hiding there and hands over the lion insignia to Ayanar, which would give the bearer instant access to the kingdom's senior-most officials. As expected, Naganandi appropriates the insignia. Mahendrar urges Sivakami to dissociate from Mamallar so that he can solemnize his son's wedding with the Pandya princess and gain the Pandyas support to win Pulikesi. Sivakami refuses.

Naganandi, disguised as a spy, enters the Pallava ministers' council and announces that the Chalukyas have imprisoned Mahendrar. Mamallar decides to attack the Chalukyas. Unfortunately for Naganandi, Mahendrar returns and imprisons him. As the emperor is addressing the ministers' council, a guard reports that the Chalukya army is approaching Kanchi. Mahendrar commands Paranjyothi to demolish the last surviving moat. The siege of Kanchi begins.

The long siege proves to be futile for the Chalukyas. Pulikesi leads a force to the banks of the Kollidam River and parleys with Jayanta Varma Pandian. Chalukya soldiers produce Vishnuvardhanan's envoy and Gundodharan, whom they have imprisoned, before Pulikesi. Vishnuvardhanan's message that mentions Harshavardhanar's plan to invade the Chalukya kingdom angers Pulikesi. The Chalukya emperor interrogates Gundodharan, who claims to be Naganandi's messenger. Naganandi's purported message elucidates the dangers looming over Pulikesi, including Harshavardhanar's impending invasion.

Gundodharan's revelation of Mahendrar's intention to impale all bikshus in Kanchi results in Pulikesi calling for a truce. He expresses the desire to visit Kanchi. Much against Mamallar's wishes, Mahendrar concedes Pulikesi's request and sends Mamallar and Paranjyothi with an army to attack Jayanta Varma Pandian.

Pulikesi watches Sivakami's soul-stirring dance at Kanchi. Mahendrar uncharacteristically reveals all the ruses he had employed to stall the Chalukya invasion and mocks Pulikesi's apathy for the arts. Sivakami and Aayanar leave Kanchi, which is barricaded, through a secret tunnel.

Mahendrar's words enrage Pulikesi, who resumes hostilities. The Chalukyas set fire to Pallava Nadu's villages and amputate the limbs of sculptors. They abduct Sivakami to Vatapi. Naganandi saves Aayanar from amputation but the sculptor ends up maimed.

The Pallavas and Chalukyas wage two battles. Mamallar and Paranjyothi, who rush back to Kanchi after defeating Jayanta Varma Pandian, repel the Chalukyas. But Mahendrar is grievously injured. Naganandi complies with Pulikesi's request to visit Vengi and stabilize the situation there after ensuring Sivakami's safety. However, Pulikesi humiliates Sivakami, and she vows to leave Vatapi only after witnessing Mamallar destroy the city.

Mahendrar learns of Sivakami's abduction. He commands Mamallar and Paranjyothi to fetch Sivakami from Vatapi surreptitiously. Mamallar visits Sivakami in Vatapi and tries to persuade her to return to Kanchi with him. Sivakami refuses, citing her vow. Meanwhile, Paranjyothi informs Mamallar that Naganandi is walking to Sivakami's palace. Accusing Sivakami of attempting to get them trapped, Mamallar leaves Vatapi with Paranjyothi.

Mahendrar, who is on his deathbed when Mamallar returns to Kanchi, enlists the ministers' council's support to invade Vatapi. He then coerces Mamallar to consent to something that the crown prince would not have agreed to under normal circumstances.

Chapter 1

Forest Residence

Once again, a lush growth of trees replete with clusters of flowers, green leaves and shoots surrounded Aayanar's forest residence. When the branches rustled in the gentle breeze, dry flowers fell to the ground, forming floral carpets at intervals. The fragrance of those flowers spread in all directions. The occasional chirping of birds provided an interlude to the silence which enveloped that area.

The lotus pond, located a short distance away from Aayanar's house, was once again brimming with water. Lotus leaves floated on the pond, and water drops resembling pearls glistened on those leaves. When the lotus leaves swayed in the breeze, the movement of those water drops was a feast to the eyes. But there was no one around to appreciate the beauty.

Previously, hundreds of disciples used to work around Aayanar's forest house. Now, not a single disciple was in sight. The sound of a solitary chisel coming from inside Aayanar's home accentuated the emptiness. Yes, the sculptor Aayanar,

1

armed with a chisel, was back at work. Nine years had passed since Aayanar's dear daughter was abducted. He had been able to survive for so long only because he focused on sculpting.

There were many more statues depicting dance postures than there had been earlier. Every statue reminded the observer of Sivakami. The colour of the paintings on the walls had faded. This confirmed that Aayanar had not yet discovered the secret of the Ajantha paint additive. Aayanar's appearance had changed immensely. His hair had turned completely white, his eyes were sunken and his face was wrinkled. It would not have been inappropriate to refer to him as the aged Aayanar.

As Aayanar was completely focused on his work, he did not hear a two-horse chariot coming to a halt outside his house. He looked around when he heard a child calling out, 'Thatha!'

Mamalla Narasimha chakravarthy and his two children entered the house. Mamallar's appearance had also changed to some extent. His previously youthful face now exuded a mature and statuesque glow. Clear thinking had replaced his youthful aggression, while his raw bravery had evolved into a firm resolve.

The eight-year-old boy and six-year-old girl both resembled Mamallar. They ran to Aayanar, who welcomed them saying, 'Come, my dears!' He embraced and petted them. Tears glistened in his eyes. Were they tears of joy or tears of sorrow, reflecting a possibility not fructifying?

The children played with Aayanar for some time, after which Mamalla chakravarthy called out, 'Kundavi! Mahendra! Go out for some time and play. I will talk to thatha and then come!' So saying, he took them by their hands and escorted them outside. He instructed the charioteer, 'Kanna! Keep an eye on the children!' The man holding the reins of the horses was indeed Kannabiran, who now sported a thick black moustache.

When Mamallar returned, Aayanar announced, 'Prabhu, I have complied with your command. I have completed sculpting the hundred-and-eighth statue today.'

Narasimha chakravarthy, who had observed Aayanar becoming increasingly disoriented after following Sivakami's abduction, had commanded him to sculpt statues depicting each of the one-hundred-and-eight dance postures. Ayanar became mentally unstable after resuming work.

'Aayanar, I have also completed my preparations. We are embarking on our campaign on Vijayadasami. We will leave for Vatapi in the evening after performing Ayudha Poojai in the morning,' remarked Mamallar.

'Aiyya, I heard of it too. Gundodharan mentioned the massive army that has now assembled at the foothills of the Thirukazhukunram mountain. It seems that this ocean-like army comprises massive contingents of elephants, horses and infantry. Apparently, several more warriors will be joining the army. I heard that mountains of swords, spears and lances have been accumulated. When Gundodharan related all this, I myself felt like visiting Thirukazhukunram.'

'Aayanar, the forces assembled at Thirukazhukunram constitute just a third of our army. Senathipathi Paranjyothi is at the head of a gargantuan army stationed on the banks of Ponnmugaliaru in the north, awaiting our arrival. The Pandya army is also marching from the south to join hands with us. I received news of this army reaching the banks of the Varaha River today.'

'Prabhu, please forgive me. I was worried that you were whiling away your time. I now understand that the efforts you've exercised are akin to that of Bhagiratha.'

'Did you compare my efforts to Bhagiratha's, Aayanar?'

'Yes, aiyya!'

'Do you remember an old incident? Mahendra Pallavar, you and I were viewing the rocks at the Kadal Mallai harbour. Suddenly, there was a downpour. One rock was hollow at the centre as though it had split into two. The rainwater that filled the hollow soon began to overflow. I observed, "The Akash Ganga is flowing!" Immediately Mahendra Pallavar remarked, "This rock is appropriate for a statue. Bhagiratha's Penance may be sculpted here." You too agreed and asked the sculptors to begin work on that rock. My father then related Bhagiratha's story to me.

'I was amazed when I heard the tale. Bhagiratha faced several insurmountable obstacles during his penance. I was astounded that he was able to overcome all of them and emerge successful in the task he had undertaken. The story my father related to me as a child has been extremely useful to me now. Aayanar, when I failed to bring your daughter back from Vatapi, I thought I could mobilize an army in three years to invade the Chalukya kingdom. That was what Paranjyothi and I had planned on our return journey from there. The task we set out to accomplish in three years has taken us nine years!'

'Pallavendra, did you say nine years have passed? It seems to me that nine eons have passed!'

'I share your sentiments, Aayanar! It seems like several eons have passed since I last saw Sivakami. But what can I do? For two years, the country was struck by famine. One year, excessive rains caused havoc. Then I was obliged to help the prince of Lanka, Manavanman. Following that,

I had to arbitrate the conflict between the Pandian and the Cheran. Whenever such incidents disheartened me, I went to the harbour and observed Bhagiratha's penance. I regained confidence and courage. Finally, my efforts, like Bhagiratha's, have borne fruit. I am going to war next week.'

'Prabhu, what's this? You're saying that you are leaving for the battlefield?' asked Aayanar.

'What else do you expect me to say, Aayanar?'

'Please say that *we* will be leaving, Pallavendra! I don't know how long I will live. I would like to see Sivakami at least once before I die.'

Mamallar wiped away the tears that filled his eyes and advised, 'Aiyya, you must live for the sake of your daughter. Don't ever think of death. I will take you if you are keen to travel to Vatapi. Please be ready to leave on Vijayadasami!'

Chapter 2

Manavanman

The Pallava army was camping in the area that surrounded Thirukazhukunram. Neither Lord Shiva, whose temple was located atop the hill, nor the eagles which partook the prasadam every day, had ever seen such a sight. The entire area to the north of the hill was occupied by elephants. It was almost unbelievable that so many elephants lived in this world! Those who witnessed this scene might well wonder if the earth would split under the weight of so many elephants assembled at a single location.

If one were to turn to the east, one would think that there were no living beings on this earth other than horses. All were high-breed horses imported from Arabia and Persia through the Mamallapuram harbour. There were white, chestnut and shiny black horses. There were also chestnut horses with white spots. Ah! While it was impossible to draw one's eyes away from the sixteen-thousand beautiful steeds, it was disconcerting to think about how many of them would return alive after the war.

Horse-drawn chariots, bullock carts and beasts of burden like cows, camels and donkeys occupied the area up to the southern horizon. Sacks of grains, clothes, daggers, shields, swords, spears, lances, tridents, bows and arrows, several other uncommon weapons, mounds of thick ropes, rope ladders, hooks, spades and torches were stocked in those carts. Numerous weapons and tools that were yet to be loaded on to the carts lay around. Observing the canopies that were heaped like a mountain in one place, one would think it was possible to cover the sky with them, without allowing a single raindrop to reach the earth.

The entire human race seemed to have congregated to the west of the hill. Countless warriors swarmed the area like bees! The strength of this infantry seemed to exceed Ravaneswaran's famed infantry. The military camp comprising the four forces of the Pallava army covered the entire region and the numerous Rishabha flags hoisted amidst the camp were fluttering in the sky.

Mamalla Narasimha chakravarthy approached this ocean-like army in a chariot. The uproar heard when he was seen arriving at a distance was akin to the turbulence of the ocean on a full moon night. The din of conches, trumpets, and drumbeats rose up to the skies and echoed in all four directions. The deafening tumult of slogans such as 'Long live, Mamallar!' 'Doom to Pulikesi!' 'Glory to Kanchi!' and 'May Vatapi be ruined!' raised by the valorous army caused the earth to vibrate.

A majestic man seated on a high-breed steed detached himself from the cheering army and rode towards the chakravarthy's chariot to receive him. Two warriors who held flags bearing the Rishabha insignia followed him. The warrior who rode towards Mamallar was the prince of Lanka, Manavanman.

Manavanman's father and Mahendra Pallavar had been friends. Like Mahendra Pallavar, Manavanman's father had been passionate about the arts and ignored matters of state. As a result of this, a vassal named Attathan had annexed the kingdom after his death, thereby preventing Manavanman from ascending the throne. Manavanman had sent emissaries to Kanchi, seeking Mamallar's help. That was when Thondai Mandalam was in the clutches of a major famine. Yet Mamallar had sent a small force to Lanka by ship. By the time that force reached Lanka, Manavanman had been summarily defeated and was hiding in a forest. Realizing that the small force sent by Mamallar was inadequate to wage war with Attathan, Manavanman had boarded the Pallava ship and come to Kanchi.

Mamallar felt a natural affection for Manavanman, as he was the son of Mahendra Pallavar's friend. The warmth and sympathy Mamallar felt for Manavanman on account of the latter reposing confidence in him and seeking refuge soon developed into an intimate friendship. They became inseparable. The relationship between them was similar to what Mamallar had hoped to strike with Paranjyothi. In truth, Mamallar and Paranjyothi had never been close friends. This was because Paranjyothi had been unable to consider himself Mamallar's peer as the latter was a descendant of an ancient royal clan. Also, ever since they had returned from Vatapi nine years ago, Senathipathi Paranjyothi had been totally involved in preparing for the invasion. He was completely focused on mobilizing an army, training the new recruits, appointing mahouts and horsemen, and procuring weapons. So, he had had no time to nurture his relationship with Mamallar.

Mamallar had felt the need for a companion with whom he could cultivate a transparent friendship. The Lankan prince, Manavanman, fulfilled that need.

When Manavanman arrived at Kanchi, Mamallar had promised to assist him by sending a large army to Lanka. But when Manavanman observed that forces were being mobilized for the Vatapi invasion, he stated that he was not willing to take away a major part of that army. He declared he would continue to live in Kanchi till the end of the Vatapi war, and then return to Lanka. Mamallar was extremely happy to hear this. He had been concerned that Senathipathi Paranjyothi would object if a large army were to be sent to Lanka at that juncture. So, Narasimhar was at peace when Manavanman opined that the Lanka expedition may be postponed. He praised Manavanman's magnanimity and selfless character to one and all.

Following this, Manavanman wholeheartedly involved himself in the preparations for the Vatapi invasion. He was particularly skilful in engaging elephants in warfare, so he focused his attention on picking and training elephants for battle. Paranjyothi and Mamallar realized that it was the strength of Pulikesi's elephant force that had given him his initial victories during his invasion of Dakshina Bharata, and that the inadequate strength of their own force had caused Mahendra Pallavar to retreat and hide in the Kanchi fort. So, they decided to mobilize a gigantic elephant force for the Vatapi invasion and procured thousands of elephants from Chera Nadu. Manavanman was extremely useful in picking the right elephants for battle and training them.

As the appointed day for the Pallava army to embark on the Vatapi expedition neared, a fierce argument broke out between Manavanman and Mamallar. Manavanman sought Mamallar's consent to accompany the invading army to Vatapi. Mamallar was unwilling to allow a guest, who had sought refuge, to accompany him to the battlefield. Another thought weighed on him; a competent person was required to oversee the Kanchi kingdom and to collect and despatch weapons and food stocks after he and Paranjyothi had left for Vatapi. No one was more suited for this task than Manavanman.

A third reason, which Mamallar harboured deep within his heart, underpinned his desire to leave Manavanman behind at Kanchi. Life is transient; it is difficult to predict when and in what form Yaman will strike. It is impossible to foresee when one's life may be in danger when one has to travel a long distance and attack an enemy. Mamallar was determined not to return to Kanchi without decimating Pulikesi and razing Vatapi to the ground. If he was unable to emerge victorious, he might have to give up his life on the battlefield. If this were to happen, a capable person was required to prevent the Pallava empire from disintegrating and to maintain its stability by coronating Prince Mahendran. Such a person should also be trustworthy.

There was no one other than Manavanman who could be trusted with the Kanchi kingdom and the prince, Mahendran. Mamallar did not particularly trust his brother-in-law, Jayanta Varma Pandian. Mamallar was aware that, at one point of time, Jayanta Varman had been desirous of bringing the entire Tamizhagam under his reign. Mamallar had sought the Pandian's assistance in invading Vatapi without betraying his distrust. Jayanta Varman had sent a large army led by his son, Nedumaran. It was this army that had reached the banks of the Varaha River. Though Mamallar had sought the Pandian's aid for the war, he had reposed his entire confidence in his dear friend, Manavanman, and had decided to ask him to stay behind at Kanchi. But Manavanman was stubborn and insisted that he would also come to Vatapi. Their argument remained unresolved.

Mamallar and Manavanman dismounted from the chariot and horse respectively. They embraced each other affectionately. Then Manavanman pointed to Aayanar, who was seated in the chariot, and asked, 'Anna, why did you bring this elderly man along? Has he come to view the invading army? Or do you intend to bring him along to the battle?'

Mamallar responded saying, 'Why do you ask, thambi? Aayanar insists that he will go to the battlefield ahead of everyone else. Prince Mahendran is competing with him to go to the battlefield. Kundavi insists that she will also follow her brother to the battlefield. It seems that our charioteer Kannan's son, armed with a dagger yesterday, declared that he would behead the Chalukyas and ended up felling most of the plants in the garden!'

Manavanman laughed and quipped, 'Do take seasoned warriors like the elderly Aayanar, junior Kannan, Crown Prince Mahendran and Kundavi devi to the warfront. Incompetent people like me can be left behind at Kanchi!'

'I will not leave you behind at Kanchi all by yourself. Mahendran is willing to stay behind in Kanchi if you're there. Kundavi is willing to follow suit if her brother is in Kanchi,' retorted Mamallar.

Manavanman immediately lifted the kumara chakravarthy and remarked, 'You're a child and so am I. Both of us will remain at Kanchi. All other menfolk may proceed to the battlefront!'

Kundavi curtly interjected asking, 'Mama, aren't you a child to your father?'

Manavanman lowered Mahendran to the ground, stood with his arms folded in front of Kundavi, and submitted with mock humility, 'Devi, how could anyone dare to open their mouth in your presence? What I said was wrong! Please forgive me!'

Everyone including Aayanar burst out laughing.

That evening, when Mamallar and Manavanman met by themselves, Manavanman asked, 'Anna, do you really intend taking Aayanar along to Vatapi?'

'Yes, thambi. There are two important reasons for my taking him along. Our soldiers will be motivated when they see the maimed elderly man and will be reminded of his daughter. If we manage to retrieve alive the woman for whose sake we are embarking on this invasion, leading a gargantuan army, wouldn't it be appropriate to hand her over to her father immediately?' asked Mamallar. He then heaved a deep sigh, which caused immense sorrow to Manavanman.

Chapter 3

Rudrachariar

The renowned city of Kanchi continued to be the joyous abode of Kalaimagal[1] and Thirumagal,[2] as it had been during the times of Mahendra Varma chakravarthy. Mansions flanked the wide streets of Kanchi, and people thronged the streets. Bullock carts, horse-drawn chariots and palanquins borne by bearers moved in proximity down the roads. Men and women adorned in fine silks and jewellery strolled around the city.

Bells heralding prayer time and musical instruments could be heard incessantly. The Vedas were regularly chanted in the Sanskrit seminaries, and so were Navukkarasar's divine Thevara Pasurams in the Tamil Saivite monasteries. The sound of chisels at the sculpture studios and anklets at the Bharatanatyam mandapams was a pleasure to art lovers. Amidst the civilian population on the streets were seen

---

[1]   Another name for Goddess Saraswati.
[2]   Another name for Goddess Lakshmi.

warriors wielding daggers and shields. When these soldiers met, they greeted each other by crossing their swords, and people congregated and cheered, 'Long live, Mamallar!' 'Doom to Pulikesi!' 'Glory to Kanchi!' and 'May Vatapi be ruined!'

Mamalla chakravarthy's chariot made its way through the vibrant streets of Kanchi and came to a halt in front of the famed Sanskrit seminary that Rudrachariar headed. Some of the teachers and students came outside and welcomed the chakravarthy with calls of, 'Jaya Vijayi Bhava!' Mamallar and Manavanman entered the seminary.

One of the most renowned art schools in Bharata Kandam, the seminary imparted training in all arts, and was located in a massive building. Classes for different art forms were in progress in various *mandapams* that were supported by beautifully sculpted pillars. Students were learning the Rig Veda, Yajur Veda and Sama Veda in separate mandapams.

It was a well-known fact that scholars who had attained complete mastery of the Vedas and Agamas taught in the seminaries of Kanchi. Research of the shastras and epics, training in the Vyakarna Shastra, teaching of Valmiki's Ramayana and the Bhagavad Gita and enactment of Kalidasa's play *Shakuntala* were all being carried out in separate mandapams.

Mamallar and Manavanman walked along these mandapams, watching the various activities. Finally, they reached a mandapam located at a corner that was enveloped in absolute silence. An extremely aged man was reclining on a cot placed at the centre of this mandapam. He sported a white, flowing beard that reached his belly. His hair was completely white. The aged man was Rudrachariar, the head of that reputed institution. Four teachers sat on the floor around his cot, listening to his explanation of the Taittiriya Upanishad.

On seeing Mamallar's arrival, they stopped the lesson mid-way, stood up, bowed to him and then went away. 'Pallavendra, I have lost the strength to stand up and welcome you. Please forgive me. Aren't you leaving on Vijayadasami?' asked Achariar.

'All preparations have been made for our departure. But the Pandya prince has not yet arrived. He is camping on the banks of the Varaha River. It seems he has fallen ill!'

'Prabhu, you should leave on Vijayadasami irrespective of whether the Pandian arrives or not. The planetary configuration that is to occur this Vijayadasami occurs only once in a thousand years. Ramabiran invaded Lanka on one such day.'

'That means I will return victorious like Ramabiran, won't I?' asked Mamallar.

'You will definitely return victorious. But I will not be fortunate enough to see the sight.'

'Gurudeva! Please don't speak in this manner!' observed Mamallar humbly.

'So what? Even if I were to leave this world and reach heaven, I will not be able to forget Kanchi and this seminary. Your majesty, your father and I will be present above this seminary on the day you return from Vatapi. Both of us will shower you with the Parijatham flowers that blossom in Deva Loka and welcome you.' Hearing this, Mamallar turned misty-eyed.

Chapter 4

Navukkarasar

That day, the Saivite monastery located in the vicinity of Ekambareshwarar's sanctum was also buzzing with activity. Thirunavukkarasar Peruman had graced that monastery with his presence for a few days. Disciples were singing his hymns and Navukkarasar was listening, his eyes brimming with tears of joy. Aayanar, who was seated beside him, also shed tears.

The bell at the Ekambareshwarar temple rang just then, signifying that the noon-time prayer service was underway. The students stopped singing the pathigams and left for lunch. Only Navukkarasar and Aayanar remained.

'Respected sculptor, ten years ago, your daughter performed abhinayams at this very place. I still remember watching her perform. I was reminded of your daughter when the students sang *"Munnam avanudaya naamam*

16

kettal"[3] sometime ago. I involuntarily shed tears,' remarked Navukkarasar.

'Adigal, I too was reminded of that performance. What you predicted that day has come true.'

'Yes, Aayanar, I remember that incident. I was concerned that your daughter, who was endowed with such divine beauty, should not face hardship in her worldly life. I shared my concern with you.'

'Swami, Sivakami had to face no mean ordeal. I too have experienced unimaginable agony. Her mother left her as an infant in my care and passed away. Till she was eighteen years old, she was the apple of my eye. We were never away from each other, even for a single day. Now, for the last nine years, I have been separated from my child. Adigal! Why is the compassionate lord testing us, who have committed no sin? What sin did we commit?' Tears flowed down Aayanar's cheeks as he spoke.

'Aayanar, don't despair. Humans find it difficult to comprehend the divine design. I too have never wilfully committed a sin in this world. Yet, my mortal body has experienced countless trials and tribulations. Respected sculptor, let me share with you the truth I have observed. What we perceive as sorrow is not so in reality! What we perceive as happiness is also not happiness! It is human bonds that give rise to feelings of happiness and sorrow. Elders have described human bonds as illusory. When we are free from illusion, we realize that neither happiness nor sorrow exists. We will then understand that only the joy bestowed by the Almighty prevails.'

---

[3] 'At first His name she heard . . .' Sivakami's Vow: *Paranjyothi's Journey*, Chapter 36 provides a translation of the entire verse.

'Swami, I understand the truth in your nectar-like words. Nevertheless, I am unable to free myself from human bonds. What can I do?'

'The way to liberate oneself from human attachment is to beseech the Lord,' advised Navukkarasar.

'Haven't I beseeched the Lord? I ceaselessly implore him. Yet, I am not free from my affection for my daughter! Every time I think of praying, I am reminded of my daughter who is imprisoned in the enemy's fort in a faraway country. The only boon I seek from the Almighty is: "God! Please protect my daughter. Please shower your mercy so that I can see Sivakami just once before I die!" What can I do?' lamented Aayanar and began sobbing.

'No, Aayanar! Don't grieve!' consoled the virtuous soul. He added, 'Isn't your wish about to be fulfilled? I heard that Mamallar has mobilized a gigantic army to invade Vatapi. By God's grace, your daughter will return. Don't worry. Till then, why don't you reside with me in this monastery? Why do you have to stay all alone in your forest residence?'

When Aayanar disclosed, 'Adigal, please forgive me. I am accompanying the Pallava army to Vatapi . . .' Vageechar was taken aback.

'What is this, Aayanar? Are you desirous of witnessing the atrocities perpetrated on a battlefield? Are you eager to witness humans shedding blood that will flow like a river? Are you desirous of seeing grievously injured and mutilated corpses?' asked the great soul.

An embarrassed Aayanar responded, 'No, adigal! Those are not the reasons for my travelling. I am desirous of meeting my daughter and escorting her back.'

Just then, a few men and women entered the monastery. Senathipathi Paranjyothi, his wife Umayal, Namasivaya

Vaidhyar and his sister came in and prostrated before Navukkarasar. After everyone was seated, Namasivaya Vaidhyar stated, 'Swami, I came to take leave of you.'

'Ah! Are you returning home? I too am desirous of obtaining darisanam of the Lord of Thiruvengadu. When I come again to Chola Nadu on a pilgrimage, I will visit Thiruvengadu,' remarked Vageechar.

'No, adigal, I am not going to Thiruvengadu. I am headed northwards to Vatapi.'

'What is this? It seems that not a soul will stay behind in Kanchi. Aayanar is going to fetch his daughter. Why are you going, vaidhyar?'

'I am going to treat the injured. Swami, a large contingent of vaidhyars is accompanying the army. I am leading that contingent. The Chalukyas are not bound by principles when they wage war. They wield poisoned swords and spears. Aren't you aware that Mahendra chakravarthy was stabbed by a poisoned dagger? When I was treating the chakravarthy, I discovered the cure for that poison. So, the Pallava Senathipathi has ordered that I too come to the battlefield!' Saying this, Namasivaya Vaidhyar shot a proud glance at Senathipathi Paranjyothi.

'Ah! Is this youth the famed senathipathi of the Pallava army?' asked Thirunavukkarasar and looked at Paranjyothi intently. 'His face exudes serenity. It appears that he will be the heir to the Saivite bhakti movement. Why is he engaged in this murderous profession?' he asked.

Hearing this, Namasivaya Vaidhyar and his sister exchanged smiles. Umayal too looked shyly at her husband and smiled slightly. Paranjyothi may have flashed a small smile too.

'Swami, we sent him to Kanchi twelve years ago to enrol at your monastery and to learn Tamil. Fate intervened to bring him to this position. Fate is also drawing me to the battlefield along with him,' replied Namasivaya Vaidhyar.

Navukkarasar looked at Paranjyothi intently once again and opined, 'You say that Fate is leading him. But his physiognomy indicates that he is endowed with the resolve to change Fate.'

At that instant, Senathipathi Paranjyothi prostrated before Thirunavukkarasar and stated, 'Gurudeva! I consider your words as a benediction!'

Paranjyothi's mother stood up and remarked with devotion, 'Swami, Umayal prostrated before you when you previously visited Thiruvengadu. You blessed her, saying, "May you be married soon." Her marriage was soon solemnized, just as you had predicted.' She then paused.

Vageecha Peruman stated, 'I am happy that my words came true, amma!'

'That which Your Holiness utters will always come true. Please bless them saying that they will bear a child,' requested that elderly woman.

Thirunavukkarasar smilingly looked at Paranjyothi and Umayal and uttered the benediction, 'A son who will be extolled in the epics and folklore will be born to them!'

Chapter 5

Mamallar's Apprehension

Mamallar and Manavanman were sitting on a crystal platform in the upper storey of the Kanchi palace, under the canopy of a star-studded sky. An uncharacteristic quiet prevailed in the city, inhabited by lakhs of people. Mamallar gazed at Kanchi and then heaved a sigh. 'This great city is peacefully asleep tonight. Tomorrow, by this time, it will be buzzing with activity. The womenfolk would have started decorating the streets. The soldiers would be getting ready to leave. Ah! No one will sleep tomorrow night!' observed Mamallar.

'Pallavendra, have you then decided to leave at the appointed hour even if the Pandian does not reach Kanchi?' asked Manavanman.

'Even if the sun does not rise on Vijayadasami, I will not tarry. Didn't you listen to Rudrachariar's prediction, prince?'

As Manavanman had not been crowned as the king of Lanka, he was addressed as 'prince'.

'Yes, I heard Rudrachariar's prediction, Pallavendra. Subsequently, I also met him alone for an astrological consultation.'

'Oh! Is that so? What did Achariar say?'

'His predictions were favourable.'

'Is that so?'

'He prophesised that I would definitely ascend the throne of Lanka one day. However, he said that I would face several obstacles and wage several wars before that.'

Mamallar smilingly asked, 'Is that all? Did he say anything else?'

'He foretold that you would return victorious from Vatapi and that two princes would assist you in this task.'

Mamallar laughingly asked, 'Who are these two princes?'

'I posed the same question to Rudrachariar. He said that it was not possible to delve into such minute details in astrology,' replied Manavanman.

'My dear friend, I will tell you! You are the one who is going to assist me in the Vatapi war even while remaining at Kanchi.'

Even before Mamallar could complete what he was saying, the Lankan prince interrupted saying, 'Pallavendra, please concede my request. Since it is unclear when the Pandya prince will arrive, is it not possible for me to accompany you? Do you expect me to lead a luxurious life at the Kanchi palace once you've left for the battlefield? Is this fair?'

'My dear friend, there is an overriding reason for prohibiting you to come to the battlefield—I have not divulged it thus far. Since you are adamant, I will tell you. If your life comes under threat on the battlefield, what will become of Lanka's royal dynasty? Wouldn't the man who unjustly captured your kingdom rule it forever? Heirs to ruling dynasties must accord the utmost importance to ensuring the continuance of their lineage. I have a son who will ensure the continuance of the Pallava dynasty; you don't. This is the key reason for my forbidding you from accompanying me to the battlefield,' disclosed Mamallar.

Manavanman shot a meaningful smile at him and remarked, 'Pallavendra, I am going to convey this to my wife, Suja, and squabble with her. Am I not being denied the opportunity of a lifetime as she has not yet produced an heir to the Lankan throne? It's because of this that I'm unable to participate in the Vatapi war, which will be a watershed moment in the annals of world history!' He then stood up.

'My friend! Please sit down. There is no rush to squabble with your wife. You may argue with her at leisure every day after I leave for Vatapi,' remarked the chakravarthy.

Manavanman sat down once again and advised, 'Prabhu, isn't it past midnight? No one is going to sleep tomorrow night. Shouldn't you sleep at least tonight?'

'Are you asking me to sleep? How can I sleep? It has been twelve years since I slept!' confessed Mamallar.

'When Lakshmanan went to the forest, his wife Urmila appropriated his sleep and slept day and night for fourteen years. Has someone appropriated your sleep in a similar manner?' asked Manavanman.

'Prince, it was also a maiden who appropriated my sleep. She did so without my consent. She seized my sleep and left. Ah! Even when that sculptor's daughter lived close by in her forest residence, she rendered me sleepless. Now, she lives a hundred kaadam away in our enemy's city, and still she has ensured that I don't sleep . . .' Mamallar suddenly looked up to the sky and proclaimed, 'Sivakami! Why do you torment me thus? I strive all day to fulfil my promise to you. Won't you let me sleep peacefully for some time at least at night? Are you sitting at the Vatapi palace, with the lantern as your sole companion, and cursing me? Even if I sleep for some time overcome by extreme fatigue, you torture me in my dreams. Sivakami, I have neither forgotten you nor my promise to you. You have been patient for so long; please be patient for some more time!'

When Mamallar looked up to the skies and spoke like one possessed, the Lankan prince was petrified. 'Pallavendra! What happened to you? Please compose yourself!' Manavanman counselled.

'My friend, you're asking me to compose myself! I wonder if I will be at peace ever again in my life. I committed a mistake ten years ago. I lost my mental balance listening to the enraged words of a helpless maiden. When the senathipathi and I went to Vatapi to fetch Sivakami, she stated that she had made a vow and that she would not return with us. The senathipathi then suggested that we ought not to pay heed to her words and that we should bring her back by force. I did not listen to him. For the last nine years, I have been recollecting my decision and regretting it.'

Mamallar lapsed into silence and was immersed in his own thoughts. He then disclosed, 'Prince, I have been eagerly awaiting the day we would embark on our Vatapi expedition. I have exercised immense effort to ensure that we leave for Vatapi at the earliest. But as the day of departure nears, I am apprehensive ...'

'What! Are you apprehensive?' asked Manavanman in a tone that betrayed disbelief and wonder.

'Yes! I am apprehensive! But the war and battlefield do not unnerve me. It's the events that will occur once Pulikesi is killed and Vatapi is captured that scare me. Sivakami has been waiting for me for the last nine years after being imprisoned by our foes. Her love for me that blossomed in her childlike heart is still intact. But what is my situation? I have married and have fathered two children. How can I face Sivakami? What can I tell her? Whenever I think of this, I am scared. I prefer dying on the battlefield!'

'Pallavendra, if you were to die on the battlefield, what will become of me, who has sought refuge in you? Didn't you promise me that you would ensure that I ascended the throne of Lanka? What will become of your promise?' asked Manavanman in a choked voice.

Chapter 6

Ekambarar's Sanctum

The clanging of temple bells and the sound of trumpets heralded the noon prayer service at the sanctum of the renowned Ekambareshwarar temple. Countless people thronged the main entrance of the temple and the street that led to the main entrance as the Pallava chakravarthy, accompanied by his family, was visiting the temple. Ekambaranathar's sanctum had never looked so beautiful. The crowns and ornaments worn by the royalty shone brilliantly in the light cast by the illuminated silver kuthuvilakkus. The men and women of the royal family were assembled on either side of the sanctum.

The chakravarthy of the Pallava empire stood in front of everyone else, majestic, sporting the crown worn by his ancestors for the last six hundred years. Even while praying to the lord with his arms folded and eyes closed, the eminence of his ancient royal lineage was evident. He was flanked by the prince of Lanka, Manavanman, and Paranjyothi. Another scion of the Pallava dynasty who had lost Vengi Nadu to Pulikesi and had sought refuge at Kanchi, Aditya Varman, stood humbly beside Paranjyothi.[4] Standing behind him were Sembian Vallavan of the Chola dynasty and the true descendant of Achutha Vikranthan, Vajrabahu. The Pallava kingdom's prime minister, Saranga Deva Bhattar, chief minister, Ranadheera Pallavarayar, members of the ministers' council and the chiefs of kottams stood in close proximity behind the royals.

The women assembled on the other side appeared to be the embodiment of the goddess of beauty. Leading the women was the chief consort of the late Mahendra chakravarthy, Bhuvana Mahadevi, whose divine form was tranquillity and devotion personified. Next to her stood Mamalla chakravarthy's consort and the daughter of the Pandya king, Vanamadevi. Close to the chakravarthini stood Princess Kundavi Devi, who was surveying the area with her dark eyes.

Next to Vanamadevi stood a devoted, virtuous and beautiful eighteen-year-old maiden named Mangayarkkarasi, daughter of the scion of the Kodumbalur Chola dynasty, Sembian Vallavan. Later on, she married Pandian Nedumaran, invited the Saivite saint Gnanasambandar to Madurai and won indelible fame amongst the Sivanadiyars. Several other women from the anthapuram were also present.

The resonant sound of the temple bells, trumpets, conches and melams echoed in unison across the expansive

---

[4] Various editions refer to this character as Aditya Varman and Achutha Varman. I have referred to him as Aditya Varman as this is historically correct.

mandapams of the temple, signifying that deeparadhanai was being performed to Lord Ekambareshwarar. Amidst these sounds, ecstatic devotees chanting 'Namo Parvathi Pathaye!' and 'Hara Hara Mahadeva!' were heard.

When the deeparadhanai was being performed, several people stood devotedly with their palms folded. It was amusing to watch Prince Mahendran and Princess Kundavi emulating the adults by vigorously patting their cheeks. At the conclusion of the deeparadhanai, the kumara sivachariar stepped out of the sanctum with some vibhuti. He stood next to the sivachariar and chanted in a loud voice:

'Tripurantakar, who defied the march of death, destroyed the three malevolent rulers along with their abodes, tore apart the elephant-headed demon and made a garment of his skin and carried fire eternally in his third eye, shall bless Pallavendrar to ensure his unequivocal victory. You will succeed in annihilating Pulikesi along with his abode Vatapi and return as an invincible warrior. Victory will surely be yours.'

The sivachariar then handed over the vibhuti to Mamallar, who received it with respect and applied it to his forehead. Even as Mamallar was doing so, the flame of the lamp that was placed next to the Shiva Lingam burned even more brightly. A spark emitted by the brightly burning lamp fell to the ground with a rustling sound. The spark glowed brightly for some time before finally going out. As everyone assembled there felt that this was a good omen indicating that the chakravarthy would be successful in his expedition, they cheered, 'Jaya Vijayi Bhava!' and 'Hara Hara Mahadeva!' The sanctum, artha mandapam and maha mandapam reverberated with the sound of people's cheers.

When the news of the Pallavendrar obtaining Lord Ekambareshwarar's sanction for the expedition spread to the people who had congregated in the outer mandapams, praharam and the streets surrounding the temple, they cheered heartily, 'Hara Hara Mahadeva!' Only one man remained silent and did not join the others in raising victory slogans. He was the Pallava chakravarthy's charioteer, Kannabiran.

Chapter 7

Kannan's Worry

Elephants fitted with beautiful ambaris were waiting outside the main entrance of the temple. Palanquins made of ivory and gold dazzled brilliantly. The chakravarthy's ornate chariot with two beautiful white steeds harnessed, also stood outside the temple. Kannabiran sat in the chariot, holding onto the horses' reins. His face wore an unusually worried expression.

People had congregated to view the beautiful chariot and the high-breed steeds harnessed to the chariot. One of them asked, 'Charioteer, why do you look so downcast?'

Kannan did not respond.

Another man retorted, 'Why ask him the reason for his worry? Doesn't he have to leave for the battlefield tomorrow? He is concerned that he will be separated from his wife and child!'

Hearing this, Kannabiran's eyes reddened with anger. He cracked the ornate whip that he had never used on the horses at the speaker.

Luckily, the man quickly stepped away and escaped unhurt. The mischief-monger stood some distance away and continued, 'Appane! Why are you so angry? If you are unwilling to proceed to the battlefield, give me the chariot! I will go!'

Yet another onlooker quipped, 'Pazhaniandi, why do you annoy Kannabiran? He is apparently worried because the chakravarthy has asked him not to accompany the contingent that is leaving for the war tomorrow!'

The onlookers sighed sympathetically.

Kannabiran rode Bhuvana Mahadevi and the others who had stepped out of the temple to the palace in his chariot and then returned home. When Kannan returned to his house after leaving the horses in the stables and patting them, he saw a novel sight. His son, who was now ten years old, was swirling a long sword around. As he did so, myriad expressions flitted across his face. Sometimes that innocent countenance exuded anger, while at other times it revealed the difficulties of being trapped in a tight corner. Sometimes the joy of decimating a foe was also apparent on his face!

Kamali sat some distance away from her son, avidly watching him. Unnoticed by her, Kannabiran entered the house noiselessly. He initially smiled happily as he watched the scene. The next instant, his smile changed into a frown. When Kannabiran angrily chided, 'Murugaiyya, stop playing!' the boy stood stunned. Kamali, who was both surprised and shocked, looked at Kannan.

'Throw away the sword! Why does a charioteer's son require a sword? If you so desire, play with a horse whip! But don't even touch the sword! Do you understand?' growled Kannan. Hearing this, the boy let the sword drop to the ground, ran to Kamali, sat on her lap and began to sob.

Kamali asked, 'What is this, Kanna? Why do you make the boy cry? Tomorrow you are leaving for the warfront. One does not know how long it will take for you to return!'

'Kamali, give up such hopes! Your husband is not leaving for the battlefield. I am going to spend my time in the city of Kanchi. This is the chakravarthy's command!' shot back Kannan.

Extreme disappointment was then evident on Kamali's face. 'What is this, Kanna? Why is the chakravarthy cheating you thus? It seems he is taking Aayanar, who is now disabled, to the battlefield!' she observed.

'Lord Rama ought to have destroyed the island of Lanka when he invaded it with an army of monkeys!' pronounced Kannabiran.

'Why are you speaking in riddles? What is the connection between Lord Rama destroying Lanka and you proceeding to the battlefield?' asked Kamali.

'There is a connection. Had Lanka been submerged in the sea then, its prince wouldn't have come here. The chakravarthy would not have commanded me to stay behind and ride the chariot for him!'

'Ah! In that case, is Manavanman also not going to war? Aren't the chakravarthy and he friends?'

'They are close friends, that's why this situation arose. If Manavanman's life is in danger on the battlefield, Lanka's royal dynasty will come to an end. Manavanman has no heirs yet. So, the chakravarthy has commanded the prince of Lanka not to go to the battlefield. I have been stopped for his sake!'

'Is that the reason? Then you don't have to worry, Kanna! The prince of Lanka and you will be able to proceed to the battlefront shortly!' quipped Kamali.

'How do you know this?' asked Kannabiran suspiciously.

'There is a reason; the princess of Lanka is to give birth to a child shortly.'

'Oh! Was this what you meant when you said that the princess of Lanka is unwell? Ekambareshwara! May a son be born to the princess of Lanka!' prayed Kannan with his palms folded, turning towards the direction of the Ekambarar temple.

Chapter 8

Vanamadevi

On the eve of the army's departure, the residents of Kanchi were transforming night into day. None of Kanchi's five lakh residents, barring the infants, slept. The street lamps across the city were shining brightly. The elephant force, cavalry, infantry and chariots harnessed with white horses assembled at Kanchi. They were to report at the palace at dawn. As the chakravarthy was leaving for war the following day, the womenfolk stayed awake all night decorating the streets and the entrances of their houses. Banana trees bearing ripe fruits, bunches of tender coconuts, festoons, fabric curtains and tender coconut shoots were used to decorate the city.

The women painted the outer walls of the houses and drew artistic kolams at street corners. Most of the kolams depicted battle scenes. Warriors riding horses and elephants and soldiers wielding swords and spears featured in those kolams. One kolam depicted the Pandavas seated in five chariots, holding bows and arrows. Another kolam portrayed

Rama and Lakshmana engaged in fierce battle with the ten-headed Ravanan. Yet another kolam illustrated Abhimanyu fighting single-handed against several warriors who had surrounded him. Ah! The Kanchi women were well-versed in both Bharata Kandam's heroic epics and the art of drawing.

The chakravarthy's palace was also buzzing with activity that night. The palace entrance and nila muttram[5] were decorated with banana trees and festoons. Thondai creepers bearing crimson flowers were suspended everywhere. At the nila muttram, the glow from the swords and spears that had been polished with ghee blinded one's eyes. The ornaments meant for elephants and horses were also gleaming.

In contrast to the exuberant thoroughfares and the palace entrance, the anthapuram was enveloped in absolute silence. The ladies-in-waiting walked around noiselessly, carrying out important tasks. When they had to speak, they whispered into each other's ears. The reason was that the chakravarthy had come to the anthapuram to bid adieu to his consort.

The chakravarthy was seated on a feather-soft mattress laid on an ivory bed decorated with blue silk fabric and strings of pearls. The empress of the Pallava kingdom and the Pandya princess, Vanamadevi, was standing deferentially in front of him. In the adjacent chamber, Prince Mahendran and Princess Kundavi were sound asleep on the silk mattress spread out on a golden bed.

Nine years ago, the Pandya princess, Vanamadevi, had wed Mamallar. Her beauty was reminiscent of that of the Pandya women described in the epics and in poetry. Her skin tone resembled the pleasing hue of a pink lotus. Her dark eyes resembled the black beetles that buzzed around the lotus flowers.

---

[5]   Loosely translated as 'moonlit courtyard'.

Uma Devi, whose beautiful form had distracted Lord Shiva from his penance and melted his heart, chose to be born in the Madurai Pandya dynasty when she incarnated on earth. Lord Shiva himself stopped dancing at the graveyard and discarded his repulsive accessories, like the human skull, and assumed a handsome form to marry the Pandya scion, Parvati Devi. Words are inadequate to describe the beauty of Vanamadevi who had been born in such a dynasty.

The chakravarthy stated, 'Devi, it's time for me to go. Tomorrow, I too will leave for the battlefield at dawn.'

Vanamadevi did not respond. A single tear that stood at the corner of her eye gleamed like a pearl.

'I don't know how long it will take for me to return. I don't even know whether I will return. Devi, I am giving you a major responsibility to shoulder. You must accord the utmost attention to bringing up Mahendran and Kundavi. You must safeguard the Pallava Empire and hand it over to Mahendran when he comes of age!'

Hearing this, Vanamadevi, who had been standing till then, sat down at Mamallar's feet and began to cry.

'Devi! What is this? Are you, a descendant of the valorous Pandya dynasty, reluctant to bid adieu to your husband who is headed for the battlefield?' asked the chakravarthy, looking slightly disconcerted.

Vanamadevi looked up at him and replied, 'Prabhu, I don't have an iota of reluctance. Nor will the situation necessitate me to oversee the kingdom and hand it over to Mahendran when he comes of age. There are several expert astrologers in my birthplace, Madurai. They have spoken at length about my marital life. There is no doubt that you will return victorious after winning over the Chalukyas and razing Vatapi to the ground!'

'Then, why are you shedding tears? What is the cause of your sorrow? You must speak frankly,' urged Mamallar.

'Swami, the astrologer who spoke of my marital life also predicted that I would attain the lotus feet of Goddess Meenakshi before you. I wept because I was concerned that this might happen before you return. I do not want to depart to heaven before seeing you return victorious.' When Vanamadevi spoke thus, her wide eyes were brimming with tears.

Mamallar lifted the beacon of the Pandya dynasty and made her sit next to him on the bed. He wiped away her tears with his angavastram. 'Devi! I too will make an astrological prediction; pay heed to me! I will return victorious after decimating Pulikesi and razing Vatapi to the ground. When I lead the victory procession around Kanchi seated in a golden chariot drawn by white horses, you will be by my side. Mahendran will be on your lap, while Kundavi will be on mine ...'

'Prabhu, I don't harbour such desires. It would suffice if I saw you return victorious from your expedition. If I continue to be alive even after you return, I will hand over this position and the joy of being by your side to the one to whom it rightfully belongs and step aside. If you so desire, I will continue to occupy a small place in this palace. If you desire otherwise, I will return to my birthplace.' Mamallar was aghast when he heard these words.

'Devi! What is this? Why are you speaking in a manner that you have not spoken in the last nine years? What have you heard? What are you thinking of when you speak thus?' asked Mamallar, looking emotionally drained.

'Swami, do you think that I could be ignorant of something that those in the palace, the residents of Kanchi and the entire kingdom know?'

'I'm unable to fathom what you're talking about. What is the mystery those in the palace and the entire country are aware of?'

'There is no mystery, prabhu. It is the reason for which you are invading Vatapi.'

'Why am I leading this expedition? What did you hear?' asked Mamallar.

'Do you want me to state the reason? You are going to free the sculptor Aayanar's daughter . . .'

'Ah! You too know about this. How long have you known? How did you come to know about it?'

'I have known for a long time. Nine years ago, when I entered this palace after marrying you, your mothers and the ladies-in-waiting used to look at me sympathetically. They used to sigh with concern. Gradually, from their conversation, I guessed the truth. Swami, within a year of becoming your chief consort, I came to know that someone else occupied your heart . . .'

'Despite knowing this, you did not broach that subject with me even once. Not even once in the last nine years did you point an accusing finger at me. Devi, I have heard of virtuous women in stories and epics. None of them match up to you,' praised Mamallar proudly.

'Prabhu, your praise makes me ecstatic, but I am not worthy of this honour,' stated the Pandya princess.

'No one but you is worthy of this honour. Despite knowing that your lawfully wedded husband had lost his heart to someone else, you did not question him about it even once. Neither did you accuse him. Can there be a woman more virtuous than you?'

'Swami, why should I accuse you? It is my father and my brother who are to blame. Weren't they the ones who insisted that you marry me? Didn't my brother, Jayanta Varman, become enraged at your refusal and invade the Pallava kingdom? You defeated him on the banks of the Kollidam River and chased him away. None of us believed my brother who returned to Madurai and claimed to have defeated you. We were happy discussing by discussing how you had humbled his pride. Even then, my brother did not spare you. He left no stone unturned to ensure that we were married so that he could substantiate his claim . . .'

'Devi! Do you still believe that I married you on account of Jayanta Varman's insistence?' When Narasimha Varmar posed this question, a smile appeared on his face.

'No, prabhu! You did not marry me on Jayanta Varman's insistence. You married me for the welfare of the Pallava kingdom. You married me because it was essential for you to befriend the kings in the south if you had to wage a war against the demonic adversary in the north. It was not my brother's duress that prompted you to marry me. You married me on your father's advice. I came to know about all this within a few days of my coming to this palace . . .'

'Still, you did not question me about this even once. Ah! How true it is when people say that the depths of a woman's heart cannot be fathomed!' thought Mamallar as he observed his consort's face closely. Her lotus-like face did not reveal an iota of rancour; only immense faith, boundless love and tranquillity were evident!

'Swami, I have never ever dwelt on your reasons for marrying me. That's because I was clear about why I had married you. When news of your defeating Jayanta Varman on the banks of the Kollidam river reached Madurai, my heart sought you out. At that moment I decided that I would marry only you, and that if I were unable to marry you, I would remain unmarried all my life. My desire was fulfilled. I was fortunate to have wed you. For the last nine years, I have resided joyously in your palace. Prabhu, I do not expect this happiness to last forever. Others should have an opportunity to live happily too. The day you return to Kanchi with Aayanar's daughter, I am prepared to relinquish my rights to the golden throne of the ancient Pallava dynasty and my role as your wife in this palace,' observed Vanamadevi in a choked voice. She then looked at Mamallar with tear-filled eyes. Mamallar understood that every emotion-laden word uttered came from an untainted heart that bore no ill-will.

Chapter 9

War Trumpet

'Devi, this ancient Pallava kingdom is extremely fortunate to have a virtuous woman like you seated on the throne! It is the fruit of the good deeds that I did in my past several births that I have you for my consort!' When Mamallar spoke thus, his deep and firm voice choked. Vanamadevi felt goosebumps. Though she wanted to articulate her feelings, she was unable to do so. The Pallavendrar continued speaking.

'Heed me, the beacon of the Pandyas! You're not just my queen consort but also the mother of Mahendra Kumaran, who will succeed me to this throne. You are the chakravarthini who mesmerized the citizens of the Pallava kingdom and won their allegiance in a moment. A few days after the death of my father, Mahendrar, the ministers' council crowned me and seated me on the Pallava throne. You were seated beside me on that very throne. Our family guru, Rudrachariar, blessed us saying that the two of us were akin to Devendran and Indrani seated on the throne in heaven. Hearing this, the courtiers cheered enthusiastically. When the courtiers recollected that, on your arrival, there was a heavy downpour in Kanchi, where it had not rained for some time, they unanimously proclaimed that you were indeed Indrani. Tamil poets conferred the title Vanamadevi on you and sang verses eulogizing you. Since then, courtiers and citizens have been proudly addressing you as Vanamadevi and Indrani. No one in this world has the right to make a lofty soul like you abdicate the Pallava throne—'

Vanamadevi interrupted him asking, 'Swami, do I have a claim just to the Pallava throne and not to your heart?'

Mamallar was taken aback when he heard this unexpected question. He composed himself and told Vanamadevi affectionately, 'Ah! You have never broached this subject with me even once despite harbouring such a doubt in your mind for nine years. You exemplify what the unerring Tamil poet, Thiruvalluvar's couplet: *"The virtuous who worships her spouse over the Creator gains such power to cause, at will, torrential rain."* Any other woman who harboured such a suspicion would have brought it up a hundred times with her husband every day and would have made life hell for him!'

'Prabhu! In that case, is what I heard in the palace and that which people spoke about across the country untrue? Is it my folly that I spent nine sleepless years fretting about this?' asked Vanamadevi, with a hint of optimism.

'Devi, rumours are not devoid of truth. All that you heard is not untrue. But it is an incident that occurred in my previous birth,' confessed Mamallar and remained deep in thought for some time. He then heaved a deep sigh and continued. 'Yes! That occurred in my previous birth. It is a dream that has waned and disappeared. In my youth, when my life as Mahendra Pallavar's only son was filled with joy and I was oblivious of sorrow, I fell in love with a sculptor's daughter. I was ready to lay my body, soul, possessions and the glory of the Pallava kingdom at her feet. But the day pride gained dominance over affection in her heart, and she obstinately disregarded my tender words when I had travelled over a hundred kaadam to rescue her, there was no place for her in my heart. I have neither forgotten her nor have I been able to forget her. The sole reason is that I have been unable to fulfil the promise I made to her. The spirit of Sivakami, who is residing in a faraway land in our enemy's fort, perpetually torments me and robs me of peace in the daytime and of sleep at night. The day I fulfil my word and free her by defeating the Chalukyas and hand her over to her father, that day the unfeeling woman's spirit will cease to torment me. That very day, I will banish all memories of her from my heart. From then on, only thoughts of you, our children and the welfare of the Pallava kingdom will prevail. Devi! Do you believe me? Or do you think that these are misleading words uttered by a deceitful man?' asked Mamallar.

That very instant, Vanamadevi stood up from the bed, prostrated before Mamallar and replied, 'Prabhu, I don't disbelieve your words. Even if I were to observe that your behaviour contradicted your words, it would be my eyes that I would distrust. I would not doubt you!'

Mamallar dwelt for some time on the difference between Sivakami's suspicion and pride-laden love, and that of the tranquil and virtuous Vanamadevi. He returned to reality with a start, held her hands, seated her next to him on the bed and observed: 'It's good that you brought up this subject now. You have removed the huge burden that has been weighing me down. In return, I am handing over the major responsibility of overseeing this expansive empire to you. Though the ministers' council will attend to matters of the state during my absence, they will consult you on important matters. Devi, besides this I am giving you the sole responsibility of performing an important task. You must promise me that you will fulfil that task.' Vanamadevi looked surprised and disturbed on hearing these words.

'Prabhu! If you believe that this helpless woman is capable of executing the task, please command me to do so. I consider it my good fortune to carry out your orders!'

'It's an extremely important task! Your brother's son, Nedumaran, who left Madurai leading a large army with the express intention of joining me in the Vatapi expedition, has not reached Kanchi yet. He has sent me a message stating that he is staying back on the banks of the Varaha River because he is unwell, that he will reach Kanchi in a week, and that I should wait for him. It is impossible for me to delay this expedition. It is imperative for me to leave on the auspicious day chosen by our dynasty's guru. Devi, I have received news that Nedumaran has fallen for the Samanars' enticing words.[6] You are aware that the Samanars are thirsting to settle scores with me. You must ensure that Nedumaran causes no harm when he reaches Kanchi.'

Mamallar had hardly finished talking when Vanamadevi majestically assured him, 'Prabhu, you may leave without worrying about this matter. I will not allow the family in which I was born to harm you. If I find out that Nedumaran harbours such evil thoughts, I will stab him with a dagger!'

Mamallar smilingly replied, 'Don't do that! Wouldn't your tender hands that resemble the petals of a jasmine ache if you were to wield a dagger? If the necessity arises, procure some

---

[6] 'Samanars', meaning 'wandering renunciates', was a term used at the time for Jains.

effective poison from Namasivaya Vaidhyar, mix it with milk and give it to him! But I don't think such a necessity will arise. My suspicion may be unfounded, but it is essential for royalty to foresee such situations and take the necessary precautions, especially when one is embarking on an expedition to a faraway country.'

Just then, there was a deafening noise that caused the palace walls to reverberate. It was not possible to fathom whether the din that enveloped the bedroom chamber came from a faraway place or from the core of the earth. The impact of that noise was felt not just by the ears but by the entire body. Mamallar stood up with a start saying, 'Ah! It's midnight! That's the war trumpet!'

The din of the trumpet that caused Mamallar to stand up with a start also brought before his eyes, gory scenes from the battlefield. Gigantic war elephants resembling massive granite hills, combatted with each other letting out shrill cries. Hundreds of chariots moved at a pace that caused the earth to reverberate, clashed against each other and shattered into smithereens. Thousands of horsemen wielding spears rode on horses that travelled faster than the wind to the middle of the battlefield and attacked each other; the gleam of the spears was blinding. Lakhs of soldiers wielding sharp swords killed each other. The bloodshed in the battlefield resembled the flow of a large river. The lifeless corpses of elephants, horses and mutilated humans floated in the river of blood. Mamallar could also visualize the pride-filled face of a woman amidst this gruesome sight! Needless to say, it was the face of the sculptor's daughter, Sivakami.

Chapter 10

Mangayarkkarasi

That night, it was not just Mamallar but the entire population of Kanchi who heard the din of the war trumpet. That sound roused diverse emotions in people. In the middle of that night, an elderly man and a beautiful young maiden were strolling in the Kanchi palace garden. That maiden's beautiful face offered stiff competition to the moon glowing in the sky. On hearing the war trumpet, the girl shivered like a wind-blown creeper. Even as she asked, 'Appa! What's that noise?' she hugged her father tight.

'My child, it's the war trumpet. The time has come for me to bid adieu to you!' declared the elderly man. The duo had been present at Ekambareshwarar's sanctum that morning. The elderly man, Sembian Vallavan, was a descendant of the Kodumbalur Chola dynasty, and the devout girl was his cherished daughter.

The Chola dynasty that had flourished for a few centuries after Karikala Vallavan had gradually become weaker and was

46

stifled between the Pandyas in the south and the Pallavas in the north. The Chola dynasty had split into a couple of branches. That branch of the Chola dynasty based in Uraiyur ruled a small kingdom. The representative of the Kodumbalur Cholas, Sembian Vallavan, had no sons, and continuance of his lineage was dependent on his only daughter. Sembian Vallavan had named his daughter 'Mangayarkkarasi', meaning queen amongst women. Even though it was her father who had named her, those who met her concurred that it was a fitting name for her. She was endowed with such exalted beauty and character.

Sembian was eager to get his daughter married to a prince from a pre-eminent royal family in Dakshina Bharata before his death. He brooded about this day and night. It was during this time that he received Mamallar's epistle directing all kings in Dakshina Bharata, along with their armies, to join hands with him in his invasion of Vatapi. He felt enthused thinking that this was an opportune moment to fulfil his desire. Despite his advanced age, he embarked on this expedition because several princes would be congregating at Kanchi at that time. He believed that he would be able to get his daughter married to one of them.

'Appa, are you really going to leave me behind and proceed to the warfront? How will I spend my time in this large palace filled with strangers? What will become of me if some harm were to befall you at the battlefield?' cried Sembian's daughter, Mangayarkkarasi.

'My child, why worry when our dynasty's deity, Muruga Peruman, is there to protect you? His spear, which smashed a mountain to smithereens, caused the ocean to dry up, overcame the sun, decimated the demon Banugopan and defended the Devas, will protect you. My child, please give me leave without losing courage.'

Hearing Sembian speak thus, Mangayarkkarasi was filled with ecstasy.

Oblivious that she was overcome by devotional bliss, her father remarked, 'Amma, not only will the spear and the peacock guide you, Mamalla chakravarthy's mother and Mahendra Pallavar's queen consort, Bhuvana Mahadevi, will also be supportive. She promised to look after you as if you were her own daughter. You lost your mother at a young age; Bhuvana Mahadevi does not have a daughter. She reassured me that she would look after you like the apple of her eye. So, you have no reason to worry, my dear daughter. Please bid farewell courageously!' As Mangayarkkarasi remained silent, Sembian Vallavan continued to speak.

'My child, an elderly man visited our residence when you were a child. He looked at you intently. He examined your tender palms and predicted, "The lines on this child's palm bear the conch and discus insignia. She will become the queen consort of a powerful king!" Those words were music to my ears. Since then, I have been anticipating the arrival of the prince. The important reason for my coming to Kanchi is to look for him . . .'

Mangayarkkarasi excitedly interrupted him, saying, 'Appa! Appa! Last night I had a wonderful dream. May I tell you about it?'

Chapter 11

Dream and Imagination

Sembian embraced his daughter and quipped, 'My child, our dreams don't necessarily come true, though some do. It is very difficult to understand the true import of dreams. But tell me about your dream. Given my limited understanding of the scriptures, I will tell you whether your dream is likely to come true or not.' Sembian thought that even if his daughter had had a bad dream, he could fabricate a favourable interpretation and bolster her courage before he left.

'Appa, that dream makes me happy and also scared. Look, even now I'm trembling . . .!' Mangayarkkarasi remarked and pointed at the goosebumps on her forearms. She continued. 'For some time now, a handsome youth has been appearing in my dreams. He often looks at me lovingly. I have never seen such a person in real life. He is even more handsome than Mamalla chakravarthy. He seems to ask me, "Don't you belong to me? When are you going to come to me?" Then my heart starts beating rapidly. I shiver. That handsome man

49

appeared in my dream last night. But I dreamt of him in horrific circumstances. Ten to twelve nude ghosts surrounded him and were screaming in a chilling manner. Each of those ghosts held a bunch of peacock feathers. Sometimes, it seemed as though the ghosts were hitting that handsome man with the peacock feathers! It seemed as though that poor man was afflicted with a malady. He shot me a piteous glance that seemed to convey, "I am trapped amidst these ghosts. Won't you rescue me?"

'I immediately turned around and ran. For a long time, I ran without knowing where I was going. Finally, I could see a temple. When I entered the temple, there was no one there. I headed to goddess Ambika's sanctum and pleaded, "Thaye! You must protect your beloved devotee!" I heard a voice from heaven say, "My child! Don't be scared! I will send my son. He will come with you and fulfil your desire!" Immediately I saw a beatific boy near goddess Ambika's idol. As the goddess had assured me that she would send her son, I thought Valli's lord would accompany me.[7] But the boy standing there sported vibhuti and rudraksha and seemed to be a devotee of Lord Shiva. That boy pronounced in his calm, dulcet voice, "Thaye! Come with me! I will rescue your Lord!" When that divine child uttered the words "Your Lord", I felt goosebumps. I immediately woke up! I feel tormented wondering if that handsome man was rescued. What is the meaning of my dream, father? Does it augur good or evil for me?'

Even before his daughter had stopped talking, Sembian enthusiastically said, 'It definitely bodes well!'

That Chola nobleman thought for some time and then observed, 'Your dream appears to be divine. You will be united

---

[7]   Valli's lord refers to Lord Murugan.

with your handsome beloved right here. From your dream, I surmise that your prospective husband may face acute difficulty, which will ultimately be resolved by the grace of our dynasty's deity, Muruga Peruman. My dear daughter! You should harbour no doubts regarding one issue. If fortune seeks you out during my absence, don't reject it! If a member of a royal family is desirous of marrying you, I give you consent to do so right away. If I return from the battlefield, I will provide my heartfelt blessings to you and your husband. If I were to lose my life on the battlefield, my soul will immediately return to bless you and only then depart to heaven.' As he spoke, Sembian Vallavan shed copious tears. Mangayarkkarasi too buried her face in her father's broad chest and sobbed.

Chapter 12

Nedumaran

It is not known if Sembian Vallavan understood the meaning of Magayarkkarasi's dream. But incidents that were unfolding at the same time ten kaadam to the south of Kanchi on the banks of the Varaha River may shed some light on what the dream foretold.

In the middle of that moonlit night, an unprecedented incident was unfolding on the banks of the Varaha River, where the massive Pandya army was camping. Flags bearing the fish insignia hoisted atop the tents were fluttering in the breeze. The landscape was filled with elephants, horses, chariots and carts. As it was the month of Purattasi and not very cold, most of the soldiers were sleeping in the open. Those who were unable to sleep sat around in groups, gossiping. Sometimes their loud laughter shattered the silence.

Their conversation betrayed their concerns. They were worried about their army camping on the riverbank for three days and not marching ahead to Kanchi, as well as the malady that had afflicted their commander, Nedumara Pandian. Some of them whispered, 'His illness is an excuse; there must be some other reason!'

When one man joked, 'Mohini has possessed the prince!' the listeners were amused.

Another soldier remarked, 'Why are you laughing? Tomorrow the Pallava army is embarking from Kanchi on its expedition. We are still sitting here, far away from to Kanchi!'

A third soldier opined, 'Probably we're returning to Madurai.'

Yet another soldier declared, 'It is preferable to commit suicide by drowning in the Varaha River than return to Madurai in this manner!'

'Ah! You've discovered the most effective way to commit suicide. If one stands upside down in the Varaha River, the water will reach his nose. You need to be extremely skilful to commit suicide by drowning in this river,' retorted a soldier.

'Come what may, I will not return. I have promised my lover that I will bring back a lot of loot from Vatapi. What will she say if I return empty-handed?' observed another man.

'Wonder how those born in the valorous Pandya dynasty can be so small-minded?' pondered one man as he heaved a deep sigh.

The handsome and majestic Pandya prince, Nedumaran, the central topic of the Pandya soldiers' conversation, was at that moment seated in his tent. He was a descendant of the Pandya dynasty, which was centuries older than the Pallava dynasty. A Digambara Samana monk was seated in his presence. A bunch of peacock feathers, a folded mat and a kamandalam lay next to the monk, who was short, squat and tonsured. Nedumaran asked him, 'Swami, how much longer do I have to wait?'

He had hardly finished speaking when the sound of an udukku was heard. Though the sound was faint, it caused one's body to reverberate. The Samana monk remarked, 'There! We've been summoned! Prince, let's go!'

Nedumaran got up without responding. Both of them stepped out of the tent and walked to the banks of the river. A boat was waiting for them. Two soldiers holding oars stood at both ends of the boat. For a moment, Nedumaran hesitated to climb into the boat. The Samanar observed this and stated, 'Prince, if you're scared, you need not come! You may return!'

Nedumaran looked at him, muttered 'Hm!', and leapt into the boat.

The Samana monk also got into the boat. The soldiers rowed the boat carefully and noiselessly. When the boat reached the opposite bank, Nedumaran asked both the soldiers to wait at that spot and walked ahead with the Samana monk.

As they walked further, the sound of the udukku became louder. That magnetic sound attracted Nedumaran. It overpowered him to the extent that he would not have been able to return even if he had so desired. Nedumaran's walking accelerated. Soon, he was running. When the Samana monk called out, 'Prince! Please stop, we have reached our destination', Nedumaran thought that he was dreaming.

Nedumaran stopped; a cave carved out of rock lay ahead of him. Two guards stood at the entrance of the cave. In reality, they were two statues carved out of stone. But the prince, who was in a trance, thought that they were human. A dim light was streaming out from within the cave. Yes! This rock and the guards have previously featured in this work. The cave was carved by the sculptor Aayanar nine years ago. The Digambara Samanars had seized it.

Chapter 13

Clairvoyance

When Nedumaran entered the cave as directed by the Digambara Samanar, the fragrance of incense made him feel slightly dizzy. He managed to suppress this feeling and continued on. As he walked deeper into the cave, he saw an extraordinary sight in the large mandapam there. Large earthen lamps placed on poles were shining brightly. Smoke was emanating from an incense holder. The light cast by the lamps and the smoke from the incense added a surreal dimension to the occurrences in the cave. Nedumaran looked intently and assimilated what was going on. Ten to twelve Digambara Samanars were sitting in a circle. All of them were chanting a prayer in a coordinated tone. One of them was playing an instrument that resembled an udukku. Another was strumming the strings of a full-length veenai. The sounds from the two instruments washed through Nedumaran's body and made his nerves throb.

Amidst the Samanars who were sitting in a circle was a boy of around sixteen. His body gently swayed to the rhythm of the prayers and the music. His eyes were half-closed. As only the whites of his eyes were visible, he looked ghastly. The Samana monk who had accompanied Nedumaran gestured to the prince not to speak and to sit quietly. Nedumaran obeyed him.

The pace of the prayers and music quickened. The boy also began swaying at a rapid pace.

Suddenly, the prayers and the music came to a halt. The boy shrieked loudly and fell to the ground. A fearsome silence prevailed in the mandapam for some time. The eyelids and lips of the boy who lay unconscious twitched slightly. The Samanar who held the veenai plucked one of its strings and asked, 'Thambi! Can you hear this sound?'

The young boy murmured, 'Yes, swami!'

'In that case, respond to my queries. Is there a difference between the place you were previously and the place you are in now?'

'Some time ago, I lay on the floor of a mountain cave. Now I am floating in the sky. I am able to go wherever I choose to in the sky.'

'What do you see in the place where you are floating now?'

'I am surrounded by dense smoke. I can dimly see several figures in that smoke. They seem to disappear and then appear.'

'Thambi, are you able to stand still at one place? Are you able to move forward and backward?'

'I am able to move in any direction I desire—forward, backward, up and down.'

The Samanar who was interrogating the boy looked at Nedumaran and asked, 'Pandya Kumara, by the grace of Rishabha Devar, this boy has obtained the power of foresight.

He is able to perceive incidents that occurred twenty thousand years ago and those that will occur twenty thousand years hence! Are you desirous of knowing anything?'

Though Nedumaran hesitated, thinking, 'Is it necessary to clear the mists that cloud the future and observe forthcoming events? Will this augur danger? Shall I leave this enigmatic cave without finding out about the future?' an incomprehensible force firmly restrained him from doing so. Nedumaran replied, 'Yes, adigal! I am desirous of knowing about the outcome of the Vatapi war.'

The Samanar asked the boy who lay on the floor, 'Thambi, please travel northwards and tell us what is happening there!'

'So be it, swami! I will travel northwards right away!' replied the boy. After some time he shrieked, 'Ah! How gory!'

The Samanar asked, 'Thambi, what gory sights do you see?'

'A fierce war is being fought. Countless warriors are attacking each other with swords and spears and are dying. Rivers of blood are flowing everywhere. Gigantic elephants are attacking each other, shrieking fearsomely. The battle is being fought close to the massive ramparts of a fort. At the main entrance of the fort, a flag bearing the varaha insignia is fluttering. Ah! The fort gates are being opened! Innumerable soldiers are exiting the fort. The war becomes even more brutal. There are numerous casualties; the entire region is filled with corpses. Ah! The sight is unbearable!'

Observing the slight twitching of the boy's eyelids, the Samana guru urged, 'Thambi! Don't be scared! No harm will befall you; observe more intently. Look around the battlefield and identify where the most vicious combats are being fought!'

'Yes, yes! There is indeed a fierce combat underway in one part of the battlefield. A warrior seated on a horse wielding two swords is battling formidably. His enemies have surrounded him and are attacking him. He is fighting all of them single-handed. The swords he is holding often gleam like lightning. He decapitates one attacker each with a swirl of his swords. Ah! A few more warriors arrive to assist him. A flag bearing the fish insignia is fluttering in their midst. They roar, "Long live, Nedumara Pandian! Doom to Pulikesi of Vatapi!" even as they pounce on their foes.'

Nedumaran, who had been a tad inattentive till then, sat upright when the boy narrated this. He was extremely eager to know what would happen next.

The boy fell silent for some time. The Samana guru prodded him again and commanded him to observe what happened next. 'Ah! The combat has come to an end. The enemies have all dropped dead. The victorious warriors surround the brave warrior and cheer, "Long live the fish insignia! Long live Nedumara Pandian!" The din of their cheering and the trumpets proclaiming victory is deafening.

'Another group of warriors is approaching. There is a chariot amidst them, and the Rishabha flag is hoisted atop it. A majestic person is seated in the chariot. The warriors accompanying him cheer, "Long Live Mamalla chakravarthy!" But their cheering is not as vibrant. The two forces meet. The person in the chariot and the person seated on the horse look at each other. Both of them dismount and approach each other. The warrior holding the flag with the fish emblem looks at the person leading the warriors holding the Rishabha flag and remarks, "Mamallar! The foes have been decimated. Pulikesi is dead. We have captured the Vatapi fort. The rest is in your hands; please give me leave!" Mamallar retorts, "You Pandya reprobate! Haven't you appropriated the glory that rightfully belongs to me?" and then draws out his sword. The warrior bearing the fish flag says, "No, Chakravarthy! No! Why do we have to fight?" The man holding the Rishabha flag, heedless, wields his sword. Aiyyo!'

The boy, who had been lying on the floor till then, sat up with a shriek, which gave all those present goosebumps. He looked around with widened eyes that conveyed fear and shock. Nedumara Pandian was shivering. He told the Samana monk, 'I wish to know what happened next. He woke up at a critical juncture.'

The monk responded, 'Prince, that's all for tonight. He will not acquire foresight again tonight. If you wish to know what happened next, you may come to the same place tomorrow night!'

Chapter 14

The Invasion Begins

When the sun rose in the eastern horizon on Vijayadasami, certain extraordinary events were unfolding in Kanchi. Mamalla chakravarthy, after performing ceremonies like the Yatra Danam and Graha Preethi at the entrance to the ancient Pallava palace, sought the blessings of the elders, including Rudrachariar, took leave of his mother Bhuvana Mahadevi, and left for the battlefield mounted on the royal war elephant.[8] The din of war trumpets blown then caused the multi-storeyed mansions of Kanchi to vibrate, and echoed through the city's mandapams.

Rows of elephants, horses and chariots that stood ahead of and behind the sovereign's elephant started moving in unison towards the northern gates of the Kanchi fort. As this procession made its way through Kanchi's thoroughfares,

---

[8] Yatra Danam means danam (charity) prior to the travel (yatra). Graha Preethi means appeasement (preethi) of the planets (graham). Both ceremonies were performed to secure success in an expedition.

beautiful women standing in the upper storeys of the mansions showered fragrant flowers and akshadai on it, cheering, 'Jaya Vijayi Bhava!' This war-bound procession, heartily cheered on by the womenfolk, reached the northern entrance of the fort in a muhurtham. The fort gates were flung wide open. Beyond the gates stood an ocean-like army. Numerous flags fluttering in the breeze amidst that army resembled the frothy white waves that rise in the ocean when strong winds blow.

Across the moat that ran adjacent to the northern gates, Mamalla chakravarthy finally bid farewell to Manavanman and his two cherished children. When he lifted and embraced Mahendran and Kundavi, he wondered when he would see them again. This thought caused tears to well up in his eyes. After lowering the children to the ground, he told Manavanman, 'My dear friend! I am leaving these children, their mother and this Pallava kingdom in your care. You have to protect them and hand them over to me when I return. As advised by Paranjyothi, I am leaving behind one part of the army that is stationed at Thirukazhukunram. If Kanchi comes under threat because of the Pandya prince, don't hesitate to use that army.'

'So be it, prabhu! Please do not worry about Kanchi,' reassured Manavanman.

'I'm glad! I was worried that you would obstinately insist on accompanying me at the last minute. Your behaviour befits that of a true friend!' remarked Mamallar warmly.

Then Mahendran pleaded for the thousandth time, 'Appa, I too will accompany you to the Vatapi war. Take me along!'

Mamallar told his son, 'Mahendra, don't be concerned about the Vatapi war. The Lanka war is going to be fiercer. You may go there, decimate the man who appropriated your uncle's kingdom and return your uncle's kingdom to him!'

After speaking thus, Mamallar abruptly dissociated himself from his children and mounted the royal elephant. That was it! That gigantic army started moving slowly as though the ocean itself was being relocated from one place to another. The clouds of dust that rose when this gargantuan army advanced in unison completely obscured the earth and the sky. Manavanman, Mahendran and Kundavi stood at the entrance of the fort and watched without batting an eyelid till the clouds of dust disappeared completely.

Chapter 15

Kulachirayar

It had been three days since Mamalla chakravarthy embarked on the expedition leading his army. The streets of Kanchi appeared deserted and devoid of gaiety. The entire city seemed to be asleep. Interrupting that abnormal slumber was a chariot whose wheels rattled as it moved rapidly and came to a halt outside Thirunavukkarasar's monastery. The chariot driver was Kannabiran.

A young man got down from the chariot. His face reflected his cultured personality, evolved wisdom and fine upbringing. Kannabiran told that man, 'Yes, aiyya! This is Thirunavukkarasar's monastery. That palanquin belongs to Bhuvana Mahadevi. It seems that the chakravarthy's mother has come for an audience with the swamigal.'

'I have to meet the swamigal immediately even if he is in conversation with the chakravarthy's mother,' declared that man as he entered the monastery.

Bhuvana Mahadevi, accompanied by Mangayarkkarasi, whom she treated as her daughter, had come for an audience with Vageechar. The swamigal was narrating the greatness of the shrines he had visited in Utthara Bharata to Bhuvana Mahadevi. Navukkarasar finally informed her that he was about to go southwards on a pilgrimage. 'Yes, thaye! I went on a pilgrimage to several shrines in the north. I went up to Mount Kailash. But the greatness of the temples in the south is incomparable. The Ekambareshwarar temple has no peers. Neither do Thiruthillai, Thiruvaiyyaru and Thiruvanaikka. I wish to travel to the south and visit these shrines again. I am leaving tomorrow!'

As he was talking, the youth who had alighted at the entrance of the monastery entered. He humbly bowed to Navukkarasar and Bhuvana Mahadevi. When Navukkarasar asked, 'Who are you, appane? Why have you come here?' he sounded slightly annoyed.

Understanding this, the youth stood with his palms together and stated, 'Swami, please forgive me. Though I knew that the chakravarthy's mother was here, I entered because of an important task. I am coming from the banks of the Varaha River. Nedumara Pandian is afflicted by high fever. Realizing that medicines administered by vaidhyars alone cannot cure him, I came to obtain some vibhuti from you. Please forgive me.' He then turned towards Bhuvana Mahadevi and said, 'Devi, you too must forgive me!'

The devi observed, 'Appane, you are very polite. But you have not yet answered the swamigal's query. Who are you?'

'I forgot in my haste, devi! I was born in Manamerkudi village located in the Pandya Nadu. My name is Kulachirai. The Madurai king appointed me to assist the Pandya kumarar in reading and writing messages,' replied that youth.

'Why should the sick Pandya kumarar stay back on the banks of the Varaha River?' asked the devi.

'A severe fever has gripped him, devi! The vaidhyars feel that he ought not to travel in this condition. We will bring him here once he is strong enough to travel. I was thinking of delivering this message at the palace. Fortunately, I met you here.'

'That's not so, appane! It does not suffice if you tell me. Come to the palace and inform Vanamadevi in person. The poor woman is extremely worried!' Bhuvana Mahadevi then stood up saying, 'Swami, please give me leave.'

Mangayarkkarasi left with Bhuvana Mahadevi. She was observing Kulachirai intently ever since he had entered the chamber. Before leaving, she took one final look at him. Coincidentally, Kulachirai also looked at her at that moment. Both their facial expressions indicated that they were thinking about some past incidents.

After the women left, Thirunavukkarasar advised, 'Appane, everything happens as per my lord Emperuman's[9] wishes. What can I, his humble servant, do? Nevertheless, I will give you some vibhuti in the name of the lord. You take it to him. Vaidyanatha[10] Peruman, who cured me of severe stomach ailment in an instant, will also cure the young Pandian.'

Kulachirayar received the vibhuti from Navukkarasar with devotion and requested again with humility, 'Swami, you should grant me another boon.'

'Ask, thambi! I am pleased with your devotion and humility,' replied Vageechar.

---

[9] Another name for Lord Shiva.
[10] Another name for Lord Shiva.

'The influence of Samanars has greatly increased in southern Pandya Nadu. Swamigal must visit Pandya Nadu with your disciples. You must prevent the citizens from falling into the Samanars' net! You must also protect the ancient Pandya dynasty from coming under the spell of the Samanars! Ah! Why did Samanam spread in Tamil Nadu like parasites on a healthy tree, swami?'

Observing Kulachirai speaking in this heated manner, Navukkarasar initially smiled. Then, the elderly soul gestured to Kulachirai to stop and remarked, 'Thambi, once upon a time I too bore a grudge against the Samana faith. But it is unfair to resent the Samana faith because of the mistakes committed by a few Samanars. The Samana faith was created to preach love and kindness. Our ancient Tamizhagam has greatly benefited from the Samana sages from the days of yore. The Samana monks caused Tamil to flourish. They authored great epics in Tamil. They spread the art of painting.'

Kulachirai lost his patience and blurted, 'That's enough, swami! Enough! I never expected to hear you laud the Samanars. I came to request you to save Pandya Nadu in the same manner as you saved Thondai Mandalam. Please come and observe the atrocities they perpetrate in Pandya Nadu!'

Navukkarasar closed his eyes and remained immersed in deep thought for some time. Then he opened his eyes and predicted, 'I neither have the wherewithal nor the desire to combat the Samanars, who are experts at wizardry. But listen, thambi. I often foresee a miracle these days. An innocent boy is going to incarnate in this sacred country and compose nectar-like Tamil verses. Several wonders will occur through him. Barren trees will turn verdant. Copper will be transformed into gold. The dominance of the Samanars in the southern Pandya Nadu will also end because of him. Saivism will flourish and the Sivanadiyars will gain strength.' As Thirunavukkarasar spoke in this manner, Kulachirayar felt goosebumps.

The Kanchi chakravarthy's palace was extremely spacious. It was divided into three sections and the entrances of each led to the nila muttram at the front of the palace. The sprawling gardens spanned the rear of the three sections. Mamallar and his queen consort, Vanamadevi, resided in the central section of the palace. Bhuvana Mahadevi, along with Mahendra Pallavar's other two wives, lived in the palace to the right. The prince of Lanka and his wife stayed in the palace to the left, which usually housed important state visitors.

Bhuvana Mahadevi had promised Sembian Vallavan, that she would look after his daughter as if she were her own and she had kept her word in letter and in spirit. No matter where she was, whether at the palace or visiting monasteries and temples, Mangayarkkarasi was always by her side.

Bhuvana Mahadevi, like her renowned husband Mahendra Pallavar, was an ardent devotee of Lord Shiva. After the demise of Mahendra Pallavar, she spent her time praying to Lord Shiva and reading the *Shivapuranam*. A Shiva lingam had been consecrated in her palace and ceremonial prayers as prescribed by the scriptures were performed every day.

Mangayarkkarasi had implored for and secured the right to make the necessary arrangements to be of service at the daily prayer ceremony. She carried out these tasks conscientiously. Mangayarkkarasi found these prayer-related tasks a useful way to spend time at a palace where she knew no one.

For three days after Mamallar had left on the expedition accompanied by his army, all the routine tasks were carried out in an orderly manner. Bhuvana Mahadevi and Mangayarkkarasi had met Thirunavukkarasar on the fourth day. Since then, Mangayarkkarasi was distracted. When the devi was performing the Shivapujai, Mangayarkkarasi handed her incense when she asked for flowers, and prasadam when she asked for incense. Observing this, Bhuvana Mahadevi comforted her saying, 'My child, why do you seem disturbed today? Are you worried about your father? Look at me, my child! I am at peace despite sending my only son to the battlefield.'

An embarrassed Mangayarkkarasi responded, 'No, amma! I am not worried!'

'Then why do you appear pensive? Is there anything in this palace that is troubling you?' asked Mahendrar's wife.

'Trouble! I did not live so comfortably even in my father's house. Nor am I disturbed by anything. Didn't a young man walk in when you were conversing with Navukkarasar Peruman? I recollect seeing him once before. I recollected certain incidents relating to this. There is nothing else worrying me,' insisted Mangayarkkarasi.

Chapter 16

Palace Garden

A week had passed since Mangayarkkarasi had seen Kulachirayar at Thirunavukkarasar's monastery. That one week had seemed like an eon to Sembian Vallavan's daughter. The palace was abuzz with the news of the Pandya prince's imminent arrival. Though Mangayarkkarasi did not feel any excitement regarding Nedumara Pandian's arrival, she was keen to meet the youth she had seen at the monastery so that she could enquire about his friend.

Mangayarkkarasi often recollected an incident that had occurred two years ago during the monsoon season, when it was raining incessantly. That day, the Pandya youth and his friend, drenched to the skin in the heavy rain, had arrived at Sembian Vallavan's palace and asked for permission to stay there for the night. Sembian Vallavan, who was renowned for his hospitality, welcomed them warmly and attended to them. The two youthful visitors claimed to be traders and were jovial. Laughter resonated across the ancient Chola palace for a long time that day.

Mangayarkkarasi's father told her in private, 'They claim to be traders but that's a white lie. Listen! They are aristocrats in disguise!' This made Mangayarkkarasi happy, as one of the youths had captivated her heart.

The two youths left the following day at dawn. But, before leaving, Kulachirai's friend promised to return one day, and also communicated more to Mangayarkkarasi through his eyes. For the next few days, father and daughter often recalled that incident. Then they dismissed it as just a dream. The handsome man who had then captivated Mangayarkkarasi now often appeared in her nightmares. So, it was not surprising that the maiden, who missed her parents' loving care, was extremely agitated.

A week later, the Kanchi palace was agog with excitement. Mangayarkkarasi came to know that Nedumara Pandian, accompanied by his retinue, had arrived in Kanchi. People said that he was staying at Vanamadevi's palace and had not completely recovered. But Mangayarkkarasi was more interested in meeting Kulachirai in private to enquire about his friend.

Bhuvana Mahadevi would send her daughter-in-law prasadam every day after completing the Shivapujai. Mangayarkkarasi offered to deliver the prasadam. Though Mangayarkkarasi's eyes scanned the palace thoroughly, she was unable to trace that youth. One day, she mustered up courage and asked, 'Amma, hasn't the youth whom we saw at the monastery the other day accompanied the Pandya prince?'

When Bhuvana Mahadevi responded saying, 'What can I say, my child! The Pandya prince's condition is worrying—' Mangayarkkarasi interrupted saying, 'Oh no! Hasn't he recovered as yet? That's why Vanamadevi appears worried all the time. Previously, whenever I took the Shivapujai prasadam to her, she would receive it with a smiling face and speak to me affectionately. Now she doesn't utter a word!'

'Yes, my child! There are several issues worrying Vanamadevi. Nedumaran has physically recovered, but the Samanars have poisoned his mind. The Pandya army, renowned for its bravery, has accompanied him. That army has been made to camp at Thirukazhukunram. I heard that the prince of Lanka and Kulachirai, whom we met the other day, are at Thirukazhukunram. My child! I pray to Lord Shiva day and night that no disaster should occur. Vanamadevi's burden is heavier. Poor thing! It seems that she has not slept for a week!' lamented Mahendra Pallavar's consort.

Mangayarkkarasi could not completely understand the possible danger in the Pandya prince's visit and why everyone was so worried. Neither did she pay much attention to this. It was only thoughts of her love interest that weighed heavily on her. She was worried that she might not be able to meet Kulachirai and enquire about his friend. This worry rendered her incapable of thinking about anything else.

It was in this state of mind that Mangayarkkarasi was plucking flowers in the palace garden one evening for Bhuvana Mahadevi's Shivapujai. Amongst the flowers she plucked and collected in her flower basket were panneer, mandarai, ponnarali, chevvarali, sampangi and malli. But her mind dwelt on one of the two youths who had visited her father's ancient palace one rainy evening and stolen her heart. It seemed that his promise to return and meet her was akin to words written on water! 'My sole companion in this world, my father, has headed to the battlefield. What will become of me now?' Tears welled up in Mangayarkkarasi's eyes.

Just then, the plants and creepers rustled as though someone was walking amidst them. Mangayarkkarasi looked in the direction from which the noise came. Yes, a man was indeed walking amidst the plants and creepers in that lush green garden. But his face was not visible. Who could he be, casually strolling around the anthapuram garden? Mangayarkkarasi had heard that all men, except Mamalla chakravarthy, were forbidden to enter here. Only women were appointed to water and tend to the plants. Given this, who was the stranger who had boldly entered the garden? Mangayarkkarasi decided that, irrespective of who it was, she ought to return to Bhuvana Mahadevi's palace. She quickly started walking towards the palace.

It was then that she heard someone saying, 'Amma, who are you? I unwittingly entered this garden. I don't know the way back. Please tell me how to go to Vanamadevi's palace?'

Mangayarkkarasi trembled on hearing that voice. It seemed as though the ground beneath her feet had suddenly slipped away. She felt as though all the plants and creepers in that garden were revolving around her. She managed not to fall down by holding on to the branches of the mandarai tree close by. The silver flower basket she was holding in her right hand fell and the multi-hued flowers in that basket lay scattered on the ground.

'Oh! Did I scare you? Please do not mistake me. I asked because I truly don't know the way back. I don't belong to this place; I'm a native of Pandya Nadu. It will suffice if you tell me the direction in which Vanamadevi's palace is; then, I will go away. As there was no one else in this garden, I had no option but to ask you. I don't even know who you are.' As the man spoke thus, Mangayarkkarasi regained courage. She let go of the branch she was holding and looked around. Her hunch was right. It was indeed he! It was the same person who had come as a guest to her father's palace one rainy night and had stolen her heart!

The Pandya prince was far more shocked than Mangayarkkarasi. He stood speechless and was only able to exclaim, 'Ah!' Both of them were surprised and stood staring at each other eagerly for some time, resembling the statues sculpted by a skilful sculptor. Finally, the Pandya prince asked in a voice choked with emotion and surprise, 'My lady! Is it truly you? Aren't you Sembian Vallavan's daughter, Mangayarkkarasi? Or am I fantasizing this too?'

Mangayarkkarasi wanted to respond but was unable to. Tears filled her eyes.

The Pandya prince eagerly walked towards her and asked agitatedly, 'My lady! What is this? Why are you crying? Did I say something wrong? What did I do?'

Mangayarkkarasi replied, sobbing, 'Aiyya, I am the unfortunate Mangayarkkarasi!'

'Why do you sound so dejected? Why are you shedding tears? Words cannot express the happiness I felt when I saw you here unexpectedly. I felt as joyful as a man who has been blind since birth regaining his vision. I, who had been so confused and worried, forgot everything else and felt so ecstatic on seeing you! But your sobbing and weeping have dampened my happiness and make me sad. What is the sorrow that befell you? Why do you claim to be unfortunate? Have I in any way been the reason for your sorrow and misfortune? As it is, I am subject to great torment and troubles. In addition to all this, if I have troubled you, what's the use in my living? I feel like giving up my life.'

When Nedumaran spoke thus with genuine feeling, the helpless Mangayarkkarasi wished to interrupt him several times. As she was not courageous enough to do so, she stood sobbing. However, when Nedumaran finally spoke about giving up his life, she somehow mustered up courage and blurted, 'Aiyya! You caused me no harm!'

'If so, why did you sob and weep when you saw me? For the last two years, I have been yearning to see you again. I used to derive joy imagining how on, seeing me again happiness would cause your face to blossom like a white lotus at sunrise. But contrary to my thoughts, your face wilted like a lotus at dusk. Why were your eyes also filled with tears?'

Without responding to the Pandya prince, Mangayarkkarasi asked, 'Aiyya, are you stating the truth? Haven't you forgotten me completely? Did you intend meeting me again?'

Nedumaran stated, 'Why do you doubt that? I was eagerly awaiting the opportunity to meet you again. That opportunity did arise. While coming to this place from Madurai, I visited the palace of Sembian Vallavan, who had offered me refuge one rainy night. I felt extremely disappointed seeing the palace locked. I felt as though the entire world was steeped in darkness. When Kulachirai told me that he had seen you here, I was at peace again.'

'Ah! Did he tell you? In that case, are you also employed by the Pandya prince?' asked Mangayarkkarasi.

A mysterious smile appeared for a moment on Nedumaran's face and then disappeared. It was then that he realized that Mangayarkkarasi was speaking to him without realizing who he was. He wanted to prolong her misconception. 'Yes! I too am employed by the Pandya prince. Do you object to that?' he asked.

Mangayarkkarasi replied enthusiastically, 'Why should I object? I will be happy if you occupy a senior post. I thought as much when I saw your friend at Thirunavukkarasar's monastery. But why dwell on the past? Hasn't my family deity brought you to me?'

Nedumaran responded with a mischievous smile, 'Nevertheless, you did not show any signs of happiness when your God brought me to your presence! Didn't you call yourself unfortunate and shed tears?'

'Swami, when I saw you unexpectedly, I stood stupefied and was unable to speak. When you spoke as though you did not recognize me, I felt like crying! Don't mock my helplessness!' When Mangayarkkarasi uttered these words, tears welled up in her eyes again.

'My dear! Please forgive me! I am so unthinking that I have made you cry again!' As Nedumaran spoke thus, he wiped away her tears with the edge of his angavastram.

After waiting for some time, Mangayarkkarasi remarked, 'Swami, a long time has passed. Soon it will be the time for prayer; I must go.'

'Do you have to go?' asked Nedumaran reluctantly.

'Yes, I do. Bhuvana Mahadevi will be waiting. If I don't return, she may send a lady-in-waiting in search of me.'

'In that case, you must come here tomorrow at the same time; you must not fail to do so. We have not discussed what we ought to do next,' urged Nedumaran.

Mangayarkkarasi looked up with a shocked expression and asked, 'If the Pandya prince leaves for the Vatapi war, will you accompany him?'

'Yes. I too will have to go. Why do you ask? Don't you want me to go to the warfront?' asked Nedumaran.

'No, I don't want you to go. I don't like the very idea of war. Why should men hate each other? Why should they kill each other? Why is it not possible to live happily and companionably?' declared Mangayarkkarasi.

Nedumaran smiled mysteriously again and quipped, 'I will convey your views on war to the Pandya prince. He may change his mind. You must definitely come here tomorrow evening to ascertain the outcome. Will you?'

'I will definitely come. It's late now, I must go.' So saying, Mangayarkkarasi bent down to pick up the flower basket that lay on the ground. Nedumaran too bent down, picked up the flowers that lay scattered, put them in the basket and returned it to Mangayarkkarasi. When he did so, he held her tender hands and touched his eyes with them, as one would do with flowers offered to God. Mangayarkkarasi, who felt goosebumps, extricated her hands from Nedumaran's grip and walked hurriedly towards Bhuvana Mahadevi's palace.

Chapter 17

Sleepless Night

Ever since Mangayarkkarasi had returned to Bhuvana Mahadevi's palace from the garden that evening, she had been delirious with happiness. An event she had not anticipated had occurred. She had never even dreamt that she would be so fortunate. She had felt that there was a void in her life after her father headed to the battlefield. There was only one incident that could fill the void and make her life joyful. That miracle had occurred that day. Her lover, who had captivated her life and soul, had gained entry to the inaccessible Pallava palace. Not only had he met her, but he had also declared his steadfast and undying love for her.

What else could make her so happy? Is it surprising that her feet no longer touched the ground and that she danced as she walked? While she was eager to confide in someone about this wondrous incident, she did not know whom to talk to. If she were to confide in someone, it would have to be Bhuvana Mahadevi, who showered so much love on her

and regarded Mangayarkkarasi as her own daughter. But
that evening, Bhuvana Mahadevi's expression and behaviour
were unusual. Mangayarkkarasi realized that it was not the
opportune moment to talk to her. During the Shivapujai,
the devi's characteristic smile and tranquillity were missing.
She even spoke to Mangayarkkarasi curtly a couple of times,
without reason. On any other day, Mangayarkkarasi would
have felt hurt at the devi's brusqueness. But on that day,
Mangayarkkarasi did not mind it. Her sole concern was that
she was unable to share her joy with the devi.

One-and-a-half jaamam after night had set in,
Mangayarkkarasi went to bed as usual in the chamber
allotted to her, which was adjacent to Bhuvana Mahadevi's.
But sleep evaded her; her eyelids refused to close. That night,
Mangayarkkarasi realized that not just sorrow and worry but
also unanticipated happiness and fervour could disrupt sleep.
After some time, she stopped trying to go to sleep and started
fantasizing about her future.

By then, the second jaamam of the night had passed and
the third jaamam had set in. Mangayarkkarasi was taken aback
when she heard a noise that shattered the pin-drop silence
that prevailed in the palace. It was only a slight noise—the
noise of a door opening. Nevertheless, Mangayarkkarasi felt
an incomprehensible fear on hearing that noise at that time
of the night.

The faint sound of footsteps from the portico outside
her room attracted her attention. Who was it who dared to
walk so close to Bhuvana Mahadevi's chamber at that time of
the night? Gripped by an inexplicable fear, Mangayarkkarasi
sat up. It seemed as though the sound of the footsteps was
becoming louder, and that they were approaching her chamber.
She was eager to know who it was. She stood up noiselessly,

walked up to the window in her chamber that was close to the portico and stood there, hiding herself from outside view. The very next instant, her curiosity was satiated. Two people were walking down the corridor. A lady-in-waiting holding a torch was followed by Vanamadevi. Yes! It was Vanamadevi. But why was she ashen-faced, as though she was possessed by a ghost?

After the duo had walked past Mangayarkkarasi's chamber, an open door in that very portico caught her attention. Ever since she had arrived at the palace, she had not seen that door ajar. She had heard that it led to a tunnel which connected Vanamadevi's palace to this palace. Vanamadevi must have come through that tunnel! Why had she come so secretively in the middle of the night?

Mangayarkkarasi understood the purpose of their visit the very next moment. The two visitors came to a halt outside Bhuvana Mahadevi's chamber. The lady-in-waiting knocked lightly on the door. A voice from inside asked, 'Who is it?'

'It's me, amma!' answered Vanamadevi.

'Coming!' announced the voice from inside, and the next instant the door opened. Asking the lady-in-waiting to wait outside, Vanamadevi went in.

Observing Vanamadevi's pallid, fear-stricken face, worry and fear gripped Mangayarkkarasi. Why had the Pallava chakravarthini's lustrous face, which resembled a full moon, changed in this manner within four days? What was the looming danger that caused her so much worry and fear? Hadn't Vanamadevi remained courageous and spirited even after the chakravarthy had left for the battlefield? Mangayarkkarasi had been impressed with Vanamadevi's behaviour. What was the danger that was about to befall Vanamadevi that had caused such a transformation? Would that danger affect only

Vanamadevi? Or would it cast a shadow on all the palace inmates too?

The innocent Mangayarkkarasi did not believe that it was wrong to eavesdrop and thus resolve her doubts. So, she stood close to the door that connected Bhuvana Mahadevi's chamber to hers and overheard the conversation between the mother-in-law and daughter-in-law. The very beginning of the conversation instilled a fear that she had never felt before and made her tremble. As the conversation progressed, she felt indescribable shock and fear. Sometimes she felt a rush of blood, and at other times she felt that her heart would stop beating. The conversation that caused the helpless girl so much dismay was as follows.

'Amma! Were you asleep?'

'My daughter! How could I have slept after you sent word? I was awaiting your arrival. But this is mysterious. Why did you come in the middle of the night? Why are you looking so pale? Poor you! It looks as if you have not slept for several days.'

'Yes, amma! Sleep has evaded me since the day Nedumaran arrived here. Thaye! Is there someone in the adjacent chamber? Is it possible for someone to overhear our conversation?'

'Why this fear, my daughter? So what if someone hears? Whom do you fear? Who should the chakravarthini of the Pallava kingdom, daughter-in-law of Shatrumallar and Mamallar's queen consort fear thus?'

'Do you ask who I fear, amma? I fear each and every employee and lady-in-waiting in our palace.'

'In that case what about the lady whom you brought along?'

'I brought her along because she is mute!'

'Why do you speak thus? What is the necessity of fearing even your ladies-in-waiting? How can you, who were born in the valorous Pandya dynasty and wedded into the heroic Pallava dynasty, be subject to fear? Isn't this ignominious?'

'Amma, this is a shame only to the Pandya dynasty and not to the Pallava dynasty. I came to know that a lady-in-waiting in my palace has been acting as a messenger between the Samanars and Nedumaran. Paying heed to the message she carried, Nedumaran attended a secret caucus of Samana siddhars yesterday, in the middle of the night.'

'My daughter, this is shocking! Are the Samanars still up to their tricks in Kanchi?'

'Yes, thaye! The Samana siddhars followed Nedumaran to Kanchi. You will be horrified if you hear of the incidents that occurred there during the time of Nedumaran's visit!'

'What happened, my daughter?'

'They are resorting to black magic to confuse Nedumaran. Poor man! Nedumaran has been completely brainwashed!'

'But what do the Samanars seek to achieve?'

'Apparently, they hypnotized a boy, claimed that he was endowed with clairvoyance, and asked him to look into the future. It seems he foresaw your son becoming envious of Nedumaran after winning the Vatapi war and killing him with a dagger!'

'Aiyyo! How cruel! Then . . .?'

'But the Samana siddhars claimed that they had the power to change what fate held in store. They also promised to crown Nedumaran the undisputed chakravarthy of the southern country at the city of Kanchi itself, should he conform to their wishes!' 'How did you come to know of all this, my daughter?'

'It seems that the chief of our espionage force, Shatrugnan, had hidden himself and observed everything.'

'Ah! The Samanars are looking for the right opportunity to seek revenge on Mahendra Pallavar!'

'Amma, apparently, they are not genuine Samanars! Vatapi spies, disguised as Samanars, are performing black magic!'

'In that case, why were they not imprisoned immediately?'

'Shatrugnan is scared that it may be dangerous to imprison them. He is concerned that Nedumaran may order the Pandya army to gain control of Kanchi, and disaster may ensue.'

'What is Shatrugnan's advice?'

'He is unable to suggest a way out, thaye! He advised that the chakravarthy ought to be informed immediately. But before my lord left for the battlefield, I had given him my word and I will definitely fulfil it. I came to secure your consent.'

'Is that so? What did you promise Mamallan?'

'I promised him that if any danger were to arise on account of Nedumaran, I myself would administer poison to him, or stab him with a dagger.'

'Ah! How sinful! How can my son leave after making you shoulder such a heavy burden?'

'Amma, he entrusted me with this task before he left. I will justify his faith in me!'

'My child, give me time till tomorrow evening. I will convey my opinion to you.'

'Amma, who is in the adjoining chamber? I think I heard a noise.'

'You don't have to be suspicious about this palace. No one here is treacherous.'

'Is that what you think? You will be surprised when you hear about what transpired this evening.'

'What happened in the evening?'

'Nedumaran left the palace, saying that he would return after strolling in the garden. As he did not return even after a long time had passed, I became suspicious. I went in search of him. At one spot in the garden where there is a dense growth of plants, Nedumaran and a girl were surreptitiously conversing. Do you know who that girl is?'

'Who?'

'That girl from Chola Nadu whom you have so affectionately adopted and taken under your wing!'

'What? Was it Mangayarkkarasi?'

'Yes, thaye! It was indeed Mangayarkkarasi!'

'My daughter! I will believe whatever you have to say about anyone else. But I will never ever suspect Mangayarkkarasi.'

'But I saw this with my own eyes, amma!'

'What did you see? You saw them both talking? That's all, isn't it? She had gone to collect flowers for the prayer. Coincidentally Nedumaran must have reached there and enquired about something. She was saying that she needed to enquire about a youth in Pandya Nadu ...'

'Their actions aroused suspicion, amma!'

'In your current state of mind, it is but natural that you're suspicious about everything.'

'Let me take your leave, amma. After confiding in you, my burden seems lighter!'

'Farewell, my child! By the grace of Goddess Meenakshi, may you feel no burden at all.'

After this conversation, the sound of a door being opened and shut was heard. Deep silence descended on the palace.

Mangayarkkarasi, who had heard the entire conversation standing still like a portrait by the door, did not sleep a wink that night. She was able to unravel many of the mysteries that had confounded her previously. She felt limitless joy and wonder when she discovered that her lover was the Pandya prince. She began to understand the meaning of the dreams she had often had about him. She feared and fretted about the peril that was about to befall him in that palace. She realized that she was the fortunate one who was responsible for rescuing him. Assailed by such thoughts, she was unable to sleep that night.

The following evening, she went to the garden slightly earlier than the agreed time. As soon as Nedumaran arrived, she cried out in agitation, 'Prabhu! Great danger awaits you at this palace. Leave this place immediately!'

Nedumaran, slightly surprised, asked, 'What are you saying? Am I in great danger? Who would want to harm this impoverished man?'

'Swami, don't think you can continue to mislead me. I have come to know that you are the Pandya prince. You are truly in great danger. Leave this palace immediately!' cried Mangayarkkarasi.

Chapter 18

Sister and Brother

That day, after sunset, Vanamadevi was searching for something amongst the gold and silver casks in the chamber where her priceless ornaments were stored. Suddenly she heard someone call out, 'Akka! What are you searching for?'

Aghast, she looked around. Unknown to her, Nedumaran had noiselessly entered the chamber. Vanamadevi's surprise heightened on seeing him. Nedumaran again asked, 'Akka, what are you searching for?' and then looked around.

Vanamadevi struggled to respond. She then enquired, 'Thambi, when did you come here?'

'I came here a short while ago. I came to ask if you were searching for this dagger!' As he spoke, he extended a small dagger that he had hidden behind him.

Vanamadevi stood staring at that dagger. Beads of sweat broke out on her face.

'Akka, if you have decided to stab me to death, please take this dagger and accomplish the task right away! It does not behove you, who were born in the brave Pandya dynasty and wedded into the valorous Pallava dynasty, to stab your dear brother in his sleep. It would be a slur on both the Pandyas and the Pallavas!'

Words cannot describe the agony Vanamadevi felt when she heard Nedumaran's speech, which was tinged with sarcasm and pity. Feelings of shame and anger gnawed her. Despite trying hard, she was unable to speak.

Nedumaran continued. 'Alternately, if you wish to kill me by administering poison, make sure that the poison is effective. I gave the poison you had secured with great difficulty to the fawn that frolics around the palace garden. It showed no signs of dying. It played more energetically than earlier!'

Every word that Nedumaran uttered pierced Vanamadevi's heart like a poisoned arrow. Unable to bear the torment, she stammered, 'Thambi! Why do you speak thus? Why would I kill you . . .'

'Akka, have you learnt to lie and be deceitful after marrying into the Pallava dynasty? Did Bhuvana Mahadevi suggest this when you went to seek her counsel last night?' asked Nedumaran.

Vanamadevi now found the pretext to express her fury. She shot back harshly, 'What I suspected is true. Wasn't it the maiden from Chola Nadu who told you all this?'

'Don't direct your anger towards that innocent girl, akka! She does not deserve it. It is true she divulged this to me some time ago. But this dagger was not lost today. Weren't you searching for it for the last two days?'

Vanamadevi again stood stunned for some time and then blurted, 'It seems that there is nothing that the Samana siddhars cannot get to know.'

'But mystic powers are not necessary to understand your innermost thoughts. It seems that Valluvar Peruman had you in mind when he composed the couplet:

The object near the mirror reflects
And the mind's travails the face reveals

'Your face revealed your intentions to me. Moreover, I was not born blind or deaf. My eyes and ears have been alert ever since I arrived at this palace. I observed that you had fastened this dagger perpetually to your waist. You absentmindedly placed it on the floor once. I did not find it difficult to appropriate the dagger then . . .'

'Ah! I am so stupid!' muttered Vanamadevi.

'You're not stupid, akka! But you were unable to bring yourself to perform this task. That's why you were walking around in a daze, unable to hide your emotions! . . . Ah! Ten years ago, when both of us lived in the Madurai palace, you showered so much affection on me. I feel such happiness when I recollect those days. My mother died when I was a child. Then, the junior queen's words were law in the palace. To me, who had not known a mother's love, you were both a sister and mother. For a long time, I used to think that you were my own sister. It was only during your wedding that I came to know that you were my half-sister.'

Vanamadevi wept copiously. 'Nedumara! Why do you remind me of all that?' she sobbed.

'How did you, who were so affectionate, acquire such a cruel bent of mind? How did you muster the courage to try and kill me by stabbing me or by administering poison?' asked Nedumaran.

'Thambi! Please forgive me. When he left for the battlefield, he handed the responsibility of running this household to me. He cautioned me that danger might arise because of you. I promised him that I would ensure that you caused no harm. But when I promised him, I did not imagine even in my wildest dreams that you would be so treacherous!' blurted Vanamadevi and wept again.

'Akka, I cannot bear to see you shed tears. I cannot understand what treachery I have committed. I also do not know what you promised your husband. If you have promised him that you will kill me, don't worry—I am ready to bare my chest; you can fulfil your vow!' So saying, Nedumaran extended the dagger to Vanamadevi and also bared his chest.

'Thambi, why are you mocking me when I'm already overcome by great sorrow? Tell me why you have come here,' asked the chakravarthini.

'Akka, I'm not mocking you; I'm stating the truth. I feel so proud of you. It is only expected that a woman born in the Pandya dynasty will be devoted to her husband. Didn't the deity of the Pandya dynasty, Meenakshi devi, disregard her father Dakshan and live under the shadow of Shiva Peruman? Should the clan of her birth cause her husband harm, it's customary for a Pandya woman to act with her husband's interests in mind. But what harm did you suspect I would cause? How did I become the object of your hatred? Please divulge that before you stab me!'

'Thambi, why do you compel me to disclose that? Didn't you conspire to capture the city of Kanchi and the Pallava throne, aided by the army that has accompanied you?'

'Why did you suspect me of such treacherous thoughts? Who told you, akka?!'

'Who has to tell me? Your expressions, behaviour and speech aroused suspicion. You mentioned that you were not sure if you would go to Vatapi. You declared that if you were given refuge, you would live in this palace permanently. You were always immersed in deep thought. Not only this, you attended a caucus of Samana siddhars in the middle of the night. The fact that you were trapped by the Samana siddhars' ruses gives enough room for suspicion.'

'Akka, don't blame the Samanars unnecessarily. It is true that they revealed certain future occurrences. But the conclusion I drew from those predictions is is diametrically opposite to what you're thinking. I did not think of capturing Mamalla chakravarthy's capital city and his kingdom during his absence. Ever since I arrived at this palace, I have been thinking of abdicating the Pandya throne, which by right is mine, renouncing this world and becoming a Digambara Samanar ...'

'Thambi! Why this disastrous thought?' asked a shocked Vanamadevi.

'What do you term as a disastrous thought, akka? Is it disastrous to assume the responsibility of ruling a kingdom and transform humankind that is endowed with a sixth sense into tigers and jackals and cause lakhs of people to kill each other? Or is it disastrous to embrace the religion of kindness and ensure that not even the most minute of living organisms is harmed?'

'Thambi, you are well-educated. I do not have the wherewithal to engage in a philosophical debate with you. Nevertheless, I do think that your becoming a Samana monk is a disastrous idea. The very thought of such an occurrence is disturbing!'

'You would rather kill me. But you find the idea of my becoming a Samana monk unpalatable! Never mind, don't worry. I will not become a Digambara Samana monk. I gave up that idea last evening itself . . .'

'Then what do you intend doing, thambi?' asked the Pallava chakravarthini eagerly.

'I am returning to Madurai tomorrow, akka! If you don't want me to take the trouble of going to Madurai . . .' So saying, he extended the dagger in his hand again.

Vanamadevi grabbed the dagger and flung it away. She then held Nedumaran with both her hands and pleaded with tear-filled eyes and a choked voice, 'Nedumara! Don't punish this mad woman anymore; don't bring up that subject again! It was a blunder to have suspected you, please forgive me!'

'I, who caused you so much turmoil, am the one who ought to seek your forgiveness. Please forgive me and bless me, akka!' implored Nedumaran.

'By God's grace, may you be blessed with all fortunes. May you soon get married to a suitable wife and rule the Pandya kingdom for a long time . . .'

'Akka, I came to Kanchi only after choosing a suitable bride. I tarried here for so long only to meet her. I attained clarity only after speaking to her in your palace garden last evening. If your blessing comes true and I ascend the Pandya throne, that maiden will be my queen consort!' confessed Nedumaran.

Chapter 19

Mother's Blessing

The following day, Nedumara Pandian visited Bhuvana Mahadevi's palace to take her leave. Mahendra Pallavar's queen consort welcomed him warmly, with a smiling face.

When Mangayarkkarasi, who was present there, was about to leave, Bhuvana Mahadevi stopped her, remarking, 'My child, why are you going? There is no confidential matter I wish to discuss with the Pandya kumaran.' Then she asked Nedumaran to sit down and observed, 'Appane, I am aware of all that transpired. Vanamadevi visited me last night itself and told me everything. Nevertheless, you caused great turmoil to that virtuous woman!' Observing Nedumaran's silence, Bhuvana Mahadevi continued, 'Your coming to Kanchi proved to be a blessing to me. I had promised this maiden's father that I would get her married to a suitable groom. The two of you made it unnecessary for me to search for a groom. Now, my responsibility in this regard is over.'

'Thaye! Please don't speak thus. Your responsibility for your adopted daughter's marriage is not yet over. There is still scope for you to play a role. Please ask Mangayarkkarasi if she will wed me and absolve you of your responsibility.'

When Nedumaran spoke thus, Bhuvana Mahadevi looked around saying, 'Why should I ask her again? She has already told me everything.' Bhuvana Mahadevi was taken aback to see Mangayarkkarasi's tear-filled eyes. She asked Nedumaran, 'What is this? Have you two children fought so soon?'

'It's not a mere fight but a war, amma! War has broken out in this palace because I have not proceeded to the Vatapi war. After driving me crazy and creating a situation that almost necessitated my sister poisoning me, she now refuses to marry me! Ask her if this is fair!' implored Nedumaran.

Bhuvana Mahadevi looked at Mangayarkkarasi. She understood that the two had brought upon themselves some trivial obstacles. 'My child, is the Pandya kumaran stating the truth? Are you rejecting the immense good fortune that has sought you out?' she asked.

Mangayarkkarasi sobbed as she prostrated before Bhuvana Mahadevi. 'Amma! When I lost my heart to him and regarded him as my husband, I was not aware that he was a Samana ...' Unable to speak further, she sobbed.

Nedumaran felt extremely worried, thinking, 'What is this? This is an unintended consequence of my action.'

Bhuvana Mahadevi enquired, 'Appane, this child was born in a Saivite clan. Aren't you aware that she worships Shiva Peruman and Parvati? You wouldn't object to that, would you?'

Nedumaran, who realized that this was an opportunity to extricate himself from a tricky situation, happily responded, 'Amma, I am not such a fanatic! Though I am attached to the Samana faith, I do not detest Saivism. My dear friend Kulachirai is an ardent devotee of Lord Shiva. When I was suffering from high fever, he came to Kanchi, obtained vibhuti from Navukkarasar Peruman and applied it on me. I did not object to that. At Madurai, he used to visit the temple thrice a day for the darisanam of Meenakshi Amman and Sundareshwara Peruman. She may follow suit, I will not object!'

Only then did Mangayarkkarasi's face glow like it had earlier.

Bhuvana Mahadevi made the remarkable couple stand in front of her and blessed them. After discussing what needed to be done next for the two of them, Nedumaran took leave and left. Bhuvana Mahadevi affectionately embraced Mangayarkkarasi and blessed her, saying, 'My child, don't worry! Didn't you relate to me the dream that often occurred to you? Your dream will definitely come true. Nedumaran will become an ardent devotee of Lord Shiva. The fruit of that good deed will accrue to you!'

Bhuvana Mahadevi's prediction about Nedumaran came entirely true. Years later, by the grace of Sri Sambanda Peruman,[11] he became a zealous follower of Lord Shiva. His views on war also changed. Twenty-five years later, when Pulikesi's son, Vikramadityan, invaded the southern country and advanced up to Pandya Nadu, Nedumaran vanquished him at the Battle of Nelveli and secured an indelible place in the history of Tamizhagam.

---

[11] A Saivite saint, one of the 108 Nayanmars.

Chapter 20

Moonlight Tête-à-Tête

Just the previous night, the banks of the North Pennai River had presented a wonderful sight when the full moon, floating in the firmament, showered its milky-white glow on the waterway, transforming the area into a dream world. One could hear the sonorous sound of water flowing and observe the entire region shining like liquid silver. Then the entire region had been tranquil. Those admiring this scene would have wondered if they had been transported to heaven to experience such joy.

But tonight, chaos prevailed on the banks of the North Pennai River. Innumerable elephants, horses, chariots and carts were crossing the waters. The golden ornaments adorning the elephants, the silver trimmings fitted to their tusks, the various jewels that embellished the naturally statuesque horses and the chariots' canopies plated with gold shone in the moonlight. When several rows of elephants and horses crossed the water at the same time, the resultant turbulence was akin to the lashing of waves in an ocean during a cyclone.

On one bank, the camp housing the infantry extended up to the horizon. The glimmer of the sharp spears the warriors held blinded one's eyes. The fluttering of thousands of Rishabha flags hoisted in that army camp could be heard. On the opposite bank, close to the river pier, stood a solitary tent. Four people seated on the ornate carpet spread on the grass by the tent were in conversation. Ten to twelve warriors armed with sharp spears and swords fastened to their waists were standing alert a short distance away from the quartet. The four were Mamalla chakravarthy, Senathipathi Paranjyothi, the king of Vengi, Aditya Varman and the chief of the spies, Shatrugnan.

The king of Vengi was Mamallar's cousin, an offspring of Simha Vishnu Maharaja's brother. That clan ruled the region to the north of the Godavari River as an independent vassal of the Pallavas. When the Chalukya emperor had invaded Kanchi, his brother Vishnuvardhanan had prevented Aditya Varman from coming to the Pallava chakravarthy's aid. Vishnuvardhanan had decimated Vengi's ruling dynasty and ascended the throne. But Vishnuvardhanan had breathed his last before Pulikesi returned to Vatapi after abruptly ending his southern expedition. The person responsible for cutting short Vishnuvardhanan's reign and life was Aditya Varman. But, a few years later, when Pulikesi had invaded Vengi leading a large army, Aditya Varman retreated to the south with whatever was left of his army and was waiting for an opportune time since. When Mamallar decided to invade Vatapi with a gargantuan army, Aditya Varman joined hands with him.

Senathipathi Paranjyothi was relating in detail his shock on seeing the massive Vatapi army on the banks of this very North Pennai River and how a disguised Mahendra Pallavar had pursued and rescued him from under the very nose of Pulikesi. The other three were listening to him with wonder. Aditya Varman was the most surprised of the three. All this information was new to him. He remarked with regret, 'Ah! I was not fortunate enough to meet that Vichitra Siddhar!'

Then Mamallar remarked, 'The prince of Lanka also rues this. I'm not boasting because he is my father, but one had to be fortunate to have even seen him. One must have committed good deeds for several births to have moved closely with him. He took me along and travelled across the southern country for three years. On moonlit nights like this, the two of us used to spend time joyfully, outside in the open. He used to take his parivadhini veenai along during his voyages. Even nature appeared to come to a standstill and listen to him when he played the veenai.'

'Anna, please stop! If you speak thus, I will lose my resolve. I feel that war and bloodshed are futile and that I would prefer to play the veenai and live my life joyfully!' remarked Aditya Varman.

Mamallar laughed heartily and revealed, 'Once upon a time, Mahendra Varmar too uttered such words. He opined that if kings lost their lust for land, the earth would be like heaven. He declared that wars were futile and that weapons like spears and swords ought not to be made. My father often used to say that the blacksmiths' furnaces should produce ploughs for farmers and chisels for sculptors. But he changed his mind completely the day he heard the news of the Chalukyas' impending invasion. The youth who had flung a spear at a mad elephant captivated him more than a thousand sculptors and sixteen thousand workmen . . .!' Speaking thus, Mamallar smiled at Paranjyothi.

'Aren't you referring to the incident that occurred on the day Senathipathi Paranjyothi arrived at Kanchi? I wanted to ask him about it,' remarked Aditya Varman.

'No one managed to win my father's confidence as much as Paranjyothi did. There were times when I felt envious of him. I have even wondered on a few occasions whether my father would overlook me and crown our senathipathi. I was prepared for that too. Even today, if our senathipathi consents—'

Senathipathi Paranjyothi interjected. 'Prabhu! Please do not speak in this manner. I do not aspire to rule a kingdom or ascend the throne. I was born in a poor family in a village. I came to Kanchi promising my mother that I would return after educating myself. Twelve years have passed, I haven't fulfilled my word yet. I continue to be illiterate. As soon as this war is over, I will fulfil the promise I made to my mother. If you feel impelled to abdicate the throne in favour of someone else, you may crown the prince of Lanka who is waiting to rule a kingdom!'

Mamallar immediately gestured with his eyes to Aditya Varman and Shatrugnan, both of whom smiled knowingly. Mamallar's immense affection for Manavanman pricked Paranjyothi constantly. Mamallar knew this well. It was the primary reason for his prohibiting Manavanman from participating in the Vatapi war. The expression in his eyes seemed to say, 'Didn't I tell you so?'

He then retorted to Paranjyothi, who sat with his head lowered, 'Well said! Are you asking me to hand over the kingdom that was once ruled by Mahendra Pallavar to that fool? Despite my telling him in no uncertain terms to oversee Kanchi, he is coming. What would be an apposite punishment for him? I'm extremely furious and feel like chasing him back to Lanka. Senathipathi, what's your opinion?'

The senathipathi thought for some time and observed, 'Why do you want to stop someone who's raring to come to the battlefield? Manavanmar's arrival will be beneficial; it will be good if he leads our elephant force.'

'I am somehow not in favour of this. Manavanman has come seeking our assistance and has sought refuge in us. Wouldn't it appear as though we won because of his support?' quipped Mamallar.

Shatrugnan, who had been largely silent till then, observed, 'Chakravarthy! Please do not think that way. You don't require anyone's help to win this war. Your skill in warfare is unparalleled. You will vanquish Vatapi and return victoriously even without the senathipathi and Aditya Varmar. Those who are fortunate to be part of this invasion are blessed. If Manavanmar participates in this expedition, people will never ever attribute your victory to him. It's an unequivocal fact that he will attain a greater stature because of his participation.'

The senathipathi and Aditya Varman wholeheartedly agreed with Shatrugnan.

'Moreover, Manavanmar has trained our elephant force very conscientiously. It's not fair to ask him not to come to the battlefield,' acknowledged the senathipathi.

'I heard that the prince of Lanka has trained the elephants in an ingenious manner. Please tell me about it,' requested Aditya Varman.

'That's true. Previously, we would use the elephants to ram into the fort gates to force them open. During the siege of the Kanchi fort, the old method did not work, thanks to

Mahendra Pallavar's foresight. When the elephants banged their heads against the fort gates fitted with spear tips, they became frenzied and hastily retreated. Now, Manavanmar has trained the elephants to force open the fort gates with iron poles, demolish the ramparts with crowbars and set the interiors of the fort ablaze by flinging illuminated torches.'

'Ah! I have never heard of anyone utilizing an elephant force in this manner till now!' remarked Aditya Varman.

Senathipathi Paranjyothi harboured no personal enmity towards Manavanman. Mamallar's deep affection for him was the reason for his discontentment. So when Mamallar spoke of him disparagingly, Paranjyothi started supporting Manavanman. 'That's why I'm saying it's not fair to send Manavanman back. Wouldn't the person in charge of the training want to lead that very elephant force to war?' asked Senathipathi Paranjyothi.

As they were speaking, the gigantic banyan that stood in the vicinity shook vigorously. Thousands of birds that had sought refuge for the night in the dense branches of that tree took to flight, flapping their wings and chirping noisily. The birds circled the tree and then returned to its branches. 'What happened to that tree suddenly? Did any wild beast climb it? Why are the birds shrieking thus?'

Shatrugnan, who had been staring in the direction of the tree, quipped, 'Prabhu, no wild animal climbed the tree. A domesticated two-legged animal is climbing down the tree!'

When he clapped loudly, one of the soldiers who was standing guard a short distance away, came running. 'Look there! Someone is climbing down that banyan tree. Catch him and produce him here!' commanded Shatrugnan. The soldiers rushed to the banyan tree, grabbed the man who was climbing down and dragged him along.

The leader of the soldiers bowed and announced, 'Prabhu! Here's the Vatapi spy!'

Mamallar and Paranjyothi burst out laughing, because the person whom the soldiers had produced was none other than the famous Gundodharan. 'Gundodhara! What's this? Why did you call yourself a Vatapi spy?' asked Paranjyothi.

'Yes, Senathipathi! I stated the truth! I meant "the spy who has been to Vatapi" when I said, "Vatapi spy". Immediately the soldiers grabbed me and dragged me along. My body still aches from their grip!' he complained.

'Fine. But what were you doing atop the tree? How long have you been sitting there?' asked the chakravarthy.

'Prabhu, I reached here last night itself. When I woke up this morning, I saw our army approaching. I immediately climbed the tree. All this time I have been counting the number of warriors in our army and wondering whether it will be adequate to defeat Pulikesi of Vatapi.'

'What conclusion did you reach? Is this army sufficient?' asked the chakravarthy.

'Swami, I have no doubt about it. But Emperor Pulikesi, who has headed to the Ajantha caves, should return before we reach Vatapi! I am worried about the proposed course of action if he is outside the fort!' announced Gundodharan.

Chapter 21

Pulikesi's Art Enchantment

When Gundodharan mentioned that Pulikesi was not in Vatapi and was headed to Ajantha, the quartet was both overjoyed and surprised. They posed a volley of questions to Gundodharan in unison, 'Is that true?' 'Has he really gone to Ajantha?' 'What work could Pulikesi possibly have in Ajantha?'

Then Mamallar observed, 'If all of us pester Gundodharan thus, how will he be able to respond?'

Gundodharan bowed to the chakravarthy and stated, 'Pallavendra, I will tell you the news I could ascertain for sure. Emperor Pulikesi has gone to Ajantha. Apparently, a Chinese traveller is visiting. I am unable to pronounce his name, people mentioned that his name is Hiuen Tsang. After visiting Kanyakubja, Kashi and Gaya in the north, he arrived in Vatapi. Apparently, he extolled Chakravarthy Harsha's reign at Kanyakubja. To demonstrate that he was in no way inferior to Chakravarthy Harsha, the Vatapi emperor

has personally accompanied that traveller to show him the
wonderful paintings and sculptures in Ajantha! Prabhu!
Apparently, Emperor Pulikesi is extremely fascinated by the
arts these days! It seems that he is carving sculptures out of
all the rocks in Vatapi in an attempt to emulate the sculptures
in Mamallapuram! I myself saw some of the sculptors from
Thondai Mandalam whose limbs were not amputated but
who were imprisoned, working on those rocks. But listen to
this joke. When Pulikesi showed the sculpted rocks to the
Chinese traveller, Hiuen Tsang, he apparently claimed, "It was
only after seeing these sculpted rocks that Mahendra Pallavan
of Kanchi attempted to replicate these at Mamallapuram.
I taught him a lesson and returned!" Do you know how I felt
when I heard this? My blood boiled. The Jayasthambam at
the Vatapi street junction that falsely proclaims that Pulikesi
of Vatapi had defeated Mahendra Pallavar of Kanchi is still
intact. Prabhu! I consoled myself thinking that this monument
would survive only for another three months and returned.
No preparations for war are underway at Vatapi. It seems that
they are not anticipating our invasion! The Vatapi army is
now scattered, with one section stationed on the banks of the
Narmada River in the north and another section at Vengi in
the east.'

When Gundodharan paused, Mamallar remarked to
Paranjyothi, 'Senathipathi, did you see? We ourselves did not
expect Shatrugnan's strategy to work so well!'

Shatrugnan then observed humbly, 'Pallavendra, why
do you call it my strategy? I only executed what you and the
senathipathi together decided!'

Senathipathi Paranjyothi responded to this, saying,
'Shatrugnan is stating the truth! Haven't the three of us learnt

all this from Mahendra Pallavar? If we do win this war, we owe the ensuing glory to Mahendra Pallavar!'

'Senathipathi, I object to your saying "If we do win this war". Why do you doubt our victory? But I don't understand what strategy all of you are referring to, it would be good if you would tell me!' remarked Aditya Varman.

'Well said, thambi! You will realize that Mahendra Varmar's training has stood us in such good stead when you understand the strategy. For the last nine years, when the senathipathi and I were preparing for this invasion, Shatrugnan's espionage force was working very skilfully. Some of our spies, goaded by Shatrugnan, started selling our military secrets to the Vatapi emperor. Initially, they sent facts and won Pulikesi's confidence. Three years ago, they sent a message that stated that the Pallava army was going to invade Vatapi. Believing it, Pulikesi was well prepared. But as the Pallava army did not invade Vatapi, he felt cheated. After being deceived thus for three years, Pulikesi angrily cast aside the old spies. The new spies sent a message saying that there were no plans to invade Vatapi this year and that more soldiers were being recruited into the Pallava army to retrieve Lanka for Manavanman. We came to know that Pulikesi believed this message. We also found out that Pulikesi had split the Chalukya army stationed on the banks of the Tungabhadra River into two and sent one section to the banks of the Narmada River and the second section to Vengi. Now, Gundodharan tells us that Pulikesi himself has headed to Ajantha. Hasn't Shatrugnan's strategy worked?'

Once Mamallar had finished speaking, Aditya Varman pointed out, 'Pallavendra, the prince of Lanka has been of immense help to us in this regard! It is only because of

Manavanman's presence in Kanchi that you were able to mislead Pulikesi!'

'After sending the Pandya kumaran, whom the Samanars had confused, back to Madurai, Manavanmar is fetching the Pandya army to war. This is no mean achievement,' remarked Shatrugnan.

Mamallar retorted harshly, 'Manavanman may have been of great help to us, but I can neither forget nor forgive him for cheating me!'

'Pallavendra! What's this? When did the prince of Lanka cheat you?' asked the senathipathi.

'I had mentioned to him the key reason on account of which he could not accompany us to Vatapi. I had told him that if he were to lose his life on the battlefield, the royal family of Lanka would become issueless. So, I forbade him to accompany us. It is in this matter that Manavanman has cheated me!' revealed the chakravarthy.

'How can he cheat you in this?' asked Aditya Varman.

When Mamallar stated, 'Within a week of our departure, the royal family of Lanka has a progeny! Apparently, Manavanman's wife was ten months pregnant when we left. On the fifth day of our departure, she gave birth to a son. In this matter, even Shatrugnan failed to communicate the truth to me!' Everyone including the senathipathi burst out laughing.

'Oh, now I know what's happening!' blurted Gundodharan.

'What have you discovered now?' asked Mamallar.

'Prabhu! When I was atop that banyan tree, I saw a large cloud of dust in the south. It seemed as though an army was advancing. From your conversation, it is apparent that the prince of Lanka is hastening here with the Pandya army,' stated Gundodharan.

When Mamallar said, 'Oh! Has he already come?' the wide smile on his face was clearly visible in the moonlight. He then asked Paranjyothi, 'Senathipathi! Notwithstanding this, what do you feel? Do you think I should forgive Manavanman's wrongdoing and take him along with us?'

In a voice tinged with hesitation, the senathipathi replied, 'Yes, prabhu! We should take him along!'

Mamallar instructed, 'In that case, the three of you cross the river tonight and make arrangements for the army's accommodation. Gundodharan and I will stay back and bring Manavanman along. There are a few issues about which I need to question Gundodharan.'

The other three, who were astute, immediately boarded the boats waiting for them on the riverbank. After they had left, Mamallar looked pointedly at Gundodharan, who stated softly, 'Pallavendra, I saw Aayanar's daughter in Vatapi, she is doing well. She is awaiting our arrival with bated breath.'

'I'm sure that unfeeling woman's well-being is under no threat. I'm the one who is suffering after losing all peace of mind,' murmured Narasimha Varmar.

Chapter 22

The Pavazhamalli Blossomed

Sivakami's life was physically quite comfortable at the Vatapi palace. But her peripatetic soul knew no peace. Years passed, and so did the seasons. Sivakami devised a method to keep track of the time. In the house where she lived, a pavazhamalli tree grew in the backyard close to the well. Sivakami had herself planted the pavazhamalli creeper close to the well the year she had arrived at Vatapi.

Naganandi adigal, while describing the mountainous province of Ajantha, had mentioned that during the months of Avani and Puraṭṭasi, the innumerable parijatham trees that grew in the region were in full bloom. The gentle breeze would spread the fragrance of these flowers across great distances, pleasantly intoxicating passers-by. Hearing this, Sivakami had requested him to fetch her one of those creepers. According the utmost priority to her desire, the bikshu had fetched a pavazhamalli plant from Ajantha. Sivakami had planted that creeper and tended it carefully.

When shoots appeared on the pavazhamalli creeper, Sivakami's heart skipped a beat. When a new branch developed, her grief-stricken heart exulted. When buds sprouted for the first time and blossomed into flowers, Sivakami forgot her sorrows and floated in an ocean of bliss. She felt happy gazing at the petals of the flowers and their deep red stalks that resembled the beaks of parrots. As the day passed and the sun travelled to its zenith, the tender flowers dried up. Her heart, which had also been temporarily soothed and felt optimistic, became hard and scorched. When the plant took firm root and put out several branches, Sivakami did not have to tend to it carefully any longer. She started counting the passing years by observing that plant.

In winter, when the chill penetrated one's bones, the leaves withered away. During spring, fresh leaf buds sprouted. During summer, the leaves matured and buds emerged. Rains would accompany the fierce westerly winds. During the months of Ani and Ati, the pavazhamalli plant oscillated precariously. Unable to bear this sight, a dazed Sivakami remained inside the house. During the months of Avani and Purattasi, the lush green leaves of the plant were covered by flowers in full bloom. During those seasons, Sivakami would sit on the stairs leading to the muttram and gaze at the plant for a long time, fondly recollecting the deities in Tamizhagam that were adorned with pavazhamalli during Navarathri and Vijayadasami. Counting them now, Sivakami realized that nine Vijayadasamis had passed since she had come to Vatapi.

Chapter 23

The Chinese Traveller

As days passed, Sivakami felt less insulted about being made to dance at the Vatapi street junctions. The prisoners from Tamizhagam found suitable jobs and settled down in Vatapi with their families. Some of them would visit Sivakami occasionally. Sivakami observed that they bore no anger or hatred. She understood that it was her naivety that had prompted her to make such a vow and that it was foolishness not to leave with Mamallar.

Nevertheless, as is characteristic of many women, Sivakami blamed Mamallar for her mistakes. 'No matter what, I was an ignorant girl! Humiliation and anger were the reasons for my making such a vow. Shouldn't a wise man like him have forcibly abducted me from here? Didn't Senathipathi Paranjyothi ask him to act thus? Why didn't he listen?' she often thought.

As the years passed, Sivakami gradually lost hope that Mamallar would return to fulfil her vow. She understood that it was a colossal task that required great effort. Sometimes she thought of sending a message to Mamallar stating, 'The vow I made was erroneous. I was ignorant in insisting that you embark on such an impossible mission. You need not pay heed to it. Please somehow just fetch me from this place!' But Naganandi's taunting words prevented her from putting that thought into action.

When the dagger Sivakami had flung found its mark on Naganandi's back, that crafty masquerader claimed, 'Ah! What have you done? I wanted to send you back with them!' Hence Sivakami's anger towards Naganandi had dissipated. She regretted her action and felt some sympathy for the bikshu. Naganandi secretly exulted that his deceitful words had had the desired impact. He had taken full advantage of Sivakami's sympathy for him. A few days after that incident, he had claimed that he himself would escort Sivakami back to Kanchi. Sivakami had not only declined his offer but also reminded him of the vow she had made. Naganandi had smiled sarcastically and asked, 'Will anyone make a vow that can never ever be fulfilled?!'

Sivakami had boldly replied, 'Why don't you wait and watch!'

Sivakami, who was in a self-imposed imprisonment in a far-off country where she knew no one, found solace in her occasional conversations with Naganandi. Conversing with the bikshu, who had travelled across the country and was well-versed in several arts, was an invigorating pastime. Sometimes Naganandi enticed her, saying, 'It's fine if you don't want to return to Kanchi. I will take you to Ajantha. You can learn first-hand about the indelible dyes your father was eager to know about!'

Sivakami would respond saying, 'I will leave this city only after my vow is fulfilled!'

Sivakami had felt ecstatic three years ago when the rumours of an impending Pallava invasion were rife. When they had turned out to be false, Naganandi's taunts hurt her even more. Nevertheless, she had not revealed her feelings and tried to uphold Mamallar's prestige by saying, 'Please be patient, adigal, please be patient! The Pallava army will invade next year, if not this year! Wait and watch!' Three years had passed since she spoke so proudly, 'Is there any point in continuing to be hopeful? How long can I deceive myself and live in sorrow? Enough, enough! Nine years have passed.' The well beside the pavazhamalli tree in the muttram of Sivakami's house seemed to persuasively beckon her, 'Come! Come! Find refuge in me!'

It was in this situation that Naganandi visited Sivakami one day, accompanied by a Chinese traveller named Hiuen Tsang. He had travelled across several countries and visited several kingdoms. After visiting one of the three renowned kingdoms in Bharata Kandam—Harsha's empire—he had come to Vatapi. After going to Ajantha in the Chalukya kingdom and the Nagarjuna mountain in Vengi, he intended to travel to the Pallava kingdom. Naganandi, who had come to know of this, had brought him along, saying, 'The daughter of the most illustrious sculptor of Pallava Nadu resides here. Her expertise in Bharatanatyam is unparalleled. Let's visit her.'

Sivakami's conversation with the Chinese traveller reminded her of her old aspirations and rendered her rapturous.

Hiuen Tsang described at length the countries he had visited and the scenic spots and artistic wonders therein.

He also asked Sivakami about the art of sculpture that flourished in Tamizhagam. When Naganandi mentioned that Sivakami's father, Aayanar, had sculpted indestructible statues of Sivakami in various dance postures, Hiuen Tsang expressed amazement. He earnestly requested Sivakami to demonstrate some of those dance postures. After nine years, Sivakami felt a genuine passion to perform the art she had learnt so assiduously. She demonstrated a few dance postures and abhinayams to the Chinese traveller. Hiuen Tsang was greatly impressed watching her dance. Naganandi was mesmerized.

When Hiuen Tsang enquired about Sivakami, Naganandi informed him about the circumstances that had led to her imprisonment and her vow offered several times to escort her back to Kanchi after obtaining the emperor's approval. She did not agree. It pains me that her wonderful art is incarcerated in this house. Sometimes, I think that I myself should set Vatapi ablaze for the sole purpose of freeing her!' declared Naganandi.

Hiuen Tsang closed his ears with his hands and pronounced, 'May Buddha bhagavan prevent such a calamity from occurring!'Then that elderly soul gave a sermon about the greatness of mercy and the ill-effects of war. He narrated the story of Buddha bhagavan stopping a ceremony to save the life of a goat. He highlighted the just rule of Emperor Ashoka. He opined that Harsha chakravarthy's reign in the current times was also just and that he had banned cruelty inflicted on animals in his kingdom.

Sivakami interjected saying, 'But adigal, you are unaware of the atrocities committed by the Vatapi emperor's soldiers in Tamizhagam. That's why you sermonize thus!'

The Chinese bikshu responded as follows: 'Thaye, I am aware that men are transformed into beasts during war! Atrocities of a much larger scale than what you witnessed might have occurred. But if one keeps seeking revenge, there will be no end to violence. To avenge the Chalukya emperor's invasion, the Kanchi chakravarthy will invade Vatapi. The scions of the Chalukya dynasty will invade Kanchi again to seek revenge. Just like a tree growing from a seed and seed-bearing fruit growing on that tree, the cycle of evil in this world will be never-ending. Someone must forget and forgive for the sake of this world's well-being. Thaye, no matter what, please do not wish for the fulfilment of your horrific vow! No one will benefit by that. Ah! There are thousands of households in this vast city. Lakhs of people reside here. Amongst them are the aged, children and helpless women like you. If this city is ablaze, won't all these innocent people suffer untold misery? Think about it!'

Listening to Hiuen Tsang, Sivakami's confusion heightened. Naganandi adigal then interjected saying, 'Sivakami! Didn't you hear what this great soul has to say? It's futile to dwell on past events. What is the benefit of seeking revenge? Isn't it enough that you've performed a penance for nine years? In two days, this Chinese elder and the Vatapi emperor are leaving for Ajantha, and I am accompanying them. Please come with us. In Ajantha, you will see wonders that cannot be seen elsewhere in this world!'

Sivakami's artistic soul was tempted for an instant. She felt like saying, 'So be it, swami! I will come!' But her lips refused to utter those words. A voice from the deep recesses of her heart questioned, 'Sivakami! Why are you thinking treacherously? After refusing to accompany Mamallar, will you go with this bikshu? Won't Mamallar be anguished if he were to come here when you are at Ajantha?'

Sivakami reined in her vacillating heart and replied, 'Respected bikshus! I am grateful for the deep concern you have for this orphaned maiden. But I am not fortunate to view the wonders at the Ajantha caves. I do accept this Chinese elder's words. Henceforth I will not pray for my vow to be fulfilled. May the city of Vatapi and its citizens flourish and not experience sorrow! I hope no harm will befall them on my account. But I will spend my life only in this house. I will not consent to leave this city under any circumstance!'

Chapter 24

The Coral Trader

After Naganandi and the Chinese traveller had left, Sivakami sat motionless like a statue for some time. Old memories flooded her mind. The breach of the Thirupaar Kadal Dam, the threat to her life on account of the flood, Mamallar arriving at just the right moment, helping her into the earthen boat and rescuing her—it all seemed to have occurred just the previous day. A slight smile appeared on her beautiful, sculpted face when she thought that she, who had not died by sinking in that deluge, was going to die by falling into the well in the muttram of her house.

She wondered how it would feel when she was jumping into the well and after she had fallen in. What would she think about when she struggled for breath in the water? Would she recollect Mamallar rescuing her when she fell off the boat at Mandapapattu? As she was thinking thus, she heard a voice in the street call out, 'Corals for sale! Corals!'

An absentminded Sivakami muttered to herself, 'Indeed! The pavazhamalli tree is growing in this house! Even after I die after jumping into the well, it will continue to blossom!'

She again heard the voice call out, 'Coral for sale!'

She could not fathom why she shivered on hearing that voice. Had she heard that voice before? Soon, the coral trader entered the house and announced, 'Amma! Do you want to buy corals? These are rare and high quality. Their hue outshines the Ajantha paints!' On hearing the word 'Ajantha', Sivakami was taken aback. She stared at the mature face that sported a thick moustache and beard. Ah! Those eyes! Those eyes that looked towards her with affection and devotion! 'Amma! Do you recognize me?' Asking this, that coral trader sat next to her and untied his bundle.

Sivakami recognized Gundodharan's voice. Nevertheless, she was unable to trust her eyes and ears. She asked, 'Is it you, Gundodhara?'

'Yes, it's me, amma! Have you forgotten me?' asked Gundodharan humbly.

'Yes, appane! I have forgotten you. How many years have passed since all of you left after saying that you would return?' asked a slightly irritated Sivakami.

'Amma, would it have sufficed if we had just returned? Didn't we have to prepare to fulfil your vow?' shot back Gundodharan.

'Ah, the vow! The disastrous vow!' swore Sivakami. She then looked at Gundodharan and declared, 'I have given up my vow, Gundodhara!'

Gundodharan stared at her uncomprehendingly. 'Amma! What are you saying?' he enquired.

'It's nothing, appa! Aren't you referring to my vow? I have renounced it!'

'Please don't speak thus, amma! The vow you made is one that Tamizhagam has also taken on. It is everyone's responsibility to fulfil it!'

'Have you come disguised thus to fulfil the vow? Is that why you're selling corals?' asked Sivakami with a mocking smile.

'Thaye, I am visiting you here like Hanuman, who in his capacity as Rama's emissary visited Sita. Ramabiran is going to come here leading an ocean-like army!' he revealed.

Overcome by emotion, Sivakami trembled. Ah! Was her nine-year wait going to truly bear fruit? Was Mamallar going to come here and fetch her to Kanchi? Was the well that was waiting to gobble her up going to feel cheated?

'Yes, amma! A Pallava army of a size not witnessed hitherto in the southern country has been mobilized. Mamalla chakravarthy and Senathipathi Paranjyothi are leading that army!' stated Gundodharan.

'Did you say Mamalla chakravarthy?' asked Sivakami, taken aback.

'Forgive me, amma! My words must have shocked you. Mamalla prabhu is now the chakravarthy of the Pallava kingdom. Several years have passed since Mahendra chakravarthy's soul departed to heaven.'

Hearing this, Sivakami shed copious tears. She had been angry with Mahendra Pallavar for several reasons. But the deep affection and devotion she had developed for him as a child remained intact. Gundodharan remained silent for some time to allow Sivakami to give vent to her sorrow.

Sivakami abruptly stopped sobbing and exclaimed, 'Gundodhara! I beseech you. I will not remain in this city even for another moment. Take me away right now!' Gundodharan stood frozen in shock. Observing this, Sivakami urged, 'What are you thinking of? This is also an opportune time. It seems that Pulikesi and the fake bikshu are leaving for Ajantha in another two days. Security is lax here these days. We can easily escape. If you're unwilling to take me along, please be merciful and push me into the deep well that stands in the backyard of this house!' Then she resumed sobbing.

Chapter 25

Thus Spoke Mahendrar

After allowing Sivakami to cry for some time, Gundodharan remarked, 'Thaye, in south Tamizhagam there's a saying, "The person who has the patience to cook the food ought to wait for it to cool down." You may have also heard of this adage. You have waited for so long. How can you lose your patience when your vow is about to be fulfilled?'

'Gundodhara, are you preaching about the virtues of patience to me? Are you lecturing about patience to me, who has been living in the enemy's city for nine years without any solace or support?' exploded Sivakami with uncontrollable fury.

'Thaye, I am not advocating patience to you. I expressed my powerlessness thus. I wish to remind you of another episode from the Ramayana. When Hanuman met Sita at Ashoka Vanam, he requested her to leave with him. He promised to take her safely back to Rama. But Sita refused to accompany Hanuman!' mentioned Gundodharan.

'Gundodhara! Why do you cite the example of Sita? I am neither Sita nor the daughter of the ruler of Mithila. I'm a humble sculptor's daughter!'

'Amma, neither am I Hanuman, though my physical form may resemble Lord Rama's emissary! But I don't possess even a minute fraction of his power. I am incapable of single-handedly setting fire to Vatapi and taking you along with me! What can I do?'

'Ah! Why do you remind me again of my cursed vow? Didn't I tell you that I've given it up? I only asked you to take me along . . .'

'Amma, didn't Mamallar, standing at this very spot in this house, plead with you to accompany him? You stubbornly refused then. You asked him to fulfil your vow and only then take you away. I stood there, listening to you. Now, Mamallar is coming, prepared to fulfil your vow. Amma, tomorrow, which is Vijayadasami, has been fixed as the auspicious day for the Pallava army's departure. If things go as planned, in exactly one month, the Pallava army will surround the Vatapi fort and lay siege. You will witness with your own eyes your vow being fulfilled. Please be patient for some more time without losing courage.'

'Gundodhara! You have failed to understand my words. Nor have you understood my intentions. I did not speak out of fear or impatience. I wish to prevent another gory war being fought because of me. Haven't I undergone enough tribulations in my lifetime? The rage I felt at that time prompted me to make that vow. Now when I think about it, I realize it's foolish. Untold atrocities will be perpetrated during the course of a war. Several people will die. Innocent people will face difficulties. How can one be confident about the outcome of war? I do not wish such difficulties to occur due to my foolish and obstinate behaviour. That's why I'm asking you to take me along!' pleaded Sivakami.

Gundodharan stood stunned, unable to respond to Sivakami. After thinking for some time, he remarked, 'Amma, even if you were to renege on your vow, Mamallar cannot abandon the Vatapi invasion. He will definitely fulfil the command Mahendra Pallavar gave on his deathbed!'

Sivakami enquired, 'Ah! What was Mahendrar's command?'

'He wanted the vow of sculptor Aayanar's daughter to be fulfilled at all costs! He forcefully insisted that only if Sivakami ammai was fetched after Vatapi was set ablaze, would the slur on the Pallava dynasty be erased. He goaded Mamallar and the ministers' council to incessantly work towards this goal!' revealed Gundodharan.

Sivakami lamented, 'Ah, was the chakravarthy so benign towards me? My opinion of him was so wrong!' and starting shedding tears again. She then enquired about Mahendra Pallavar's death and the goings-on in Kanchi for the last nine years. Gundodharan gave her a detailed account. But there was one subject he did not broach. He was unable to muster the courage to speak about it.

When it was time for Gundodharan to leave, Sivakami asked in a yearning voice, 'Appane! Will Mamallar definitely come? Or are you deliberately misleading me?'

Gundodharan replied, 'He will definitely come to uphold the honour of the Pallava dynasty!'

She scoffed, 'True! For him, upholding the honour of the Pallava dynasty is of utmost importance. That's why he is coming after so many years. If he were coming on account of his affection for me, he would have done so long ago and taken me back.'

Gundodharan thought to himself, 'Ah! Pleasing women is an arduous task. Why do some people almost kill themselves trying to please such women? Isn't this sheer madness?'

Then Gundodharan asked, frankly, 'Amma, didn't Mamallar come incognito here one day, placing his affection for you above the honour of the Pallava dynasty? Didn't he plead with you to accompany him?'

'Yes, Gundodhara! I did commit a blunder then. Please inform Mamallar that I've undergone enough punishment for this during the last nine years. Please also tell him that I've been holding on to my life for so long only to meet him once and seek his forgiveness!' acknowledged Sivakami.

Fortunately, that helpless maiden was unaware of the harsh tribulations that lay in store for her. Had she foreseen these, would she have continued to live?

Gundodharan hesitated as he was about to leave. It seemed as though he wished to say something but was hesitant to do so. Sivakami emboldened him, saying, 'If you have anything else to say, don't hesitate!'

'Devi, I have nothing else to say. There's a belief that women cannot keep secrets. One such episode features in the Mahabharata too. Amma! Please don't get angry; the news of my visit here and Mamallar's impending invasion should not be disclosed!'

A sad smile appeared on Sivakami's face. 'Gundodhara! Haven't I caused enough hardship to Mamallar for so long? Will I betray him to these vengeful oppressors? Here, I know no one but Naganandi bikshu. So you may return peacefully!' stated Sivakami. Then she advised, 'Gundodhara, you called yourself Hanuman. Your conduct should befit the name. You must stay by Mamallar's side always and protect him! These scoundrels are venomous. They kill people by wielding poisoned daggers. Aiyyo! Should he be in danger again because of my foolish obstinacy?'

Gundodharan, at that moment, understood why Sivakami did not wish for a war to be waged. He realized that the reason was her concern that some danger may befall Mamallar on the battlefield. His respect and regard for Sivakami grew multi-fold.

Chapter 26

The Rise of Neelakesi

Sivakami felt overwhelmed after Gundodharan's visit, as several thoughts tormented her. Time hung heavy on her hands. Every moment seemed to be an unending eon. She repeatedly recollected every word that Gundodharan had uttered. She frequently wondered if she had spoken to him appropriately. She also often worried about what he would relate to Mamallar. Whenever Sivakami recollected Gundodharan cautioning her not to divulge Mamallar's impending invasion, a smile appeared on her sorrowful face. But she was soon to understand how crucial that word of caution was.

Three days after Gundodharan's visit, exuberant chaos prevailed in Vatapi. Sivakami came to know that Emperor Pulikesi was leaving for the Ajantha Art Festival on that day, and that his procession would pass through the highway that ran close to her house. She knew that she could watch the procession from one of the windows in her house. Finally, the emperor's procession passed by in the third jaamam of the afternoon. Emperor Pulikesi was seated majestically on the royal mount. Naganandi bikshu and the Chinese traveller followed him in a palanquin.

The emperor's three young sons were seated in a beautiful golden chariot. Travelling ahead of and behind the emperor in several carriages were the kingdom's senior ministers, feudal lords and army chiefs. The euphoric cheering of the citizens accompanied by the sound of musical instruments had a deafening impact. Seeing this, Sivakami was reminded of Mahendra Pallavar leaving for the Mamallapuram Art Festival. Ah! Previously Pulikesi had been completely devoid of artistic sensibility—he had now undergone a complete transformation! Was he influenced by his visit to Kanchi?

Whenever Sivakami thought about that procession, she felt irritated. She consoled herself thinking Pulikesi's ostentatious ways and arrogance would soon come to an end. It was possible that Mamallar would reach Vatapi before they returned from Ajantha. Wouldn't they be terror-stricken when they came to know of the impending invasion? Sivakami then felt that it was wrong on her part to have told Gundodharan that there was no need for a war. There was another reason that heightened her anger. It seemed that the bikshu who was seated in the palanquin had turned around and looked at Sivakami's house for a moment. Her expectation that Naganandi would come again to bid farewell before he embarked on the voyage did not fructify. She thought, 'How arrogant the fake bikshu is!' This thought served to fan her fury further.

That evening Sivakami was very surprised to see Naganandi ride to her house on horseback. 'Swami! What is this! I thought you were en route to Ajantha! Aren't you going?' she asked.

'I'm definitely going, Sivakami! I have an important chore to perform in Ajantha, you're connected with it. I rushed back because I wanted to tell you about it. Tonight itself, I will reach the place where the emperor is camping!' Without allowing Sivakami to speak, Naganandi bikshu asked, 'Did you watch this afternoon's procession?'

'Yes, I did. I was reminded of Mahendra chakravarthy leaving for Mamallapuram from Kanchi for the art festival. It seems that Emperor Pulikesi will outshine even Mahendra Pallavar,' quipped Sivakami.

'There is no doubt he will outshine Mahendra Pallavar. The Vatapi emperor is not the blood-thirsty Pulikesi of old. He is the new Pulikesi who is passionate about and appreciative of the arts,' stated Naganandi.

'In that case, the Ajantha Art Festival will be a lavish event,' retorted Sivakami.

'There's no doubt about that too. The bikshus in Ajantha have made the necessary arrangements to welcome and host the chakravarthy appropriately. It seems that acharyas from Nalanda, Sri Parvatham and several other seats of Buddhism have come to participate in the festivities. You must be aware that it was the Ajantha sangramam that gave refuge to the Vatapi emperor and protected him during his youth. Despite this, the emperor did not extend any assistance to the Ajantha sangramam for a long time. The Jain monks did not allow that. They insisted that all state assistance must be extended only to Jain monasteries and temples. But now the emperor has had a change of heart. He is awarding state grants to exponents of sculpture and painting irrespective of their faith—Samanam, Buddhism, Saivism, Vaishnavism or Sakthar. Hence in all of

Bharata it is in the Chalukya kingdom that the arts flourish most. Vatapi has overtaken Kanyakubja and Kanchi!'

When Naganandi proudly spoke thus, Sivakami listened with genuine interest.

Naganandi asked, 'Sivakami! Do you know who was responsible for the Vatapi emperor's change of heart?'

Sivakami promptly responded saying, 'There's no doubt it was the exponent and connoisseur of all arts—Naganandi adigal!'

Naganandi's face was far more genteel than it had been nine years ago. The cruelty that had been evident in his face previously had now disappeared. Sivakami's response made him smile and further enhanced the glow on his face. He smiled as he looked at Sivakami with his gentle and captivating eyes and enquired, 'Kalaivani![12] What you say is true. It was I who converted the blood-thirsty warmonger Pulikesi into a connoisseur of arts. But before that, can you guess who transformed me into someone who was obsessed with the arts?'

Sivakami thought that the bikshu was referring to her. Nevertheless, she asked, 'How would I know, swami?'

'Yes, you would not know. I have not told you thus far. Aren't you aware that there are several divine paintings on the walls of the Ajantha caves painted with indelible dyes? Amongst those paintings is a portrait of a maiden performing Bharatanatyam. It was that portrait that ignited the spark of artistic appreciation in me. Sivakami, you must see that wonderful painting one day ...'

'I don't harbour such futile desires. I will never ever be fortunate enough to view the wonders in Ajantha in this birth!' muttered Sivakami.

---

[12] Another name for Goddess Saraswati.

'Don't speak thus! In a certain sense, I am not unhappy that you're not accompanying us this time. That's because neither you nor I will be at peace should you come with us. This might change soon, as change is the only permanent phenomenon in life.'

Sivakami was startled when Naganandi spoke thus. She observed Naganandi cautiously when she asked, 'How and in what manner will there be a change?'

'The time may come for you to be liberated from this cage and freely travel across the cosmos, singing joyously!'

'That day will never come,' countered Sivakami, and heaved a deep sigh.

'In that case, aren't you hopeful that your vow will be fulfilled?' asked Naganandi.

Sivakami gritted her teeth and claimed, 'No; I lost that hope long ago!' But she felt fear and confusion within. Was this treacherous bikshu suspicious? Was he trying to extract the truth from her? Perhaps Gundodharan had been trapped by him.

'Sivakami, you've lost hope that your vow will be fulfilled. But you will not leave this city without your vow being fulfilled. Isn't that the case?'

'Yes, swami. That's how it is!' responded Sivakami boldly. That was when she gratefully recollected Gundodharan's words of caution.

'Ah! I will never ever consent to your being in such a situation, Sivakami! I have to act in the manner I mentioned I would to the Chinese elder yesterday. If Mamallar does not fulfil your vow, I myself will do so. I myself will set this city on fire!'

'Ah! Why do you speak thus? Why do you have to perpetrate such cruelty to satiate this mad woman's obstinacy? No, never.'

'In that case, you must give up your meaningless vow.'

Sivakami, who wanted to change the course of the conversation, asked, 'Swami! You have spoken a lot about me. That's enough. Tell me about yourself, tell me about Ajantha!'

'Yes! I came here primarily to speak about myself. I am going to be born again in Ajantha. I will not return as an ochre robe-clad bikshu. I will return as Neelakesi maharaja, draped in the finest silks!' When Naganandi uttered these words, Sivakami looked at him with surprise.

Chapter 27

The Conflagration Within

Naganandi adigal, whose eyes were as mesmerizing as a snake's, gazed pointedly at Sivakami, who was staring at him with indescribable surprise. 'Sivakami! Don't you believe me? If only I could open my heart and show you . . . If only I could show you the fire raging within all day and night . . .' Speaking thus, the bikshu punched himself hard on his chest twice. Immediately, he grabbed the small dagger fastened to his waist, removed it from its sheath and was about to stab himself. Sivakami quickly held his hand and prevented him from doing so.

In the brief span of time in which Sivakami held Naganandi's hand, she underwent two amazing experiences. She realized that Naganandi's hand and his entire body were trembling. Nine years ago, Sivakami, who had the same feelings for the bikshu as she did for her father, happened to accidentally touch his hand a few times. Then, she had thought, 'His physique is taut like a diamond. His body is not made of mere flesh, blood, nerves and skin. It seems as though his entire body is made of bones. He must have undertaken extremely harsh penances to harden his body thus.' It surprised Sivakami that the same bikshu's body had lost its rigidity and was supple.

Naganandi, while continuing to hold the dagger, stared at Sivakami for some time. Then, like someone who had regained his consciousness, he flung the dagger away. Immediately, Sivakami too let go of his hand. 'Sivakami! I suddenly lost my mind and became mesmerized! Please remind me of what I mentioned and why I unsheathed this dagger,' asked the bikshu.

Sivakami responded, 'Swami, you stated that you were giving up your monkhood and that you were going to ascend the throne and rule the kingdom,' and then hesitated.

'Yes, Sivakami! I stated the truth. I'm going to Ajantha for this very purpose. Thirty-five years ago, I assumed the vows of a monk on the banks of the Ajantha River. I am going to renounce my vows on the banks of that very river and return. I am going to seek liberation from that very venerable guru who ordained me as a bikshu. Do you consent to this?' asked Naganandi adigal.

Sivakami, who was gripped by an incomprehensible fear, shrieked, 'Swami! What is this? Why do you have to renounce Buddhism—a faith you've practised for all these years? As a consequence of your action, wouldn't you develop worldly attachments? The penances you have observed all these years will be futile. How do you stand to gain by your action?'

Even as she spoke, she instinctively knew that she was committing a blunder by asking these questions and that she had fallen into that bikshu's trap. The bikshu asked her in turn, 'Do you ask how I stand to gain?' and laughed out aloud.

'Don't you know? In that case, I will tell you. Pay heed to me! It is for your sake I'm going to give up my penances as a monk, Sivakami! It is solely for you! As prescribed by the Ajantha tradition, I am going to seek the guru's consent to my giving up my vows and publicly renouncing my monkhood. Actually, I violated my vows several years ago. I flouted my vows on the very day I saw you at your father's forest residence. You were a live statue among those wonderful lifeless ones. But I don't regret it. I am prepared to spend sixteen thousand years in hell in exchange for living with you for one day. I am ready to forego enlightenment in lieu of being the recipient of your affection for one moment ...'

Sivakami trembled with fear. The suspicion that had been smouldering within her all these days had turned out to be true! But why had the fake bikshu concealed his emotions for so long? Why had he spared her for so long and not troubled her in any way? She got the answers to these questions the very next instant.

'Sivakami, an opportunity arose nine years ago for me to redeem my soul and for you to safeguard your happiness. I would have probably upheld my vows had you accompanied Mamallan when he came here to fetch you, or had you given me the opportunity to unite the two of you. You too would have led a happy life thereafter. But you unnecessarily suspected me, and aimed the poisoned dagger at my back without understanding my true intentions and injured me. The poisoned dagger did not kill me that day. But if that very poisoned dagger were to be wielded on me today, I would not live beyond half a nazhigai! Sivakami, when you held my hand some time ago, a doubt arose in your mind. You were shocked that my hand, which had been hard like iron and stone nine years ago, is now so soft. You are the reason for that change,

Sivakami! I hardened my body by observing harsh penances. I converted my blood into poison by consuming venomous herbs for a long time. Those days, a poisonous snake would meet its death if it were to to bite me. No harm would befall me. All the poisonous snakes in the vicinity would slither away quickly on sensing the odour of my sweat, unable to bear its intensity. You yourself have observed this several times . . .'

When Naganandi adigal mentioned this, both of them were reminded of the incidents that had occurred at Mandapapattu ten years ago on a full moon night.

'By consuming therapeutic herbs and undergoing treatment, I have transformed my previously steely body into a soft one. I have removed the poison that had mingled with my blood. It was in these efforts that I have been engaged for the last nine years. This was the reason for my not meeting you for several days at a stretch. Sivakami, I am capable of leading a householder's life like a thirty-year-old youth. After all this, you cannot reject me. You will have to atone for the sin of causing me sorrow through your rejection for several hundred rebirths hereafter! Even then you will not be absolved of your sin!'

Sivakami felt that her head was about to explode. When the bikshu sat in front of her and spoke in this manner, she also wondered if it was a dream for a moment. The comfort and happiness provided by such a thought disappeared the very next instant. No, this was not a dream but horrific incidents occurring in reality in her presence. It was a fact that the bikshu was staring at her with his bloodshot eyes.

As soon as Sivakami realized that danger was looming large, her mind attained clarity. There was only one way to escape from this lunatic. She had to buy some time from him by being humble and pleading with him. If God were kind to her, Mamallar would have freed her and taken her along with him before this frenzied bikshu returned from Ajantha. Otherwise, she would have to employ an alternate tactic. So Sivakami opened her mouth to beg and plead with the bikshu.

The bikshu prevented her from doing so by saying, 'No, Sivakami! You don't have to say anything today. You don't have to respond in haste. I initially thought of discussing these issues with you after returning from Ajantha. But by the time we stopped for the night at the state guest house on the outskirts of Vatapi, I decided that I ought to divulge my innermost feelings to you, and that it was only fair that I give you enough time to think through everything and come to a decision. I am neither going to force you nor pressurize you. I will never ever ask you to act in a manner that is contrary to your wishes. But I will tell you what I have to say in a single breath; please pay heed to me patiently. You can communicate your decision to me once I return from Ajantha.'

When Sivakami heard these words, she became somewhat placated and less agitated.

Naganandi started relating his tale again from the beginning. 'The instant I saw you at your father's residence, you usurped the place in my heart that had previously been occupied by my brother and the Chalukya kingdom. Since then, all my thoughts and actions became flawed. The Vatapi emperor's invasion of the southern country was not a success only on account of those mistakes. Ah! Your tender heart would melt if only you knew how much mental torture I experienced those days. On the one hand, the fiery love I felt for you scorched my heart. At the same time, the intense envy I felt towards those associated with you, your friends and those whom you loved seared my mortal body. You would have been shocked had you been aware of the ferocious conflict, akin to the war between the devas and the asuras, that was raging in my heart then. At one point of time, I felt an uncontrollable fury and urge to kill all those associated with you. But I lost the courage to do so as I feared that you would lose your affection for me if you came to know of it. I had several opportunities to kill Mamallan and Mahendra Pallavan. But they survived because I was scared of the consequences should you come to know of it. Didn't Paranjyothi rescue you from the mad elephant the day he arrived at Kanchi? It was for this reason I helped him escape from the prison and brought him to your house. I could not bear the sight of you expressing your gratitude to him. Kalaivani! I was also jealous of your father's influence over you. But as he was fortunate enough to beget you, I saved him from the soldier who was about to wield the sword on him. Since then, I have been proud of my hands, as they saved your father.'

Hearing this, Sivakami's heart truly melted. 'This bikshu may be a merciless demon; his heart may be the abode of a devil, the blood flowing in his veins may contain snake venom. But didn't he save my father's life on account of his love for me?' thought Sivakami.

Understanding Sivakami's train of thought, the bikshu spoke further, like one possessed. 'Listen to me, Sivakami! I saved Aayanar because he gave birth to you. Let me cite an example to illustrate how I sought revenge on those who antagonized you. Haven't you lived fearlessly in Vatapi, unaffected by any danger all these years? You may have probably guessed the reason for this. It was only because everyone knew that you were living under my protection that no one approached you. One woman in the palace was envious of this. She was the chief consort's sister. That woman, who was endowed with a venomous mind, tried hard to seduce me. As she was not successful, she started bad-mouthing you. "Do I lack the beauty of the artiste from Kanchi?" she asked. The following day, when she neared me, I held her hand and scratched her with my fingernail. She slept that night, woke up the following morning, and looked at herself in the mirror. That was it, she lost her mental stability and became deranged! She was looking so hideous. She left this city without informing anyone and loitered around the mountains for a long time. Now she has joined the kabalikas and is feeding herself by engaging in cannibalism . . .'

Sivakami was again gripped with fear; she wished that this frenzied bikshu would leave soon.

'Sivakami, a few days ago I inadvertently met that embodiment of Kali. Do you know what she said? "Swamigal! You are bound to hand over your lover, Sivakami, to me one day. My hunger will be satiated only if I consume her body!" insisted that mad woman. She thinks that I will hand over your body to her for her to consume. She did not realize that my hunger for you is a hundred times more intense than hers! How will she understand the ardour that grips me every time I see you that makes me want to gobble you up?'

Suddenly, it seemed to Sivakami that Naganandi bikshu was approaching her like a python with its mouth wide open and its forked tongue protruding out with the intention of swallowing her up. As she hurriedly moved back with her eyes tightly shut, she shrieked, 'Aiyyo!'

Naganandi laughed and quipped, 'Sivakami! Did you get scared? Open your eyes and see. It's me, the bikshu, who is speaking!'

Sivakami opened her eyes. She realized that the sight she had just seen was an illusion. Nevertheless, her eyes were filled with fear.

Naganandi stood up and pleaded, 'Sivakami, think about all I just said. You seem to think that I've gone mad. Fortunately, I have not yet become mad. I still possess clarity of thought. But if the love I bear towards you is not reciprocated, I may become crazy in a few days. Then, I cannot predict my actions. Sivakami, I will take leave of you. You must strengthen your resolve and communicate your decision to me when I return. For your sake, I am about to perform a sacrifice, the magnitude of which far exceeds all other sacrifices I have made for you thus far. You will come to know about it before I return. Once you come to know about it, you cannot but feel mercy for me.' After speaking thus, Naganandi gazed at Sivakami with uncontrollable eagerness for some time. He then abruptly walked towards the entrance.

Long after the bikshu had left, Sivakami continued to tremble.

Chapter 28

Festivity and Disaster

The sight of centuries-old lush green banyan trees standing tall with widespread branches was breath-taking. The aerial roots of such ancient banyan trees that grew close to the parent trees gave the illusion of them being independent trees themselves. Likewise, the two beliefs that developed as offshoots of the Sanathana Hindu dharma and rooted firmly as distinct faiths were Buddhism and Samanam. In ancient times, these two faiths were instrumental in significantly augmenting the artistic treasures of Bharata.

Two thousand years ago, bikshus had started carving chaithyams and viharams out of the granite rocks that lay on the banks of the crescent-shaped river, whose precipitous flow tore across the inaccessible Ajantha mountains. The exquisite arts of sculpting and painting had flourished in that secluded province for almost six centuries up to the times of Emperor Pulikesi II. Sculptures carved out of indestructible boulders and portraits painted with indelible paints abounded. The

Brahmas[13] living in the chaithyams had created gods and goddesses, valorous men and women, and handsome males and females who were beauty personified, captivating the eyes and hearts of the viewers.

During the thirty-sixth year of the reign of Emperor Pulikesi, a festival—the grandeur of which had never been witnessed by that province—was conducted. That year was also the last year of the Chalukya emperor's reign. In ancient Bharata Nadu, the influence wielded by the various faiths waxed and waned with the rise and fall of the patronizing dynasties. As in the present times, in those days too there lived narrow-minded people deeply attached to their respective faiths, who lacked religious tolerance and in whom prejudices ran deep. Periodically, great souls who viewed all faiths equitably and who caused the arts to flourish also emerged.

During the times of this epic, foremost amongst the kings who possessed such forbearance were Harshavardhanar in the north and Mahendra Pallavar and Mamalla Narasimha Pallavar in the south. Emperor Pulikesi of Vatapi, after returning from his Kanchi expedition, gradually joined the ranks of such broad-minded kings. He encouraged the arts by endowing sizable grants to the Ajantha Buddha Sangramam. Due to this, the Ajantha bikshus, for the first time in six centuries, decided to invite the reigning emperor—Pulikesi—to preside over a festival commemorating sculptures.

A highway was constructed across the forests and mountains to receive the emperor and his retinue. They, along with minsters and strategists, army commanders, famous poets and art connoisseurs of the Chalukya kingdom and foreign

---

[13] The artists who created the sculptures and paintings are being compared to the creator, Lord Brahma.

dignitaries, travelled on elephants, horses and palanquins to Ajantha to participate in this art festival. The Ajantha bikshus accorded a royal welcome and warm hospitality to the visitors, who divided themselves into groups and visited the chaithyams and viharams and appreciated the sculptures and paintings. As it was possible to clearly view the lifelike paintings on the inner walls of the viharams only during noon when the sun was shining brightly, arrangements were made for the guests to stay overnight so they could see the paintings the following day, and then return.

Evening set in, the sun was setting behind the imposing mountain peaks in the west. As time passed, the shadows cast by those mountain peaks extended towards the east. These shadows chased the golden glow cast by the sun on the high peaks further eastwards. The crescent-shaped Vadora River sang, danced, frolicked, leapt, tripped and rose again as it swiftly flowed. Parijatham trees covered with lush green leaves, flowers and buds that grew on the sloping rocks extended up to the horizon. They were interspersed by konrai trees covered by their bright yellow blossoms. Two statuesque men were conversing, sitting on a rock by the riverside. They were Emperor Pulikesi and Naganandi bikshu.

The brothers were seated on that very rock on the banks of the Vadora River, on which they had sat thirty-five years ago, sharing their fantasies about the future and delineating their strategies for capturing the Chalukya kingdom and taking it to great heights. But the difference in their appearance and the course of their conversation between then and now was stark. The river that had reflected their innocent faces thirty-five years ago now mirrored their line-ridden, wrinkled and cruel faces. Their faces now manifested the maturity endowed by age, worldly experiences, inner turmoil and deep-rooted passions.

Importantly, intense anger was evident in Naganandi's blood-shot eyes. Every word he uttered was akin to an agniastram (a weapon emitting fire). 'Ah! Thambi, you ask me what I wish for. Shall I tell you? A horrific earthquake should erupt this very instant, consume Ajantha mountain and push it deep down. I wish that a thousand thunders simultaneously strike, destroying the chaithyams and viharams, the bikshus residing here, you and your retinue and myself!' cursed Naganandi.

Hearing this, Pulikesi observed in a laidback manner, 'Adigal! Our Ajantha trip has been truly beneficial. Words are inadequate to express my happiness. For some time now, you were becoming a very docile person. Only today, you seem to be the Naganandi bikshu of old!' So saying, he smiled.

'Yes, thambi, yes! Today, I have become the old Naganandi. Careful, or you will face the consequence of this transformation!' hissed the bikshu like a snake.

'Anna! What do you propose to do to me?' asked Pulikesi.

'I am going to stab you with this poisoned dagger tonight when you're asleep . . .' Pulikesi burst out laughing. Then he enquired in a mocking tone, 'Then what will you do? In other words what do you intend to do with my corpse?'

'I will fling it into this river.'

'Then? What will you tell those who enquire about me?'

'No one will ask!'

'Why not? Won't the citizens of the Chalukya kingdom enquire how their Emperor vanished in the dead of the night?'

'They will not! Only if they come to know of the emperor's disappearance will they enquire. No one will come to know of that.'

'How is that possible?'

'I once saved your life by donning your robes, I was beaten up and tortured. In another instance, I disguised myself as you, combatted Mahendran in the battlefield and killed him by wielding a poisoned dagger. Our identical appearance will help me. People will never come to know of your disappearance. The disappearance of Naganandi bikshu will not even cause a ripple. By right, this Chalukya kingdom is mine. I wholeheartedly gave this kingdom to you. For the last thirty-five years, I thought of nothing but your welfare and progress. But you humiliated me in front of several people today. You are merciless, ungrateful and devoid of fraternal affection! Ah! I am extremely shocked that this earth has not yet split into two and consumed you!'

'Anna! Anna! What are you saying? How did you bring yourself to curse me thus? In what manner did I humiliate you?'

'There can be no greater insult than this. What can be more degrading than you commissioning an indelible dye portrait of Sivakami prostrating before you and seeking your forgiveness? Is this why you brought me here? Is this the reason behind your organizing this art festival? Ah! You wicked beast! Hell awaits you for using one art to degrade another!'

'Anna! What has come over you? How did that dancer from Pallava Nadu mesmerize you? What power does she possess to separate two brothers, who despite having two distinct physical bodies shared a soul? Anna! Anna! Look at me and speak! Recollect our intimate friendship of thirty-five years and speak! Thirty-five years ago we sat on this very rock and built castles in the air. You have achieved most of what we dreamt about. Keep this in mind and speak! Tell me with this divine Vadora River, Akasavani and Bhoomi Devi as witnesses!

Has that maiden from Kanchi become more important to you than me? Are you cursing me thus on account of her?'

The bikshu asserted in a tone that was even harsher and angrier than earlier: 'Yes, yes! I speak with the lotus feet of Buddha Bhagavan as witness! I swear by the Sangam and Dharmam. Sivakami is far more important to me than you. You, your kingdom, sons and friends are not equal to a speck of dust on her foot. Doom will befall your descendants and you, who disgraced her! Do you know what became of the artist who painted the picture of her seeking refuge?'

'Adigal! What did you do to that unfortunate man?'

The bikshu laughed in a blood chilling manner and quipped, 'Wait and watch! Soon, someone will inform you!'

'Anna! I have realized one thing. It is a blunder to uphold the vows of celibacy and monkhood from a very young age. One must renounce the world only after experiencing the joys and tribulations of worldly life. People who embrace monkhood during their youth fall for the charms of a temptress later in their lives and become crazy like you!'

'Pulikesi! I have been patient all along! I will no longer tolerate you uttering even a word against Sivakami.'

'Adigal! You are so merciful to Sivakami and strive hard to defend her honour. Does she reciprocate your feelings? Does she feel one-thousandth of the allegiance you feel for her?'

Naganandi felt that Emperor Pulikesi's questions were akin to a sword smiting his heart into two; the bikshu's face betrayed his anguish.

Nevertheless, he overcame that intolerable sorrow very quickly and retorted confidently, 'You don't have the right to ask that question but I will tell you. Sivakami is not as hard-hearted as you are. She also feels affection for me.'

'Anna! I never imagined even in my wildest dreams that you could be deceived thus!'

'Thambi! I have not been deceived; Sivakami saved my life the night we embarked on our journey to Ajantha.'

'How did that happen? What danger befell you for Sivakami to rescue you?'

'I was about to stab myself with this poisoned dagger. Sivakami held my hand and saved me.' When the bikshu spoke, that incident appeared in his mind. Tears filled his eyes.

Pulikesi smiled and exclaimed, 'Aiyyo! Have you, a genius, changed thus? Do you know why Sivakami saved your life? She wants you to be killed by her lover, Mamallan. That foolish girl still harbours such fantasies!'

An incident that occurred that afternoon formed the background of the brothers' conversation. Emperor Pulikesi, the bikshu, the Chinese traveller and luminaries of the Chalukya kingdom had been viewing the amazing paintings at Ajantha in a group. The divine life of Buddha Bhagavan and incidents from his previous incarnations were depicted on the interior walls of the chaithyams and viharams. Scenes from the social life of those times were portrayed on the outer walls of the verandahs. The dominant theme amongst the contemporary paintings was the life of Emperor Pulikesi. One such painting showed Emperor Pulikesi, seated majestically on his throne, receiving tribute from emissaries of the Persian King.

It is not surprising that this painting enthused all the viewers. However, another painting not only caused discomfort amongst the viewers but was also instrumental in triggering a disaster later. That doomed painting depicted a dancer prostrating at the feet of Emperor Pulikesi and seeking his forgiveness. There was no doubt that the artist who had painted this portrait was very gifted as he had used all his imagination to paint the image of Pulikesi. In that portrait, Pulikesi resembled an angry Devendran who was about to decimate his foes. The artist had captured the intense sorrow very well and the beseeching expression of the maiden who was prostrating before him. The scared and pitying expressions of the ladies-in-waiting served to highlight the dancer's surrender.

The artist had also depicted a bikshu worriedly rushing towards this scene. On observing the depiction of the bikshu, the viewers understood that he was hastening to save the dancer from the king's punishment. When the person who was explaining the paintings uttered a few words about the philosophy underlying the painting, everyone looked at Naganandi in unison. For an instant, Naganandi's face resembled a snake with its hood raised. The very next moment, Naganandi realized that a hundred eyes were observing him closely. Immediately, his expression changed, and he smiled. 'Wonderful! Wonderful! This painting is peerless. The expressions and imagination are exquisite. Who is the artist who painted this? He needs to be duly rewarded!' announced Naganandi.

Chapter 29

Traitor

The conversation between Pulikesi and the bikshu on the riverbank was becoming increasingly contentious. Emperor Pulikesi tried hard to talk Naganandi out of his obsession of Sivakami. But the emperor's words only served to fuel Naganandi's anger. The more disparagingly Pulikesi spoke of Sivakami, the more passionate and laudatory became the bikshu's defence of her. When the combative conversation between the brothers escalated and there were signs of an impending physical attack, a gory incident that occurred in the vicinity caught their attention.

A man shrieking, 'Aiyyo! Aiyyo!' in a bloodcurdling manner ran to the banks of the Vadora River, that was flanked by perpendicular cliffs, and stood there for a moment. He again screamed, 'Aiyyo!' rushed towards the river and jumped into it. He sank into the river. Shortly thereafter, his head resurfaced above the water some distance away from where he had jumped. A horrific scream that caused rocks to shatter was heard. The man sank into the water once more, never to rise again. There were no signs of his sinking there. The Vadora River continued to flow with a tinkling sound along its mountainous course.

Emperor Pulikesi observed this incident that had transpired in a few seconds with rapt attention without batting an eyelid. When the man who jumped into the river resurfaced shrieking and sank again, he felt his chest tightening. After staring intently for some time at the spot where the man had sunk, Pulikesi turned around and looked at Naganandi. The smile that then appeared on the bikshu's face caused Pulikesi to shiver.

'Anna! What did you do to that resident of the chaithyam?' asked Pulikesi.

The bikshu let out a ghastly laugh and replied, 'What did I do to him? Nothing at all! I blessed the man who painted such a portrait. When he bowed to receive my blessing, I scratched the rear of his neck with my little finger slightly. He must have felt a burning sensation when the poison in my nail mingled with his blood. Shortly thereafter, he must have felt that his entire body was on fire. His brain must have also felt the heat. To cool his body and brain, he ran in that manner and jumped into the river. Along with his body and brain cooling down, his life also left him!'

'Aiyyo! Anna! When did you become such a cruel demon? After joining the sangam of Buddha, who is the very embodiment of mercy, and donning ochre robes, how could you commit such heinous acts?' asked Pulikesi.

Naganandi stared at Pulikesi and hissed, 'Oh! Did you realize that I am a merciless demon only now? Didn't I commit crueller acts than this for your sake and for the sake of your kingdom? Why did you not come forward to preach justice to me then? Have you forgotten that you had happily agreed when I suggested that we poison Kanchi's drinking water and kill all its residents?'

'Yes! Yes! I have not forgotten all that; but that was in the past!' admitted Emperor Pulikesi and heaved a sigh. After staring at the river for some time, he looked at Naganandi.

'Anna! I have not forgotten all the assistance you have rendered me. My life is yours and so is this kingdom. I have done nothing for you in return for all the support you have extended to me all these days. I intend doing so now. I have experienced the pleasure of sitting on the Vatapi throne and ruling the kingdom for thirty-five years. I have had enough. You may assume the pleasure of ascending the throne and the responsibility of ruling the kingdom from now. I will spend the remaining days of my life in the Ajantha Sangramam, donning the ochre robes you're currently wearing. You spent your youth in the Ajantha mountains, which is the abode of Prakrithi Devi[14] and Kalai Devi.[15] I will live here during my old age. You may assume the burden of ruling the kingdom henceforth . . .'

When Pulikesi spoke thus, the bikshu understood that these were genuine words that came from his heart. A smile replaced the fury that had been raging on his face thus far. When Pulikesi paused and remained silent, the bikshu built castles in the air. His face reflected his joyous dreams.

'Anna! What do you say? Do you agree to this?' asked Pulikesi. Though the bikshu completely trusted his words, he asked again to reconfirm Pulikesi's intention, 'Thambi! Are you stating the truth? Or are you mocking this mere ochre-clad bikshu?'

---

[14] Mother Nature.
[15] Goddess of Art.

'Anna! I swear by the holy name of our grandfather, Satyasraya Pulikesi, that I'm stating the truth. I am prepared to prove my intention this very instant. I will renounce the world and become a bikshu today itself. I will also speak to the acharya bikshu and release you from monkhood. But on one condition. You must give up that dancer from Kanchi.'

The glance that Naganandi shot at Pulikesi resembled that of a tiger staring at the hunter who had killed its mate! Pulikesi might have met the same fate as the artist who had painted the portrait 'The Dancing Maiden's Surrender'. But at that point of time, the duo observed seven to eight people hastening towards them from the opposite bank of the Vadora River. They were not civilians; they included ministers and commanders. It seemed as though they were coming to communicate an important and urgent message to the emperor. Observing this, the bikshu controlled the fury raging within and remarked, 'Ah! I suspected that there was some treachery in your offer to abdicate the kingdom in my favour. My hunch was correct!'

'Anna! Think before you speak! How can a sculptor's daughter ascend the throne that was once occupied by Satyasraya Pulikesi? I will never ever consent to this. Chase away the temptress who caused a rift between you and me, ascend the Vatapi throne and rule the kingdom for as long as you live!' pleaded Pulikesi.

Like earlier, Naganandi hissed like a cobra and cursed, 'You malicious man! You sinner! May doom befall you! May your capital be set on fire and be reduced to ashes! Your kingdom will be ruined! Even if I were to secure Devendran's position, I would not give up Sivakami. Do you think I will sacrifice her to secure this lowly Chalukya kingdom? Never! You are going to soon face the consequences of your ungrateful and treacherous behaviour. From this moment, our relationship stands severed. I will never ever meet you again. Here I leave. I will take Sivakami along and leave your kingdom. Look at those people! They bear news of your destruction!'

As Naganandi was sprouting these fiery words, those on the opposite bank crossed the bamboo bridge that spanned across the river and were walking towards the rock on which the emperor and the bikshu were seated. True to his words, Naganandi took two steps forward and then hesitated as though he was struck by an afterthought. It seemed as if he wanted to confirm the news the courtiers were about to convey.

The emperor was shocked when he saw the anxiety and fear writ large on the faces of his courtiers. He asked, 'All of you have come as a group. What's the occasion? Is there some important news?'

'Yes, prabhu! Indeed it's important news. But I feel hesitant to convey implausible news like this!' blurted the prime minister of the Chalukya kingdom.

'What's the important news? Who bore the message? From where did he come? All of you are pallid with fear. Are our enemies invading the Chalukya kingdom? Tell me quickly!'

'Mahaprabhu! You have just stated the news!'

'What are you blabbering? What did I say?'

'Didn't you ask if enemies are invading our kingdom?'

'Is that so?'

'Yes, Emperor!'

'It's indeed unbelievable news. Who is the aggressor? It cannot be Harshavardhanar from the north. Recently I received a cordial invitation from him. We do not have foes in the west and east. Our attacker would have to come from the south. Is Mamallan of Kanchi invading us?'

'That's the news, prabhu!'

'I cannot believe this. Even if that were the case, why are all of you so unsettled? Nothing is lost!'

'Perumane! A large part of our army is stationed on the banks of the Narmada River. Yet another chunk is in Vengi . . .' stated the prime minister hesitantly.

'So what? Can't we bring our forces to Vatapi before Mamallan leaves Kanchi?'

'Mamallan is not in Kanchi, prabhu! The Pallava army crossed the North Pennai River a week ago. It must have neared the Tungabhadra River by now!'

'How miraculous! Who brought this news?'

'They brought this message from Vatapi. They rushed non-stop without even halting at night!' remarked the prime minister and produced two emissaries before the emperor.

'Who sent you? Have you brought a written message?' asked a shell-shocked Pulikesi.

'No, Perumane! There was no time to even pen a message. The chief of the Vatapi fort asked us to communicate this message orally to you. Six of us left Vatapi five days ago. Four people fell on the way. The two of us managed to reach here.'

'Minister! Could they be stating the truth? Didn't we hear that Mamallan was constructing ships for the Lanka invasion?'

'Yes, prabhu! This news is difficult to believe. But they do bear the insignia of the chief of the Vatapi fort. It seems that another group of emissaries is following them with a detailed scroll. If they're stating the truth, the Pallava army must have crossed the Tungabhadra River by now. As famine has broken out in the province on the banks of the Tungabhadra River, we redirected the army stationed there to Vengi only a few days ago.'

Pulikesi stood stunned for some time. The truth must have struck him suddenly. He looked at Naganandi who stood a short distance away listening to this conversation.

Pulikesi again looked at the prime minister and asked, 'Minister! What was our espionage force doing? Why wasn't the news of Mamallan's invasion conveyed to us before? Why didn't the news of the Pallava army leaving Kanchi reach us when we were still at Vatapi?'

The prime minister bowed and replied, 'Prabhu! The chief of our espionage force was removed from service one year ago. Our bikshu assumed his responsibilities. You should ask the adigal!'

The gazes of everyone assembled there including that of the emperor fell on the bikshu.

Pulikesi asked, 'Adigal! Were you aware of Mamallan's impending invasion? Did you intentionally hide this news from me?'

'Thambi! Do you want me to respond to your query in the presence of everyone assembled here?' asked the bikshu.

'Adigal! Have you forgotten what you had stated some time ago? Didn't you say that the relationship between us has ceased to exist? Now, why do you profess its existence? Please state the truth immediately!'

'In that case, I will speak. I was aware of Mamallan's invasion beforehand. I did not report this development to punish you, an ungrateful sinner!' roared Naganandi.

When the emperor commanded, 'Imprison this traitor!' the eight people present there surrounded the bikshu.

The bikshu immediately drew out the small, curved dagger fastened to his waist and warned, 'Careful! The person who nears me will immediately go to Yama Loka!'

The eight people drew out their respective swords from their sheaths.

'Well done! The eight of you, who are the epitome of bravery, will together kill a lone bikshu. Emperor Pulikesi's fame will spread all over the world. Mamallan too will be impressed and return,' quipped the bikshu in a mocking tone.

Hearing this, Pulikesi commanded, 'Stop! Don't tarnish your swords by killing that debased traitor. Give way!'

The eight people, obeying the command, made way. But they continued to be watchful thinking that the bikshu might attack the emperor.

Emperor Pulikesi told the bikshu, 'Adigal! It would be a mistake to kill you. It is not an adequate punishment for you who betrayed your brother, who had reposed his faith in you, and your country. You must live for a long time and atone for the monumental sin you have committed. You must recollect your treachery and shed repentant tears. You wicked ghost in human form! Go! Go to Vatapi and take your Mohini along! Uphold at least this promise of yours! I don't want to see you as long as you're alive! You depraved man who dared to betray a kingdom for the sake of a woman! Go! May you live long and repent recollecting your betrayal!'

Naganandi stood like a statue listening to Pulikesi's emotional outburst. When Pulikesi stopped speaking, he started walking eastwards along the riverbank without uttering a word.

Pulikesi, who stared intently in the direction of the bikshu, immediately turned around after he left and wiped away his tears. Then he looked at those present and remarked, 'Minister! Senathipathi! The message the emissaries have conveyed must be true. There is no room for doubt. I ignored your words of caution regarding the bikshu. Though all of you and I are going to face the consequences for this, nothing is lost. We will teach Mamallan that it's no joke to intentionally trifle with a tiger. We will butcher all the Pallava soldiers who crossed the Tungabhadra River and will ensure that no one returns. All these days, I regretted that I was unable to secure a definitive victory in my invasion of the southern country. Now there is an opportunity to redress the regret. Pallava Nadu is going to be annexed to the Chalukya kingdom.'

Chapter 30

The Great War of Vatapi

More than a month had passed since the extraordinary art festival at Ajantha had drawn to an abrupt and awkward closure. During that one month, fierce competition had broken out between the Chalukya army that was rushing from the north and the invading Pallava army that was marching from the south to reach Vatapi. It was the Pallava army that won the battle of speed. When the Chalukya army was still six kaadam to the north of Vatapi, the ocean-like Pallava army had already reached Vatapi without impediment and had surrounded that expansive city's fortress from all sides.

The citizens of Vatapi were alarmed by this unprecedented disaster. Vatapi's residents, who were extremely proud of Emperor Pulikesi's brave deeds and of his fame spreading far and wide even across the high seas to far-flung nations, had not even imagined that their country would be invaded. The Pallava invasion, akin to thunder striking across clear skies, numbed and shocked the people. Everyone was aware that their emperor was not present in the city at that point of time and that the forces deployed for the fort's security were inadequate. Hence, most of the city's womenfolk felt extremely apprehensive. The Samanars, Saivites and Sakthars who were inimical to the Buddhists opined, 'The Ajantha Art Festival, in reality, is a plot hatched by the Buddhists!'

The chief of the fort, Bhimasenan, also had to provide additional security to the viharams and monasteries which were the targets of the citizens' angry attacks.

Commander Bhiman had also made arrangements to read out the messages sent by the emperor through his emissaries to help the citizens allay their fear. The emperor had stated in that epistle that he was rushing to Vatapi along with the massive army stationed at the banks of the Narmada River and that another large force stationed at Vengi Nadu was also marching towards Vatapi. He insisted there was no need for the citizens to lose heart should the Pallava army lay siege to the Vatapi fort ahead of his reaching Vatapi and that he would teach the Pallava army a lesson by decimating it and liberating Vatapi very soon. After hearing the above epistle read out at street junctions, the Vatapi residents managed to somewhat overcome their fear and muster courage.

When Emperor Pulikesi, accompanied by the large army that was stationed on the banks of the Narmada River, was four kaadam away from Vatapi, he received news of the Pallava army reaching Vatapi ahead of him and surrounding the fort. He immediately stopped marching ahead. As the army from Vengi had to cross several forests, mountains and rivers on its way, it came to be known that it would take time to reach Vatapi. In the circumstances, Emperor Pulikesi decided after discussions with his ministers and army chiefs, not to engage in war immediately and to wait for some time. He decided to launch a ferocious

attack against the Pallava army once the forces from Vengi
arrived and to tarry at the same place till then. But the doyens of
warfare, Mamalla chakravarthy and Senathipathi Paranjyothi,
did not allow him to execute his decisions.

The Pallava army chiefs debated at the minsters' council
whether to attack the Vatapi fort or to confront the massive
army led by Pulikesi first. Manavanmar and Aditya Varmar
opined that as their mission was to capture Vatapi fort, they
ought to attack the fort immediately. Senathipathi Paranjyothi
felt Pulikesi ought to be attacked and slaughtered before the
forces arrived from Vengi, that the Vatapi fort was not going
to disappear and that the longer the Vatapi fort was under
siege, the easier it would be for the Pallava forces to capture it.
The chief of spies supported the senathipathi. After deploying
a small force to continue the siege at the Vatapi fort, a major
portion of the Pallava army started marching northwards.

Emperor Pulikesi came to know of this. He realized
that if he retreated at this juncture, the Chalukya kingdom's
honour would come to naught. He prepared himself for war.
Three kaadam to the north of Vatapi, the two mammoth
armies locked horns. The gory battle continued for three days
and nights. Thousands of warriors, stabbed by swords and
pierced by spears, met their end on the battlefield. Corpses
of soldiers who had died fighting bravely, their arms, legs and
heads mutilated, lay in mounds on the battlefield.

The dead elephants that lay on the battlefield resembled
black granite hills. The corpses of humans and those of horses
were all piled together. The pathetic moaning of humans, the
horrific shrieking of elephants and the sorrowful neighing
of horses that were on the verge of death mingled together
to form an intolerable din. Rivers of blood flowed in all four
directions. The mutilated limbs of warriors floating on the

rivers of blood presented an excruciating sight. It is impossible
to provide an accurate description of that war in which lakhs
of warriors and thousands of elephants and horses were
deployed. Only great playwrights like Valmiki, Vyasar, Homer
and Kambar[16] could do that.

It was possible to estimate the relative strength of
both sides from the very beginning of the war. Those who
understood the intricacies of warfare could surmise the
outcome of the war. The Chalukya army that had travelled a
long distance nonstop was unable to withstand the assault of
the invigorated Pallava army, which had had the opportunity
to rejuvenate itself after reaching Vatapi. A key contributory
factor to the weakness of the Chalukya army was that a major
part of its elephant force was stationed along with its army at
Vengi.

At the dawn of the third day, the victory of the Pallava
army and the defeat of the Chalukya army had become a
certainty. That afternoon, the Chalukya commanders and
ministers surrounded Pulikesi and forcefully impressed upon
him the need for him to retreat to a safe place till the arrival
of the forces from Vengi for the welfare of the kingdom.
The chakravarthy, realizing that there was no alternative,
acquiesced. It was decided that the emperor escorted by what
remained of the cavalry would retreat when that day drew
to a close. But a major disruption occurred in the evening.
The Pallava army had saved the elephant force that had been
specially trained by Manavanmar for the very end. That
evening they launched an attack by that force.

---

[16] Valmiki and Kambar are the authors of the Ramayana in Sanskrit and
Tamil respectively. Vyasar is the author of the Mahabharata.

When 5000 ferocious elephants armed with iron poles pounced on the Chalukya cavalry, those unsuspecting horses were taken aback. The horses dispersed and fled in all four directions. The remaining Chalukya soldiers fled even faster than the elephants. For the whole of the third night, the Pallava soldiers pursued the fleeing Chalukya soldiers and hunted them down. The following dawn, the battlefield in which a terrible war had raged during the last three days, was filled with the corpses of the Chalukya soldiers. Not even a single living Chalukya soldier was seen.

Amidst the blowing of trumpets and conches and the sound of victory slogans reaching the skies, the Pallava chakravarthy and his commanders garlanded and congratulated each other and celebrated the conclusive victory secured by the Pallava army. Despite the uproarious celebrations, a small worry lingered in the bottom of their hearts. They wondered what had become of the Chalukya emperor, Pulikesi. It was not known whether the Vatapi emperor had battled till the very end and embraced heroic death or if he had taken flight after observing several Chalukya soldiers fleeing the battlefield. If he had died on the battlefield, they would need to accord his mortal remains the honour due to a powerful emperor. If he had fled, it was possible that he would mobilize an army again and attack them. After debating for a long time about Pulikesi's fate, the Pallavas decided that it was futile to engage in such discussions. After making arrangements for a force headed by Shatrugnan to comb the battlefield thoroughly for Pulikesi's corpse, Mamallar and the others headed to Vatapi again.

Chapter 31

The Bikshu's Vow

One night after the Great War of Vatapi came to an end, an extremely sorrowful incident unfolded in the vicinity of the kabalikas' sacrificial altar that lay some distance away from the Vatapi fort. The just rising moon's rays streamed through the trees and fell on the bare rocks, which along their pitch-black shadows resembled huge ghosts, heightening the eeriness of that rocky terrain.

A hideous female form was seen walking by the rocks, sometimes in the shadow of the rocks and at other times in the moonlight. That apparition was carrying a body on her shoulder. The stiff manner in which the body lay on her shoulder indicated that it was a corpse. As she walked in the moonlight, her shadow resembled that of a demon's. One would have thought that it was a demon who was carrying his prey.

She looked even more frightening from close quarters. Her tanned thick skin, short reddened tresses and fiery eyes made her look like an ogress. But the male corpse, which that woman carried on her shoulder, was not so frightful. He looked regal. Who was it? Probably it was . . .

When this unsightly fiend turned around the corner of a rock, she was taken aback to see someone walking towards her. She hesitated. Why was she shocked? Was it fear? Could she too be subject to fear? Or was there some other reason? The person walking towards her did so without any hesitation. The man approached her asking, 'Ranjani, is that you?' His voice sounded like the bikshu's. Isn't it surprising that the repulsive monstress had a beautiful name like Ranjani? Nevertheless, in the past, the woman had possessed a captivating appearance befitting the name Ranjani [17] It was the bikshu who had transformed her into a repulsive kabalikai. [18]

It seemed as though the kabalikai was even more shocked when she heard the bikshu's voice. Observing her standing like a statue, the bikshu asked again, 'Ranjani! Why this silence? Where did you go to hunt?'

It seemed as though the kabalikai had overcome her shock. 'Adigal! Is it truly you?' she asked in a surprised and suspicious tone.

'What kind of a question is this? Why do you doubt that? Who else but I would come in search of you in the middle of the night? Since I could not find you in your cave, I came here looking for you! What is that? Whom are you carrying? Which sinner's corpse are you bearing? Nowadays you seem to have no dearth of prey!'

Even as the bikshu was speaking in this manner, the kabalikai dropped the corpse she had been carrying for so

---

[17] In Sanskrit, Ranjani means pleasing/charming.
[18] Female kabalika (cannibal).

long with a thud. She exclaimed, 'What fun!' and let out a terrifying laugh.

'What is the fun? Where did you find the corpse?' asked the bikshu.

'Adigal! I wept nonstop thinking of you as I walked for two kaadam. All my tears were in vain!' complained the kabalikai.

'Did you weep? Why should you shed tears thinking of me? What kind of a joke is this?' asked the bikshu.

'It is a big joke. I will narrate the joke from the beginning, listen to me!' So saying, the kabalikai narrated her story.

'I had gone to derive some amusement by watching the war. I was watching the war from the top of a hill that stands some distance away from the battlefield. My God! What a war it was! How many casualties! How many humans were sacrificed! The kabalikas sacrifice one human being every month at this spot! That's nothing! There, lakhs of human beings and thousands of elephants and horses were sacrificed. The sacrifices continued day and night for three days. Finally, one side started fleeing while the other side was pursuing them. I did not even observe who was chasing whom. I took to flight fearing that they would capture me. Today, I surreptitiously walked through the forest during the daytime. In the evening, I could hear the sound of a horse galloping. I ran even faster thinking that someone was coming to seize me. For some time, the horse also continued galloping. When darkness had set in, I hid myself behind a tree to find out who was chasing me. The horse that was chasing me suddenly fell. The man who was mounted on the horse lay immobile; he did not get up. When I went close to the horse, I realized that it was on the verge of death. It seemed that the man who lay on the horse had been dead for a long time. As his legs were fastened to the stirrups, he must have lain on the horse without falling off. I bent down and looked at his face, it was exactly like yours. Am I not a mad woman? I thought it was you, carried him on my shoulder and came here weeping . . .'

The bikshu seemed to be suddenly struck by a thought then. He bent down and stared intently at the corpse's face in the moonlight. When the bikshu shrieked, 'Thambi! Pulikesi!' it echoed across that vast rocky area. 'Ranjani! Go away! Leave me alone for some time! Don't stand here!' ordered the sobbing bikshu. Hearing this, the kabalikai became scared and walked away to stand behind a rock.

The bikshu sat down and placed Pulikesi's corpse on his lap. 'Thambi! What became of you? Is this how you died? Isn't it because of this sinner that you were reduced to this state?' lamented the bikshu and repeatedly beat his chest and forehead. 'Aiyyo! Thambi! Didn't you pass away thinking that I had betrayed you? My brother, you are dearer to me than my own life! Would I betray you, who lived along with me in our mother's womb for ten months? I had conspired to wreak revenge on Mamallan! You died before I could divulge my intention to you!'

The bikshu again punched himself on the chest and swore, 'You base bikshu! May your anger be doomed! May your love be destroyed! Your Sivakami! Ah! What will Sivakami do? Thambi! I did not betray you. Neither did I betray our nation. Had both of us exercised some patience at Ajantha that day, this disaster would not have occurred! I would not have allowed this war to break out! I would have starved everyone from Pallava Nadu to death! I would have slaughtered Mamallan! Aiyyo! Things have come to such a pass . . .'

The bikshu gently lifted Pulikesi's corpse from his lap and placed it on the ground. He stood up, lifted both his hands towards the skies and shrieked in a manner that gave the kabalikai hiding behind the rock goose pimples. 'Thambi! Pulikesi! I will avenge your death! I swear by the lotus feet of Buddha Bhagavan! I swear by the vengeful Rudran[19] who bears a kabalam.[20] I also swear by the bloodthirsty Shakti Bhadrakali[21] that I will seek revenge on those who killed you!'

---

[19] Manifestation of Lord Shiva.
[20] Skull.
[21] A ferocious manifestation of Goddess Parvati.

Chapter 32

The Kabalikai's Love

The bikshu, after swearing by the names of several Gods with his face tilted skywards and his hands raised, sat down and placed Pulikesi's lifeless body on his lap again. 'Thambi! You have not died. All these days though we lived in two separate bodies, we shared the same soul. Like our soul, our bodies have become one now. Henceforth you are me, I am you! We are not two separate people!'

After speaking thus in an emotion-laden voice, the bikshu sobbed and cried in a manner that caused his body to shake.

It seemed as though he had lost his self and had immersed himself in an ocean of grief. The night was passing quickly. The moon was rising higher and higher. The shadows of the rocks and trees became progressively shorter. The kabalikai, who had been standing for a long time behind a rock, finally lost patience.

She went and stood behind the bikshu and gently placed her fingers on his shoulder. Taken aback, the bikshu looked around. 'Ranjani! Is that you?' he asked. 'Yes, it's me!' replied the kabalikai. 'Haven't you left yet?'

'If that's your order, I will do so.'

'No, stay! You are the only one in this vast world who bears affection for me.'

'There is not a soul to shower affection on me.'

'Ah! Ranjani, why do you say so? Am I not there?' asked the bikshu.

The sorrow that had been evident in his voice some time earlier had disappeared without a trace and had been replaced by deceptive affection. 'Adigal! Why are you trying to deceive this helpless woman? Who would feel affection for this hideous form?' asked the kabalikai.

'Haven't you heard that love is blind? No matter how unsightly you may be, in my eyes you are Rathi!' remarked the bikshu.

'You treacherous bikshu! Why do you intentionally prevaricate? You were the one who made me look repulsive. If you bore affection towards me, would you have behaved in this manner?' questioned that repugnant kabalikai.

'Ranjani! Haven't I explained this several times to you? Had you resided in the Vatapi Palace looking as beautiful as an Ajantha painting, wouldn't some prince have won your hand? That's why I acted in this manner.'

'You yourself could have won my hand. Who would have prevented you?'

'I have also explained that to you a thousand times. I will state the reason again: I had some tasks to execute. Foremost was securing my release from the Buddha Sangam.'

'You've been saying this for a long time. When will you be released?'

'Ranjani, I have been released! The great obstacle that prevented you from fulfilling your desire no longer exists. Are you happy now?' asked the bikshu gently.

'Are you stating the truth?' asked Ranjani.

'I swear I'm stating the truth. The necessity for me to seek my release did not even arise. The members of the Buddha Sangam excommunicated me. This must have happened on account of your penances.'

The kabalikai asked suspiciously, 'Why did they excommunicate you? How did the members of the Buddha Sangam dare to excommunicate the all-powerful Naganandi bikshu?'

'That's a long story, I will tell you later. We now have an extremely important mission ahead of us. We must cremate this corpse immediately. If anyone comes to know of this, everything will go awry. Ranjani! Why don't you bring the logs and build a pyre right here?'

'I will not do it!'

'Why not? Won't you help me?' asked the bikshu.

'I will help you only if you tell me why they excommunicated you from the Buddha Sangam.'

'I will tell you briefly, listen! I was aware of Mamallan's impending invasion. But, for certain reasons I did not reveal this to my brother. When this fool came to know of this, he thought that I had betrayed him and the nation. He told me, who had saved his life by risking my own and had orchestrated his rise to such a powerful position, "I don't want to see you as long as you're alive!" and sent me away. On account of his behaviour, he is now lying here as an orphaned corpse. You and I must cremate him!' confided the bikshu and took a deep breath. He continued, 'The bikshus at the Ajantha Sangramam came to know of this. They, who had accepted all the assistance that came to them through me, on realizing that I had fallen out of favour with the emperor, cursed and excommunicated me. They also faced the consequences of their behaviour. Ranjini! Those who oppose Neelakesi will not survive, they will face doom.'

'What became of the Ajantha bikshus?' asked the kabalikai.

'Nothing at all. Within a week of the incident occurring, the bikshus had to shut down the Ajantha Sangramam and flee for their lives. A rumour had spread across the country that the Ajantha Art Festival was a conspiracy hatched by the bikshus to assist Mamallan of Kanchi. I was the one who sowed the seeds of this rumour. The citizens were prepared to march up to Ajantha and destroy the Sangramam and the sculptures and paintings that lay within the Sangramam. When the bikshus came to know of this, they closed all the secret routes that led to Ajantha and started fleeing northwards to Harsha's kingdom. After that, I myself tried to go to Ajantha again. I too was unable to trace the route. I decided to tackle this problem later and returned. I came at the right time. Ranjani! Stand up! Do as I bid quickly! Build the pyre right away! Bring the fire!'

'What are you going to do after cremating the emperor?'

'Ranjani! You must not divulge anything about the emperor's death or his cremation to anyone. You must not reveal this even to the wind. You must keep this matter extremely confidential. Do you understand?'

'Why the secrecy, adigal?'

'I will tell you later. Ranjani! We don't have a moment to waste.'

'You treacherous bikshu! You don't have to tell me the reason. I know what it is.'

'What do you know?'

'After cremating this corpse, you are going to head to Vatapi through the secret tunnel! You're going to proclaim that you are the emperor. You are going to ascend the throne with the temptress from Kanchi by your side . . .'

Naganandi stood up in anger and announced, 'I will act in the manner you just described. Go to hell! Henceforth I will have nothing to do with you . . .'

Before he could speak further, the kabalikai fell at his feet and pleaded, 'Adigal! Please forgive me. I will obey you.'

'But you don't trust me. What is the use of telling you?'

'There is one way to instill trust in me!'

'What is that?'

'Hand over that dancer to me!'

'Ranjani! You have waited for so long. Please be patient for some more time. Wait till the siege of Vatapi comes to an end. Haven't I told you that I have a reason for safeguarding Sivakami? The time has now come. When I wreak revenge on Mamallan, I will hand Sivakami over to you. Then the emperor of the southern country will be Neelakesi! You will be the Empress! The Chalukya, Pallava, Chola, Pandya and Vengi kingdoms will lie beneath our feet!'

When Naganandi alias Neelakesi uttered these words, his eyes glowed like fire in the moonlight.

The kabalikai appeared assuaged. In deference to Neelakesi's words, she brought the logs from her cave and started building a pyre. Then she muttered to herself, unheard by Neelakesi, 'Perfidious bikshu! You're trying to cheat me again. But your plans are never ever going to fructify. That temptress Sivakami will not give you a second look no matter how much you beseech her and even if you give her Devendran's position. Finally, you will have to fall at my feet!'

Chapter 33

Ministerial Consultation

A week had passed since the Pallava army had conclusively won the Great War of Vatapi. Some distance away from the main entrance to the Vatapi fort, a gigantic Rishabha flag fluttered majestically in the sky. At the tent pitched beneath the flag, Mamallar's ministers' council had congregated. The faces of the ministers sitting around Mamallar revealed their pride on winning a decisive victory in a major war tinged with worry. However, Mamallar's valorous and handsome face exuded fire and brimstone. A message sent by the Vatapi chieftains seeking to surrender ignited a debate at the ministers' council.

On returning from the battlefield, the Pallava army had been divided into two forces. One force was strategically stationed two kaadam to the east to attack the Vengi army that was marching towards Vatapi. Preparations were underway to deploy the second force to attack and capture the fort. It was a matter concerning the proposed attack of the fort that had made Mamallar furious. He was not even willing to give the soldiers who had returned after winning a major war time to relax. He rushed the senathipathi and the others. He mounted a horse and rode around the fort motivating the soldiers. Mamalla chakravarthy himself explained to the soldiers how to cross the moat in one go, how to climb the ramparts of the fort, how to wield the spear and kill the guards stationed on the fort walls and what they should do on entering the fort. Mamallar's behaviour made Senathipathi Paranjyothi angry and sad. He asked, 'Why don't you leave these tasks to me? Don't you trust me?'

Mamallar's urgency in initiating the attack on the fort stemmed from his concern that the enemy might call for a truce even before the attack started. His fear was not unfounded. When it was decided that the attack on the fort would be launched the following day, a white flag signifying a truce had been raised at the main entrance to the fort. Two people had climbed down the ramparts using a rope ladder. They had submitted the two messages to Senathipathi Paranjyothi and returned.

One of the messages was written by the chief of the fort, Bhimasenan, to the chakravarthy. The message stated that the Vatapi chieftains had held discussions and decided to relinquish control of the Vatapi fort to the Kanchi chakravarthy without any opposition—that all the wealth in the Vatapi palace and the elephant force and cavalry stationed within the fort would be surrendered to him and that they were willing to comply with any other conditions he might have. The message requested Mamallar to show mercy and refrain from attacking the fort and to allow the city's womenfolk to retain their houses, wealth and freedom. The message concluded stating that if Mamalla chakravarthy were to acquiesce to their request, the chief of the fort, Bhimasenan, along with his men were prepared to surrender.

This message calling for truce gave no room for suspicion; it was the truth. The residents of Vatapi who stood in the mandapams atop the ramparts observing the proceedings had also come to know of the Great War that had been fought between the Pallava and the Chalukya armies. As it was clear that the Pallava army had won the war, the Vatapi citizens were struck with fear. Wailing and lamenting filled the streets and homes. Everyone had come to know that they did not possess adequate forces and weapons to safeguard the fort and that they had not accumulated sufficient food supplies to sustain them should the siege continue any longer. If the siege were to continue for a month, the citizens would have to starve. If the enemy forces were to attack the fort and forcibly enter, then the citizens could not expect mercy from them. Lakhs of women, children and aged people would be rendered helpless.

Taking all this into account and in the absence of an alternative, the Vatapi chieftains and the chief of the fort, Bhimasenan, called for a truce. Mamallar had summoned the ministers' council to discuss the offer of truce. That day, Mamallar was impatient and short-tempered, a phenomenon that had never occurred in the past. The very sight of the message made him furious. When the message was read out, sparks of fire flew from his eyes. Those assembled understood from the chakravarthy's body language, facial expression and manner of speaking that he was not favourably inclined towards the truce. Despite this, when the chakravarthy sought their opinion, those assembled truthfully stated that they were in favour of accepting the truce and safeguarding the city and its residents.

The chakravarthy's fury escalated. When each one supported the truce, Mamallar reacted caustically, exclaiming, 'Is that so!' and 'Oh!' Paranjyothi and Manavanmar refrained from voicing their opinions. 'Why are you standing quietly without saying anything? Senathipathi! What's your opinion?' asked Mamallar pointedly.

'Prabhu! I too believe that the hostilities must cease. What's the use of innocent people suffering? Moreover, when they are begging for their lives by surrendering to the chakravarthy, what other option exists?'

'Senathipathi! What are you saying? Have you too started proselytizing about justice and fairness? Have you forgotten the atrocities perpetrated by Pulikesi in our country? Aren't you aware that we are duty-bound to set this city ablaze and reduce it to ashes? Do you speak thus despite being aware of everything? What has suddenly come over all of you? Are you all tired of war? Does the sight of blood scare you? Have you become so attached to your lives and possessions? Manavanmar! I hope that at least you are on my side! Or have you too joined the ranks of Buddha Bhagavan's foremost disciples and become a pacifist?' demanded Mamallar fierily.

Manavanmar understood Mamallar's state of mind very well. He realized that Mamallar would go to any length to fulfil his promise to Sivakami and if the surrender were accepted, Mamallar would not be able to keep his word. Truth be told, Manavanmar was extremely surprised that Senathipathi Paranjyothi had supported the armistice. Also, the thought that if the offer of ceasefire were accepted, there would be no opportunity to unleash the elephant force that he had specially trained to attack the fort lurked in a corner of Manavanmar's mind.

Assessing the situation, Manavanmar remarked, 'Prabhu! When all the valorous commanders of Pallava Nadu unanimously favour a truce, I was hesitant to offer a contradictory opinion. Specifically, I was unwilling to dispute the senathipathi!'

Mamallar roared in a commanding tone, 'Illavarasey! If it's mandatory that everyone must voice unanimous views, then there is no need for a ministers' council. Everyone may boldly state their opinions here. There's no need for anyone to be afraid!'

'Prabhu! I will state my opinion if you command me to do so. I believe that we ought not to accept the armistice. Does surrendering set right all the untold atrocities that have been committed?'

Senathipathi Paranjyothi interrupted saying, 'What sin did the citizens of Vatapi commit? How can they be held responsible for the barbarian Pulikesi's actions?'

Manavanmar responded saying, 'The senathipathi speaking thus surprises me. Didn't these people happily witness the atrocities perpetrated by Pulikesi? Did they ever attempt to prevent him from behaving unjustly? They are the ones who strengthened the savage Pulikesi. They are the ones who shared and enjoyed the loot Pulikesi plundered and brought back. They are the ones who enslaved and extracted work out of the men and women, who Pulikesi imprisoned and brought back to Vatapi. Haven't the Vatapi citizens insulted and earned the indelible enmity of the Pallava kingdom by making the sculptor Aayanar's daughter dance at the street junctions? Has our valorous senathipathi forgotten all this?' When Manavanmar spoke thus, Mamallar shot a sharp look at Paranjyothi.

Then Senathipathi Paranjyothi observed, 'Pallavendra! It's impossible for me to forget the events that Manavanmar recalled. I was desirous of discussing this with you separately. But as Manavanmar has raised the subject of Sivakami Devi, I too will voice my opinion here. The emissaries who delivered the offer of armistice handed over another scroll separately to me. Here is the message penned by Sivakami Devi. Please read this scroll!' So saying, he removed a message from the sheath of his sword and handed it over to the chakravarthy. When the Pallavendrar read the message, his already reddened eyes blazed and resembled ignited coal. The intense anger he felt made his hands tremble. As soon as he read the message, he was about to tear the bunch of palm-leaf scrolls into shreds. The Senathipathi interjected, 'Pallavendra! The message was for me. Please be merciful and return it to me!'

Chapter 34

Sivakami's Missive

The message that Sivakami had written to Senathipathi Paranjyothi was as follows:

> This message is for the brave commander of the Pallava forces and my dear brother, Paranjyothi, from Aayanar's daughter, Sivakami. I am indebted to you and the Pallava Kumarar for not having forgotten this helpless maiden despite nine years passing and for invading this country to uphold my vow. News of the Great War fought to the north of this fort has reached here. People here are wondering if the Vatapi emperor lost his life in that war.
>
> The chief of the Vatapi fort, Bhimasenar, visited and requested me to pen a message. Acquiescing to his request, I have willingly written this missive. The objective behind the expedition initiated by you and the Pallava Kumarar has been achieved. The Chalukya army and the Vatapi emperor have been decimated. I beseech you to end the hostilities and accept the offer of truce extended

by the citizens of Vatapi. I no longer harbour the desire that the Pallava Kumarar should keep my word. Then innocent citizens of this large city will lose their homes and belongings and will be put to untold hardship. I don't wish them to be subjected to such torture. No one stands to benefit from violence.

It is evident that there have been several casualties on both sides during the war. I regret the disastrous slaughters that have occurred on account of me. My dear brother! When I was living all alone in this city for the last nine years, my mind ceaselessly recollected our last meeting. I realized that I had committed a blunder by refusing to accompany you and the Pallava Kumarar back to Kanchi when the two of you came to Vatapi to rescue me. I regret my foolishness in stubbornly insisting that I will leave the city only when the Pallava Kumarar had ensured that my promise was fulfilled. Isn't it sheer madness that humans who are endowed with a sixth sense kill each other in the name of war?

Is it right for humans to kill living beings created by God? When we are incapable of creating even a minute organism, isn't it sinful to slaughter thousands of people? The more I think about these issues, the more remorse I feel for instigating this horrific war. There exists a God to mete out punishment and forgive erring humans. Elders believe that even a particle does not move in this world without God's knowledge. This being the case, why do humans have to take the initiative to punish other humans?

Anna! Let bygones be bygones. At least now the bloodshed should end. Please forgive me for my obstinacy and all the difficulty I have put you through. Please inform the Pallava Kumarar that I implore him to stop the war. Ever since a siege was laid on the fort, the residents of the city have been extremely respectful to me. Should the Pallava Kumarar accept their surrender, they are prepared to seat me in a palanquin and send me back with all honours. Please make all this known to the Pallava Kumarar. I am extremely eager to see all of you. I hope that I will be fortunate enough to meet you and the Pallava Kumarar by sunset today. I hereby prostrate to the lotus feet of my dear father.

Given Mamallar's state of mind, the rage he felt on reading Sivakami Devi's message was easily comprehensible. When Mamallar was about to tear the message up, the senathipathi pointed out that the message was meant for him. This made Mamallar even more furious. 'Is that so? Take your message, Senathipathi! Take it by all means. Please pray to this great scroll that preaches justice!' So saying, he flung the manuscript down.

The senathipathi reverently picked up the scroll and declared, 'Yes, Pallavendra! This indeed is a great message for me. I came to Kanchi to be educated by Thirunavukkarasar Peruman. I was not fortunate then. But today, I was fortunate to have read Sivakami Devi's sermon. Isn't Sivakami Devi the daughter of the sculptor Aayanar, my preceptor?'

Mamallar felt an uncontrollable rage. He, who had never mentioned Sivakami's name in public, now spoke arrogantly in the presence of his council. 'Senathipathi! I have committed two blunders in my life. I attempted to seat the sculptor's daughter on the throne. I failed in that attempt. I made you, who had come to learn Tamil and sculpting, the senathipathi of the Pallava kingdom! That has now become the second blunder. The sculptor's daughter has proved that she is unfit to ascend the throne. You have proved that the son of a vaidhyar, who treats peoples' ailments, is unfit to lead the army of a nation ...'

Tears welled up in Senathipathi Paranjyothi's eyes. Humiliation and anger overcame him. He started saying, 'Pallavendra ...'

When Mamallar roared, 'Senathipathi! Stop!' he was rendered speechless. Till then, Mamallar had never spoken to him thus. He had never uttered an insulting or hurting word. Paranjyothi was unable to comprehend this new anger-filled incarnation of Mamallar, who then attacked him with sharp words. 'Who did you think I am? Who did the sculptor's daughter think I was? How dare she write this message? How long have you two been conspiring to bring disgrace to the Pallava dynasty? When this foolish girl unthinkingly insists, we ought to prepare for war and when she condescends to command us we have to end this war. Does she think that she is the raison d'être of the Pallava kingdom? Did she write this message thinking that the citizens of Pallava Nadu and the Pallava chakravarthy are her slaves? I did not mobilize this massive army and prepare for this war for the last nine years to keep my end of the pact with the sculptor's fickle daughter. You need to understand this. I came to defend the honour of the Pallava dynasty. I embarked on this expedition to abide by the command Mahendra Pallavar issued on his deathbed. I came to ensure that the world does not mock Narasimha Pallavan, who won the title of Maha Mallan at the age of eighteen. I did not come to uphold the vow of the sculptor's short-sighted daughter. I did not come here to listen to her preach justice and to attain enlightenment. Since it is evident that you are unwilling to conduct this war further, I relieve you of the senathipathi's post this very instant!'

Mamallar, who spoke looking at the senathipathi, turned to the prince of Lanka and declared, 'Illavarasey! Foreseeing that our senathipathi would betray me at an opportune moment, I brought you along. Fortunately, at least you are willing to obey me! Prepare to attack the fort immediately. We must start the attack tonight itself!'

Pin-drop silence prevailed after Mamallar's fiery speech, which resembled a prolonged bout of lightning, came to an end. Everyone stood stunned. They had believed that Mamallar and Paranjyothi were inseparable friends who shared a common soul. Hearing Mamallar speak to Paranjyothi so harshly, they were in turmoil.

Manavanmar thought sadly, 'What is this? This is an undesirable and unintentional outcome! Haven't I antagonized the senathipathi and made a permanent enemy of him?'

As he stood still, Mamallar rebuked him, 'Illavarasey Why are you standing still?' Manavanmar looked at Paranjyothi.

The senathipathi, who had been standing dazed like the others till then, stepped forward and requested in a choked voice, 'Pallavendra! I seek a boon from you on the strength of the twelve years of service I have rendered to the Pallava kingdom!'

As Mamallar did not respond, Paranjyothi spoke further. 'Prabhu! You and I made a pact standing beside Pulikesi's Jayasthambam that is visible from here. We swore to demolish that false Jayasthambam, erect a memorial commemorating the Pallava invasion in its place and free Sivakami Devi. We have toiled day and night for the last nine years to keep our word. Please permit your humble servant to continue as a Senathipathi till we uphold the vow!'

The anger in Mamallar's face disappeared and he smiled. 'Why do you have to use such roundabout means to seek a boon? Senathipathi! That's my desire too. Start the attack immediately!'

'Please forgive me. I have another request, prabhu! If we begin our attack of the fort, we must emerge victorious within one day and one night. Please give us three days to make the necessary arrangements!' asked the senathipathi humbly. Mamallar's silence indicated his reluctant acceptance of the senathipathi's request.

Chapter 35

Vatapi Ganapathi

There are two types of people in this world. The first consists of people quite indifferent to the recurring acts of cruelty they witness. With time, it becomes their habit to not just watch, but also to indulge in such vicious acts. Incidents that initially arouse pity fail to evoke any emotion over a period of time. The second type comprises people who are not indifferent, but feel more and more enraged at such acts of brutality. They are affected by others' sufferings. The more they witness injustice and violence, the firmer their resolve becomes to eradicate these evils. Senathipathi Paranjyothi was of the second type. He did not belong to the demonic tribe of humans who became increasingly bloodthirsty when they witnessed gore. At the Vatapi War, he observed rivers of blood flowing in the battlefield, mountains of piled-up human corpses and the moans of those who had been grievously injured and were on the verge of death. This led Paranjyothi to think, 'Why should such atrocities occur? Why do humans have to engage in barbaric acts and kill each other?'

Sivakami's message reached him when he was in this state of mind. He had felt that every word written in that message was true. He thought that God himself had preached thus through Sivakami Devi to prevent him from engaging in such brutal acts. If this were not the case, why did Aayanar's daughter have to write to him instead of writing to Mamallar directly? Paranjyothi thought that as Sivakami Devi had herself declared that there was no necessity to fulfil her promise, Mamallar would immediately acquiesce. Who stood to gain by tormenting the citizens of Vatapi in retaliation for the brutality perpetrated by Pulikesi at Pallava Nadu ten years ago? Moreover, there was no guarantee that the violence would end with this. 'We are avenging the injustice committed by Pulikesi a decade ago by torturing the citizens of Vatapi now. Similarly, the Chalukyas may seek revenge on Pallava Nadu in a few years from now. When sovereigns seek vengeance to uphold their honour and their dynasty's glory, innocent people on both sides are put to untold misery.'

Senathipathi Paranjyothi was thinking along these lines. Intermittently, he also recollected Mamallar's scornful words, which made him sad. Wasn't he under the delusion that Mamallar's emotions and intellect functioned in unison? Not only was Mamallar extremely dismissive of his suggestion, but he had also humiliated him. Wasn't this trait characteristic of royalty? Ever since the Prince of Lanka had come to Kanchi, Mamallar's character had undergone a complete transformation. All these troubles were because of Manavanman. Senathipathi Paranjyothi had sought three days' time, to make preparations to attack the fort. It was a valid reason. Senathipathi Paranjyothi had learnt from experience that it was preferable to make due preparations and complete a task in a day rather than embarking on a task unprepared and complete it in ten days' time. So, preparation was primary in his war strategies.

However, there was another important reason for Senathipathi Paranjyothi seeking time. He was desirous of safely fetching Sivakami Devi, who was still residing within the fort, to the Pallava army camp before the attack began. How could one be sure that no harm would befall Aayanar's daughter if she were to remain inside the fort when the Pallava army attacked it? Mamallar and Paranjyothi had discussed this issue previously. Shatrugnan and Gundodharan were commissioned to ascertain if there was a secret tunnel that led inside the fort so that a few people could be sent in ahead of the attack. The senathipathi had sought three days' time to see what would become of their efforts.

The third day was drawing to a close; the sun was setting. If Mamallar were to pass orders that night, the attack would have to start. But Shatrugnan and Gundodharan had not returned yet. How can this tricky situation be resolved? Paranjyothi hoped Mamallar would change his mind and accept the truce without engaging in combat. If not, how can we ensure that no danger befalls Sivakami Devi?

The Pallava senathipathi was riding by the ramparts of the fort considering possible outcomes. It seemed that there was some disturbance within the fort. Dead silence had prevailed within the fort all these days. But at that point of time, all kinds of noises were heard. Paranjyothi felt heightened confusion on account of this. He brought his horse to a halt when he reached the main entrance of the fort. To attack the fort, it was imperative to first demolish the gigantic gates fitted to the massive main entrance. Only then would it be possible for all the soldiers to enter the fort at the same time and capture the city within a short period of time. Though arrangements for this had already been made, the senathipathi wished to take one final close look before commanding the warriors of the elephant force to launch the attack.

So, he dismounted from the horse and walked towards the entrance. It was then that the exquisitely carved sculptures at the entrance of the Vatapi fort caught his attention. Amongst those sculptures was an idol of Ganapathi. Paranjyothi stood close to the idol with his arms folded. He prayed silently as follows: 'Vinayaka Peruman, remover of all barriers! Please bless us so that our mission is accomplished! Please be with us so that we may safely hand over my guru's daughter, Sivakami Devi, to her father, Aayanar. Please grant this prayer of mine, I will ensure that you're not harmed when we attack this fort. I will take you back to my native village, build a temple, consecrate you in that temple and perform daily prayers.'

The instant Paranjyothi finished praying, commotion broke out amongst the Pallava soldiers who were stationed some distance away from the fort entrance. They looked at the top of the fort entrance and exclaimed in surprise. As this attracted the senathipathi's attention, he looked towards the soldiers. One of them called out, 'Senathipathi! The white flag has been lowered!' The senathipathi hurried to the spot where they were standing and looked at the the fort entrance. The flag of truce that had been fluttering for the last three days no longer remained hoisted.

Chapter 36

'Victory or Death'

Senathipathi Paranjyothi stood rooted to the spot for a moment, wondering what the lowering of the white flag meant and what the reason could be for this occurrence. As if in response to the queries that rose in his mind, there occurred a miracle in the vicinity of the fort wall just then. On the wide and long fort walls that had been vacant all these days stood warriors armed with spears. Their steel helmets, copper armours fastened to their chests and the tips of the spears they held, gleamed in the yellow evening sun.

These warriors cheered in thundering voices, 'Long live Maharajadhi Raja,[22] Chaluka Kula Thilaka,[23] Tribhuvana Chakravarthy[24] Satyasraya Pulikesi!' This was followed by thousands of voices hailing, 'Jaya Vijayi Bhava!'

---

[22] Maharajadhi Raja—Great King of Kings.
[23] Chaluka Kula Thilaka—the Pride of the Chalukya Dynasty.
[24] Tribhuvana chakravarthy—Emperor of the Three Realms.

Senathipathi Paranjyothi stood shocked for some time as he observed this astonishing sight. A soldier close to him pointed to the top of the fort's main entrance and called out, 'There! There!' A tall majestic figure stood there surveying the surrounding area. Ah! There was no doubt that it was Emperor Pulikesi.

Paranjyothi, at that point of time, clearly understood why the white flag had been lowered. Emperor Pulikesi had escaped from the battlefield and had gained entry into the fort either through a secret tunnel or by evading the Pallava soldiers and climbing over the ramparts at night. Now there was no scope for peace. A war was inevitable; attacking the fort was imperative. The blood of thousands of men would be shed. The city of Vatapi would be set ablaze. As the senathipathi was thinking thus, an arrow swiftly flew from the fort entrance. The Pallava soldiers exclaimed in shock as the arrow was heading towards Paranjyothi's head. For a moment it seemed as if all their hearts would cease beating. Fortunately, the arrow flew one span above the senathipathi's head and hit the ground behind him.

While everyone else was disconcerted, the senathipathi remained unperturbed. He smilingly commanded that the arrow, which had struck the ground, be removed. A tiny scroll was fastened to its tail. Paranjyothi read the message which stated, 'Victory or Death'. Paranjyothi felt as though a big burden had been lifted from his chest. The conflict within him had been resolved. The responsibility for starting the war again and causing bloodshed had fallen on Pulikesi. The attack on the fort could now be conducted without guilt.

When Paranjyothi reached this conclusion, he asked the warrior standing next to him, 'Sadaiya! Do you see the idol of Ganapathi at the fort entrance?'

'I do, swami! I observed you standing close to the idol and gazing at it!' replied Sadaiyan.

'Good! I am entrusting an extremely important task to you. Once the sun sets and it is pitch-black, you and ten other warriors must approach the fort entrance unseen by the Chalukya soldiers. You must remove that idol of Ganapathi without causing any damage to it and bring it to my tent. Do you understand? Your bringing that idol back safely will be a precursor to our winning the war!' commanded the senathipathi.

'So be it, senathipathi! I will exercise the utmost caution in bringing the idol of Vinayakar[25] to your tent!' remarked Sadaiyan.

Immediately the senathipathi turned his horse around and rode swiftly to Mamalla chakravarthy's tent.

The other commanders had already assembled in the chakravarthy's tent. They had come to receive their final orders from the chakravarthy, who was awaiting Senathipathi Paranjyothi's arrival. Mamallar wore a serene expression and was calmly conversing with those around him. Those at the tent were not yet aware of the white flag being lowered and the Chalukya warriors standing on the ramparts prepared for war. When they had heard the Chalukya soldiers chanting war slogans, they thought that it was the Pallava soldiers who had done so.

Paranjyothi entered like a storm into the chakravarthy's tent, which till then had been tranquil, and bowed to the chakravarthy. He exclaimed, 'Prabhu!'

Mamallar interrupted asking, 'Senathipathi! Why are you so agitated? After thinking for the last three days, I have come

---

[25] Vinayakar—another name for Lord Ganapathi.

to the conclusion that your suggestion was fair and just. I have decided to accept the offer of truce and bring the war to an end.'

The senathipathi became even more flustered. Tears welled up in his eyes. He admitted in a choked voice, 'Prabhu! I'm a fool. My suggestion was ridiculous. Your initial command was both fair and just. Delaying the attack for three days was a blunder. Prabhu! The white flag at the entrance of the fort has been lowered. Armed Chalukya warriors are standing atop the ramparts prepared for war ...'

All those assembled in the tent were extremely shocked and furious on hearing of this development. The chakravarthy leapt up from his throne and roared, 'Senathipathi! Are you stating the truth?'

'It's the truth, prabhu! I saw it myself! I headed straight here after witnessing this sight.'

'Are you able to deduce the reason for this change?' asked Mamallar.

'There's no need to deduce, prabhu! Pulikesi did not die on the battlefield. He managed to survive and has somehow entered the fort. I also observed the Vatapi emperor standing atop the fort entrance, surveying his army. Here is Pulikesi's message, which leaves no room for doubt. I found this message fastened to the tail of an arrow that was shot from within the fort!'

As he spoke, Paranjyothi submitted the tiny scroll on which 'Victory or Death' was written.

'This is good news; the responsibility and blame for Vatapi's destruction will rest on him!' quipped Mamallar in an enthusiastic voice. He then asked, 'Senathipathi, do you harbour any uncertainty? May we start attacking the fort now?'

'I am no longer unsure, prabhu! We are prepared. Our elephant force will start demolishing the fort gates in one muhurtham. Our soldiers will also start scaling the ramparts and entering the fort!' announced the senathipathi. He then told the assembled army chiefs, 'All of you head to your respective forces. Please remind our soldiers how they ought to conduct themselves once they enter the city. Be prepared to start attacking once you hear the trumpets.'

The army chiefs, on hearing this, bowed to the chakravarthy and senathipathi and left in high spirits. The chakravarthy, his security guards, Manavanmar and Senathipathi Paranjyothi were the only ones in the tent. Mamalla chakravarthy asked, 'Senathipathi! What have you commanded the soldiers to do after entering Vatapi?'

'Prabhu! I have commanded them not to harass children and women. All the menfolk, who oppose us, ought to be killed while the ones who surrender ought to be imprisoned. All houses in Vatapi without exception must be set on fire and reduced to ashes. I have instructed the soldiers to kill those who attempt to extinguish the fire. I have asked them not to stop those citizens who are fleeing the city but they ought not to carry any of their belongings with them. I have ordered our soldiers to collect and hand over to us all the valuables they can find. Half the valuables secured by each of our soldiers will be returned to the finders. If you wish to convey any other instruction, please let me know,' replied the senathipathi.

'Senathipathi! I have nothing to add. You have acted with foresight!' acknowledged Mamallar.

'Prabhu! An important task is pending. I have earmarked this task for the prince of Lanka, you should command him!' remarked the senathipathi.

Before Mamallar could reply, Manavanmar stated, 'I am waiting for the senathipathi's orders!'

'I have heard that the wealth in the Vatapi emperor's palace far exceeds that in any other sovereign's. Harshavardhanar distributes his wealth amongst his citizens every five years. The avaricious Pulikesi does not behave thus. The wealth that Pulikesi has accumulated in the last thirty years, which is comparable to Kubera's,[26] lies in his palace. Manavanmar should assume the responsibility of carefully bringing those treasures from the palace to our army camp. The palace should be set on fire only when it is stripped of all its wealth. I have set aside 5000 warriors to assist Manavanmar in this mission.' The senathipathi spoke thus looking at Mamallar.

'Senathipathi! Manavanmar will fulfil your wishes. But besides the treasure in the palace, is there no other treasure in Vatapi worth safeguarding? What arrangements have you made for that?' When Mamallar asked this question, his voice choked. Paranjyothi understood that the chakravarthy was enquiring about Sivakami Devi.

'Prabhu! I have retained that responsibility for myself. I do not wish to delegate this to anyone else,' he confided.

'Very good. Is there no news from Shatrugnan yet?'

'I am expecting his arrival.'

'Senathipathi! You have assigned tasks for everyone. But you have not delegated any task to me. What am I supposed to do?'

---

[26] Kubera—the God of Wealth in Hindu mythology.

'Prabhu! I beseech you to stay right here in this tent.'

'Am I not required to even enter Vatapi?'

'If the necessity arises, I will send you a message. Then, you must be prepared to come to Vatapi immediately. Please allow Kannan to accompany me along with the chariot.'

'You may take him along. I will be very anxious here.'

'Prabhu! By Vinayaka Peruman's grace, everything will turn out well. Please do not worry. If necessary, I will send a message. Please give me leave now.'

'Farewell, Senathipathi! As usual, may you return victorious!'

The senathipathi rushed out of the tent. After he left, the surprised chakravarthy wondered, 'How has he suddenly become so devoted to Lord Vinayaka?'

Chapter 37

Shatrugnan's Fear

The war trumpets were blown one muhurtham after sunset, just as the senathipathi had informed the chakravarthy. The Pallava soldiers, who had surrounded the Vatapi fort from all sides, started marching towards the ramparts. It seemed as though the ocean-like army along with its flags fluttering in the wind would inundate the Vatapi fort. The Pallava army elephant force marching towards the four fort gates resembled black granite hills moving.

The earth trembled under the weight of the elephants that had been specifically trained to carry iron poles and sturdy wooden masts with their trunks in this mission. Clouds of dust rose up to the sky and disappeared. The din caused by one lakh warriors and ten thousand elephants moving forward in unison resembled the uproar in the ocean during a raging cyclone. For some time that gargantuan army marched in darkness. Suddenly, illuminated torches became sporadically visible. Shortly thereafter, these multiplied to thousands and their light blinded the eye. The smoke from these torches spread in all four directions, creating a surreal sight that instilled fear.

Senathipathi Paranjyothi stood outside his tent and was looking around. He was pacing to and fro impatiently and drawing patterns on the ground with his sword, anticipating the arrival of someone. It was in this situation that Sadaiyan and four others reached the tent carrying the idol of Ganapathi. Paranjyothi commanded them to place the idol inside the tent. Paranjyothi followed them into the tent and asked Sadaiyan, 'Appane! You and your men stay here and safeguard the Ganapathi idol. I have prayed for the Almighty's guidance to bring Sivakami Devi unharmed out of the Vatapi fort. I have, as a token of my gratitude, promised to build a temple in my village, instate this Vinayaka Peruman and conduct prayers thrice every day!'

He reiterated, 'Sadaiya! If you stay here and guard the idol, you will lose your share of the loot from our plunder of Vatapi. I will compensate you for that!'

'Swami! We will abide by your command!' averred Sadaiyan.

Senathipathi Paranjyothi then stood with his arms folded and eyes closed for some time in front of the Ganapathi idol and prayed. At that moment, the sound of someone running towards the tent was heard. The next instant, a dishevelled Shatrugnan entered the tent. His face was ashen as though he had seen a ghost. Paranjyothi asked him, 'Shatrugna! Why are you in this state? Why do you look terror-stricken? Are we in grave danger? Were you unsuccessful in your mission?'

'Senathipathi! I have faced several grave dangers during my lifetime. But the dangers I faced yesterday and today were unprecedented,' declared Shatrugnan and looked at those present.

The senathipathi, understanding the gesture, asked everyone else to leave. As soon as they had left, he commanded, 'Shatrugna! The attack on the fort has begun. There is no time for delay. Tell me what happened quickly! Were you successful in your mission? Tell me about it first!'

'Senathipathi! There is a secret underground tunnel that leads into the fort. I have found out where it is. But it's no mean task to enter the fort through that tunnel. The attack on the fort has begun. Now, entering the fort through the tunnel does not serve our purpose. I came here to seek your advice!'

So saying, he related his tale.

Chapter 38

Gruesome Cave

The tale that the chief of spies, Shatrugnan, related to Senathipathi Paranjyothi with uncharacteristic agitation was as follows: Shatrugnan and Gundodharan, as commanded by the chakravarthy and the senathipathi, had combed the area surrounding the fort to ascertain if there was a secret tunnel that led into the fort. They carefully searched the rocky terrain close to the kabalikas' sacrificial altar thinking that it was highly likely that the entrance to the secret tunnel would be located there. One night, when they were engaged in this reconnaissance, they observed something burning and walked towards that spot. A man and a woman were standing close to the fire. It was evident that the man was Naganandi bikshu and that the woman was a ghastly looking kabalikai. Shatrugnan and Gundodharan tried eavesdropping on their conversation but could not comprehend anything clearly. But they heard the names of Pulikesi and Sivakami being mentioned often. It was clear that Naganandi was seeking the

kabalikai's assistance. Just as dawn was setting in, the bikshu
and kabalikai pushed away a rock that sealed the entrance to
a cave and entered it. As soon as they got in, the entrance to
that cave was closed again.

After waiting for a long time, Shatrugnan and
Gundodharan decided to remove the rock and enter the cave.
Fortunately, they observed someone moving the rock from
inside just then and hid themselves. The kabalikai came out.
They waited for her to leave the place so that they could enter
the cave. All day, she did not budge from the entrance of the
cave. Only in the evening did she leave the place.

After asking Gundodharan to stand guard outside the
cave, Shatrugnan alone entered the cave. Oh God! The
macabre sights in that cave would render one sleepless for the
rest of their life. Human skulls and skeletons lay heaped in
that cave. The stench was unbearable. As it was pitch-black
inside the cave, Shatrugnan was unable to find out if the
entrance to the tunnel was located therein. Suddenly, the dim
light that pervaded the cave disappeared. Shatrugnan looked
around to locate the entrance of the cave. The entrance to the
cave was no longer visible. A chill went down his spine when
he thought the kabalikai may have sealed the entrance from
outside. He lost sense of the time he spent in the dark and
stinking cave filled with skulls and skeletons. Despite trying
hard, he was unable to locate the entrance to the cave.

For what seemed to be four eons, he paced around the
dark cave in vain. Suddenly light streamed in from one
side. The entrance to the cave opened and the kabalikai
immediately entered. She was carrying a human skull and
bones. Shatrugnan went to the farthest corner of the cave and
stood with his back against the wall. After carefully keeping

the skull and bones aside, she sat on the ground at the centre of the cave and removed a large boulder. When she lowered herself into the aperture the boulder had covered, Shatrugnan realized that it was the entrance to the tunnel. Shatrugnan was happy when he thought that all the time he had spent inside the cave withstanding hunger and thirst had not been futile. It seemed that the kabalikai after entering the tunnel had changed her mind.

She exited the tunnel, closed the entrance, and lay there talking to herself.

From her soliloquy, Shatrugnan came to know that she had been in love with Naganandi bikshu on account of which she hated Sivakami; that Pulikesi had died and it was his skull and bones she had brought into the cave some time ago; that Naganandi was going to masquerade as Pulikesi and was desirous of ascending the Vatapi throne and making Sivakami his empress—an occurrence the kabalikai was determined to prevent at all costs. After talking to herself in this manner for a long time, the kabalikai fell silent. Shatrugnan, thinking that she had fallen asleep, decided to escape. He inched his way to the entrance of the cave. As soon as he reached the entrance, he swiftly jumped out. As he was jumping out, someone grabbed his hand from inside the cave. A shocked Shatrugnan looked around. The kabalikai, who was standing inside the cave, had grasped his hand. She then let out a blood-curling growl. Shatrugnan froze in shock and thought that death loomed over him. Nevertheless he tried extricating his hand but was unable to free himself from the kabalikai's iron-like grip.

The kabalikai then shrieked, 'Lambodhara! Lambodhara!'

Shatrugnan was rendered speechless with shock when he observed Gundodharan come running from behind a rock, calling out, 'Here I come, thaye!' As Gundodharan came running towards Shatrugnan, he gestured with his eyes.

The kabalikai who was standing inside the cave ordered, 'Lambodhara! Hold on to this stealthy spy. I will bring a dagger. You won't let go of him, will you?'

'I will never do that, amma! I will be the first person to behead him!' So saying, Gundodharan held on to Shatrugnan tightly. The kabalikai went inside the cave. Immediately Gundodharan gestured to Shatrugnan and loosened his grip. Shatrugnan extricated himself and fled. Gundodharan raised a hue and cry as he pursued Shatrugnan. After running in this manner for some time, they came to halt behind a rock. 'Swami! I became this kabalikai's disciple only to find out what became of you. Don't worry about me, I will stay here and manage her. You rush back. Our army must have started attacking the fort by now!' suggested Gundodharan.

'The entrance to the tunnel lies inside the cave, Gundodhara! I will inform the senathipathi and return with a few men. Till then, you have to somehow manage this ogress. Don't let her enter the tunnel!' advised Shatrugnan and then ran swiftly to inform the senathipathi.

Shatrugnan was unaware of what had become of Gundodharan after that.

After listening to the shocking and fearful tale, Senathipathi Paranjyothi remarked in a worried tone, 'Shatrugna! You have brought such important news at a critical time. We do not even have the time to consider this development. The attack on the fort has started. We will enter the fort before dawn tomorrow. You take a hundred warriors along and go to that kabalikai's cave! Please ensure that no one uses that tunnel as an escape route. If possible, you and Gundodharan enter the fort through that tunnel. As soon as the fort gates are thrown open, I will head directly to Sivakami Devi's house. With Lord Ganesha's[27] blessings, we will rescue Sivakami Devi and hand her over to Aayanar.'

---

[27] Another name for Lord Ganapathi.

Chapter 38

The Destruction of Vatapi

Mamalla chakravarthy stood outside his tent watching the massive Pallava army nearing the ramparts of the Vatapi fort. He realized that the most important event in his life was unfolding in front of him. On account of the Pallava army launching a fierce attack on the fort that night, he secured a pre-eminent place in history and came to be known as 'Vatapi Konda Narasimhan'[28] for several thousand years thereafter. But would the primary goal that prompted him to mobilize this gargantuan army and invade Vatapi be achieved? It was a foregone conclusion that he would fulfil the promise he had made to Sivakami either that night or on the following day. The Vatapi fort being demolished, and the city being set ablaze within three days was a certainty. But would Sivakami be alive to witness this? Ah! Of what use was it even if that unfortunate woman were to witness Vatapi on fire before

---

[28] The narasimhan who won Vatapi.

leaving the city? Would she be able to lead the joyful life she had previously led? No, never. All her fantasies had become a shattered dream. It was possible for Sivakami to experience moments of happiness even in that shattered dream; even that fortune was denied to Mamalla chakravarthy. Henceforth his life would be akin to a barren desert. In that seemingly endless desert, only mirages would offer him solace.

Mamallar was immersed in such thoughts when he saw Paranjyothi, who had taken leave from him, walking towards him. He was surprised. When Paranjyothi came close to him, he asked, 'Senathipathi! Is there a fresh development?'

The senathipathi replied, 'Yes, prabhu! Shatrugnan has returned,' and then related what Shatrugnan had told him in brief.

Mamallar after listening to Paranjyothi asked, 'Is there any change in our plans due to this news?'

'Nothing significant, prabhu! But it has now become imperative to attack the fort at the earliest. Isn't a snake slithering past our feet more dangerous than a tiger that attacks us from the front?'

'It seems that you believe the kabalikai's tale. Do you suppose that it was Naganandi bikshu and not Pulikesi who sent you the message proclaiming war? In that case, we ought to be even more worried about Sivakami Devi. May I accompany you into the fort right away?'

'No, prabhu! I believe that it's best that you remain here.' Senathipathi Paranjyothi was determined to ensure that he would be the first person to meet Sivakami Devi. He had not forgotten the disastrous consequences of Mamallar meeting Sivakami first and speaking to her nine years ago. He considered it his duty to prevent such an occurrence again.

Mamallar too was not desirous of meeting Sivakami immediately for several reasons. So, he quipped, 'As you say, Senathipathi! Don't forget one thing. Your statement that a snake is more dangerous than a tiger is entirely true. Don't show any mercy to Naganandi. As long as that fake bikshu is alive, the two of us can never be at peace. You will not forget this, will you?'

'I will not forget, prabhu!'

Observing the senathipathi hesitantly continuing to stand there despite the conversation having ended, Mamallar asked, 'Is there any other news?'

Paranjyothi stated, 'Yes, just one more thing. You haven't changed your mind about your command to set Vatapi on fire, have you?'

'Senathipathi! Enough! I am heading to the fort entrance this instant. Trusting you henceforth is futile. You may smear yourself with vibhuti, wear rudrakshas and perform Shiva Pujai!'

'Prabhu! The Peruman who smeared himself with vibhuti reduced Tripuram to ashes. Burning Vatapi down is a facile task for him. You will witness the city of Vatapi burning tonight itself!'

'In that case, why the hesitation and questions?'

'I wanted to confirm your wish for sure. You had ordered the city to be set on fire once our army entered the fort. I wish to act differently. First, we will begin destroying Vatapi. I am going to command our army to throw illuminated torches from outside the fort into the city.'

'What is the necessity for this?'

'I have announced that our soldiers would be awarded half the wealth they brought back from the city. So, when they see the city ablaze, their ardour will increase multi-fold. Prabhu!

We must enter the fort before dawn tomorrow. If we delay further, it will be impossible to rescue Sivakami Devi. Please be prepared by dawn. I urge you not to sleep tonight and to watch Vatapi being destroyed!' After speaking thus, Paranjyothi swiftly left without waiting for the chakravarthy's response.

Just as the senathipathi had promised, the destruction of Vatapi began at around midnight. Scaffolds were erected outside the walls of the fort. Pallava soldiers, specially trained for this purpose, stood on the scaffolds and flung illuminated torches and sulphur bombs into the city. The wind fanned the flames of the torches further. The places where those torches fell, caught fire instantly. The sulphur bombs exploded and served to spread the fire. By the third jaamam of that night, fire enveloped the city of Vatapi, which was inhabited by lakhs of people, from all sides. Vayu Bhagavan[29] also came to the aid of Agni Devan.[30] The raging wind further intensified the fire, which in turn gobbled up the mansions and towers of Vatapi.

Clouds of smoke that accompanied the fire spread in all directions and reached the skies. At the same time, the Pallava and Pandya soldiers surrounded the fort from all sides and attempted to scale the ramparts. The Chalukya soldiers stationed on the ramparts prevented them from doing so. Thousands of Tamil warriors, attacked by swords, spears and arrows, lost their lives. Like the waves that lash the shore in quick succession during a storm, successive contingents of Tamil warriors attacked the fort.

The four entrances to the fort were also subject to brutal attacks. When ten to fifteen elephants wielding massive wooden masts and iron rods ferociously attacked each

---

[29] Vayu Bhagavan—the God of Wind.
[30] Agni Devan—the God of Fire.

of the fort entrances in unison, the gates were smashed to smithereens and fell apart. Just as Senathipathi Paranjyothi had assured the chakravarthy, by the time the fourth jaamam of that night drew to a close, the Pallava soldiers entered the city of Vatapi that was already on fire. The Pallava soldiers who had attacked the ramparts started jumping into the city from all four sides. The rising sun was witness to the historic scene of the city of Vatapi succumbing to fire.

Chapter 40

Fury

Sivakami had felt a raging fury since the time the Pallava soldiers surrounded the Vatapi fort on all sides. She was angry that she was unable to see Mamallar and Aayanar despite their camping only a short distance away from the fort walls. She fretted about the outcome of the war. She wondered how she ought to behave with Mamallar and what she ought to tell him when she met him for the first time after the Pallava army had won the war. These thoughts tormented her. When Sivakami heard that Pulikesi had been killed in the war that had been fought to the north of Vatapi, her heart swelled with pride. She was also worried as to how the Chalukyas would treat her in the aftermath of the Pallava victory.

When the commander of the fort, Bhimasenan, had requested her to write a message to Mamallar, she felt a pride she had never felt before. In deference to his wishes, she wrote a message to the senathipathi. She mentioned in that epistle the decisions she had made after exercising deep thought and had also sent her entreaty. But the missive did not reflect the true emotions that lay buried deep in her heart. The desire to seek revenge on the city and its residents, who had insulted her and her art, lay in the deep recesses of her heart. So after sending the scroll, she thought, 'Why did I write that message? What right do I have to pen such a missive? What will Mamallar and the senathipathi, who have mobilized such a massive army and undertaken the invasion, think? Will they mock at the fickle nature of the female mind? Even if they were to agree with what I had written, will they chide me later on?'

Certain incidents that occurred after she sent the message caused her to regret her action. After the commander of the fort visited Sivakami, crowds of people often congregated outside her house. The people who had almost forgotten Sivakami till then were reminded that she was the reason behind the grave disaster that had befallen them. They stood in groups outside her house and spoke of her disparagingly. When Sivakami looked out of the window on hearing the noise, they jeered at her, laughed loudly and made faces at her.

Sivakami's lady-in-waiting, who knew what the matter was beforehand, forcefully dragged her away from the window. Then Sivakami could hear the crowd's raucous jeers and mocking laughter. The fiery anger that had previously raged in her heart and subsided was now ignited again. 'If Mamallar were truly a brave man, he would tear the message I had written in a helpless situation to shreds and enter this city with his army. He will uphold my vow. He will turn this city into hell and will cause these beasts who don't possess an iota of civility to wail and flee. I will feel placated only when I witness that sight!' she thought. She derived happiness by visualizing that sight in her mind.

As time passed, crowds thronged the street, which became noisier. A few enthusiastic men in the crowd flung stones at the roof and main door of Sivakami's house. When these stones found their mark, the mob laughed tauntingly. In the evening, the crowd suddenly fell silent for a moment. Then the sound of drums shattered the silence. As soon as the playing of the drums ceased, a thundering voice proclaimed, 'The emperor has returned to the fort! He is going to decimate the Pallava forces and hoist the flag of victory! Everyone is ordered to return to their houses. Men well versed in warfare must congregate outside the palace with their weapons!'

Immediately the crowd enthusiastically cheered, 'Long live the Vatapi emperor! Doom to Mamalla Pallavan!' The mob dispersed as it continued cheering passionately. Miraculously, the very next instant not a soul lingered outside Sivakami's palace. Shortly thereafter, twenty Chalukya soldiers arrived at that desolate place. They stood guard outside Sivakami's palace and on both sides of that street.

Sivakami felt somewhat composed when her lady-in-waiting explained what transpired. As Pulikesi had survived and returned to the fort, the outbreak of war was a foregone conclusion. Sivakami was keen to witness her vow being upheld at all costs. Anticipating that the brutal citizens of Vatapi and the demonic Pulikesi may harm her, Sivakami armed herself with a dagger. She had decided long ago that she would give up her life if her honour was threatened. In addition to the dagger there was also a well in the backyard!

The Pallava army had started attacking the Vatapi fort. That evening a fearful din akin to that of a tumultuous ocean amidst cyclonic winds and torrential rains was heard. Hundreds of war trumpets, thousands of drums and conches played in

unison. This was accompanied by thousands of soldiers raising
victory slogans and lakhs of people enthusiastically cheering.
When the ramparts of the fort, the mandapams and the
towers echoed these sounds, the listeners felt as though their
nerves were being stretched and their hearts being filled with
rage. By sunset, the ten lakh residents of that large city were
more or less in a stupor, oblivious of what they were doing
and what they were saying. The fury that Sivakami felt was far
more intense than what the citizens of Vatapi felt.

She was unable to sit still even for a moment. But she
was also unable to leave the house. For some time, she paced
around the house. Then she looked out of the window. Frenzied
people were running from east to west and from west to east.
She went to the upper storey of the house and looked around.
It was evident that the city was in disarray. As the ramparts of
the fort were close to the backyard of her house, she was able
to see the soldiers stationed on the fort walls prepared for a
combat. She was also able to see the soldiers marching down
the roads and civilians running helter-skelter.

Sivakami went downstairs again and instructed her lady-
in-waiting to find out what was happening at the entrance
of the house. The lady-in-waiting returned bearing the news
that the Pallava army was going to attack the fort that night.
She also refused to stay with Sivakami that night as she was
scared of the war and was leaving to be with her relatives.
Sivakami's pleading with her was in vain. She took the second
lady-in-waiting along and left the house. When the duo
opened the palace doors and left, Sivakami heard the soldiers
posted outside, who had grown impatient, wonder why they
had to stand guard outside the house. She closed all the
doors in her house firmly and locked them. The front doors
of that mansion were large like the main doors of a temple.

Embedded in one of the front doors was a smaller door that was large enough to let an adult inside. It was fitted with a separate latch and lock. The two ladies-in-waiting left the house through the smaller door.

Ever since Sivakami had come to Vatapi, she had slept fitfully. That night she did not sleep a wink. Her heart and her nerves throbbed with eagerness to know what was happening outside and what was going to happen. She heaved deep sighs, her heartbeat quickened, her stomach churned. Around midnight, Sivakami stood in the upper storey of her mansion and observed houses in several parts of the city ablaze. She realized that the vow she had taken nine years ago was being fulfilled. While Sivakami experienced the contentment she had not felt thus far in her life, she also felt an inexplicable sorrow.

The fire spread in all four directions. The great chaos, which had prevailed in the city that evening, assumed another form by nightfall. Spirited slogans of victory changed into shrieking and wailing. The citizens' proud gait was transformed into fear-stricken fleeing. As time passed, one could see many more women and children fleeing. When Sivakami witnessed this, the contentment she felt vanished. Instead, she felt distressed. Finally, she went downstairs, unable to witness that ghastly sight.

'Ah! Hasn't this disaster occurred because of me? What will be the outcome? Is this large city truly going to be destroyed by the fire? Are the lakhs of men, women and children living in this city going to meet their end? Aiyyo! What is this? What will become of me?' Thousands of such thoughts rose and ebbed within Sivakami like waves. Then she paced around the main hall of the house as she was unable to bring herself to go upstairs. She paced around till her legs started aching. She lay down with her face on the bare floor. She thought that she would feel better if she wept. But she was unable to cry; it was as though something was blocking her tear glands and preventing her from shedding tears. The dim light characteristic of midnight pervaded the muttram of her house. At that point of time, a thundering noise was heard outside the house.

A thought suddenly struck Sivakami. Was it Mamallar who had come? After ensuring her vow was fulfilled, had he come to take her back to Kanchi? It would be good if it were so. The destruction of this vast city could be stopped at least now. She intended to fall at his feet and plead, 'Prabhu! That's enough, please stop!' Thinking thus, Sivakami got up and ran swiftly. When she neared the door, she hesitated. She decided to open the smaller door embedded in the main door. The sight that met her eyes on opening the door instilled shock and fear in her. Neither Mamallar nor the Pallava soldiers stood there. Only an angry mob of Vatapi citizens were standing outside the door. A few people in that mob were arguing with the guards.

The instant Sivakami's face appeared at the entrance, hair-raising sounds resembling a hundred cheetahs and tigers roaring were heard. Several people in that gang pushed the guards aside and rushed towards the entrance. Sivakami understood the situation. She immediately closed the door. In her haste and fear, she forgot to latch the door. She then rushed to the backyard of that mansion without any concrete plan. Her natural instinct to flee from the frenzied mob gave her legs adequate strength to run swiftly towards the backyard.

When Sivakami crossed the doorstep of the rear entrance, in the dim-lit dawn she observed a ghastly female form sporting a garland of skulls and bones. Her blood froze for an instant. She felt her hair standing on end. On seeing Sivakami, that female apparition laughed heartily. Then that apparition asked, 'Beautiful Sivakami! Artistic Sivakami! You temptress who mesmerized Mamallar and Naganandi! How will your beauty aid you now? Will your mesmerizing eyes and glowing face save you now?' and laughed. 'Sivakami! I too was endowed with enthralling good looks like you at one time. I am in this state because of you. I have waited for so long to seek revenge!' exclaimed the kabalikai gritting her teeth as she took the dagger fastened to her waist and aimed it at Sivakami.

At that time, Sivakami could neither think nor try to escape. She was shell-shocked. Nevertheless, God has endowed every living being with a self-preservation instinct. Spurred by that instinct, Sivakami took one step back. At that moment, unknown to the kabalikai a figure suddenly emerged behind her. That figure, which had entered through the rear entrance, firmly held the kabalikai's hand that was aiming the dagger.

The iron-like grip forced the kabalikai to loosen her hold on the dagger, which fell to the ground. The enraged kabalikai looked around and asked, 'You sinner! Have you come at the right time?' Sivakami closely observed the figure that had suddenly appeared and saved her life. Sivakami was astonished when she realized that it was the Vatapi emperor, Pulikesi. Ah! Didn't the citizens claim that the emperor had died! Was this his ghost? Or . . . had the bikshu disguised himself as the emperor as he had done in the past?

Chapter 41

'Here Is Your Lover!'

Naganandi adigal, disguised as Emperor Pulikesi, saved Sivakami's life in the nick of time. Sivakami, on seeing the angry mob at the entrance of her palace, shut the doors and rushed inside. The very next instant the sound of horses swiftly galloping towards her palace was heard. Most of the people assembled there quickly dispersed, thinking that Pallava warriors were coming. The few people who stayed behind and the guards were shocked when they saw emperor Pulikesi. The citizens of Vatapi were disconsolate, observing the misfortune that had befallen their king, who till ten days ago had reigned over their expansive kingdom spanning the area from the Narmada to the Tungabhadra, as undisputed monarch.

On seeing the emperor, the few people who remained there started wailing and complaining loudly. The emperor, understanding the situation, whispered something to a warrior close to him. After calming down the chaotic crowd, the soldier announced in a loud voice, 'Respected citizens! The emperor is grateful for the loyalty you have demonstrated during this dangerous period. This calamity has befallen us due to unexpected acts of treachery. The emperor is determined to seek revenge at the appropriate time. The emperor has come here to accord apt punishment to the maiden from Pallava Nadu, who is also a reason for the occurrence of this disaster. He requests you to allow him to perform that task and asks all of you to find ways and means to safeguard your lives. The merciless Pallava demons are engaged in unjust warfare and have set fire to your houses. Please try to save your families and possessions; please go to your houses immediately!'

Hearing this, the citizens started wailing and complaining even more loudly as they started leaving Sivakami's palace. Then the emperor told the security guards posted outside the palace, 'You have performed your duty well. I am very happy. Now, try to save your lives. I command all those who survive to come to Nasikapuri! I will reach there soon and meet you!' Hearing the emperor speak thus, the soldiers' eyes brimmed with tears. They bowed to the emperor, and left. Then the emperor looked at the chief of the cavalry who had accompanied him and asked, 'Dhananjaya! Do you remember all that I told you?'

'Yes, prabhu! I remember,' replied Dhananjayan.

'I repeat; leave this place immediately. Leave the city loudly cheering, "Glory to Mamalla chakravarthy!" Go to the forest that's in the vicinity of the kabalikas' sacrificial altar. I will reach there ahead of you!' the emperor again whispered to the chief of the cavalry. 'There is a mad kabalikai in the cave close to the sacrificial altar. Kill her ruthlessly!'

The very next moment Dhananjayan and the other horsemen rode away. Then, the street was desolate.

Naganandi, disguised as Pulikesi, reached the door of Sivakami's residence and knocked softly. He then pushed the door of the smaller entrance and it opened. He immediately entered the palace and latched the door. He attentively scanned the front quarters of the house and realized that it was empty. He headed to the backyard and arrived just in time to firmly grasp the kabalikai, who was holding a dagger aloft and rescue Sivakami. When the kabalikai blurted, 'You sinner, have you come?' the bikshu observed her closely with his magnetic eyes. He instructed, 'Ranjani! Please come here!' and walked further down. Sivakami was amazed to see the enraged ogress obediently following him.

The bikshu ushered Ranjani behind a pillar. He asked in a low tone so that Sivakami could not hear, 'Why are you behaving thus?'

'Bikshu! What wrong have I done? Seeing the city on fire, I was worried about you. I came here to rescue you and take you away!'

'Is that so? I'm very happy. But why were you on the verge of killing that maiden from Pallava Nadu?'

'That was also to save you. How can one be sure that no danger will befall you on account of her? Isn't she from our enemy state?'

'You fool! How can she put me in peril?'

'Bikshu! Isn't love far more dangerous than all other perils?' retorted the kabalikai.

'You're not yet rid of your stupidity. When you're there, will I even look at another woman?'

'In that case, why are you so concerned about her? How does it matter to you if I kill her?'

'You idiot! You have no reason to wreak vengeance on Sivakami, only I have. How many times have I told you that I'm carefully safeguarding Sivakami to seek retribution against the Pallavan?'

'Bikshu! Nothing has gone wrong even now.'

'No, not really. In a way, you rushing here is for the good. Ranjani! You must help me now. If you act as per my instructions now, I will behave in the manner you desire for the rest of my life!'

'Bikshu! Are you stating the truth?'

'How many times have I promised you? What will you do if I promise you now and break my promise later on?'

'I know what to do.'

'Do that. But for now, do what I ask you to!'

'Tell me, adigal!'

The bikshu lowered his voice further and told the kabalikai what she had to do. 'Do you understand what I said? Will you follow my instructions?' he asked.

'I will definitely do that!' assured the kabalikai. Then she asked with a grisly smile, 'Bikshu! After you have sought your revenge, may I seek mine?'

The bikshu's face fell. 'Ah! It seems that you will never be rid of your suspicion. How many times have I told you that you may do so! Leave quickly! I can hear a chariot and horses approaching!'

The kabalikai headed to the front quarters of the house and approached the main entrance. She unlatched the smaller door and hid herself close by, hid her right hand that held a dagger behind her and waited like a tigress about to prey on an unsuspecting goat. A murderous rage was evident in that ogress' eyes.

After sending the kabalikai to the front quarters of the house, Naganandi bikshu approached Sivakami. 'Do you still doubt me, Sivakami? Do you still have no faith in me?' When the bikshu asked this in a gentle tone, Sivakami became even more confused. She started saying 'Emperor!' and then paused hesitantly. 'Oh! It's my mistake!' admitted Naganandi and removed his crown.

Sivakami's doubts were cleared. 'Swami! Is that you? In this garb!' she exclaimed.

'Yes, Sivakami! Once earlier, I assumed this disguise and saved your father's life . . . Had I arrived even a moment later, that ogress would have killed you! She wouldn't have killed just you, but also the art of dancing that enthrals this cosmos . . .'

'But . . .' remarked Sivakami hesitantly.

'Why are you hesitating, Sivakami? Ask what you want to quickly!'

'Nothing! I am surprised at the influence you wield over that kabalikai!'

'That's the power of love, Sivakami! That ogress is in love with me! That is why she obeyed my command so quickly.'

Seeing Sivakami smile, the bikshu spoke further, 'But don't think that she has always looked so appalling! I mentioned this before, do you remember? Once upon a time, she was the most beautiful woman at the Vatapi palace. One day, she spoke ill of you. So, she was reduced to this state.'

'Aiyyo! What a cruel punishment!'

'She was at least spared after this punishment. Do you know what became of the artist who painted a portrait of you prostrating before Pulikesi? I touched his neck and blessed him! That was it! He felt as if his body was on fire.

Soon thereafter, that artist jumped into the river. He did not resurface after that!'

'Aiyyo, how cruel! Why did you act thus?' asked an extremely agitated Sivakami.

'Ah! These were not the only things I did for your sake, Sivakami! This massive city of Vatapi is on fire today. Do you know who responsible for this is? Do you know who is responsible for the Pallava soldiers entering the city and committing atrocities and lakhs of citizens running around aimlessly in a frenzied manner? It is this sinner who betrayed his nation and his clan!' confessed the bikshu and punched his chest hard. He looked at Sivakami who stood stupefied by his behaviour and revealed, 'Sivakami! Even as I was leaving this city and heading to the Ajantha Art Festival, I came to know that the Pallavan was invading us. Despite that, do you know why I hid this news from my brother, Pulikesi, and accompanied him to Ajantha? It was solely for your happiness. I behaved thus so that you could witness your vow being fulfilled and then leave this city. It was solely for this purpose I sacrificed the life of my brother, who was dearer to me than my own life. This sinner is responsible for the death of the Vatapi emperor!' admitted the bikshu and punched his chest again.

Sivakami trembled; she firmly held the bikshu's hand and prevented him from punching himself. Naganandi calmed down the instant Sivakami held him with her tender hands. 'Sivakami! Forgive me for causing you distress!'

'What is there to forgive, swami? You once saved my father's life. Today, you have saved mine. Am I not indebted to you for all this? But you need not have undergone so much difficulty for this helpless maiden ...'

'Sivakami! I have not saved you yet. If you feel even an iota of gratitude for all the assistance I have rendered to your father and to yourself, you must help me now!'

'What should I do, swami?'

'Trust me and come with me!'

Suddenly, Sivakami became suspicious and hesitant. She asked, 'Where do you want me to come? What's the purpose?'

'Sivakami! You're not yet completely out of danger even though that ogress' attempt to kill you has been thwarted. The Pallavas have set this city on fire, which has spread to the neighbouring street. In another half a nazhigai, the fire will spread to this house, too. Not only that, didn't you observe the enraged mob congregated outside this house? They will not hesitate to cut you to pieces in their fury. They hold you responsible for the calamity that has befallen this city!'

At that point of time, a noisy commotion erupted outside the house. The sounds of a door being opened and shut, someone shrieking and something falling down with a thud were heard in quick succession. Sivakami shuddered. 'Don't you hear the commotion caused by the hysterical people outside, Sivakami? Do you want to remain here and allow the frenzied mob to kill you? Won't you come with me?' pleaded Naganandi.

Sivakami believed that Naganandi was stating the truth. 'Adigal! Where and how will you be taking me?' she asked.

'Anticipating such a danger, I had a tunnel built from this house. Trust me! If you accompany me, I will lead you outside the fort in half a nazhigai!'

'Swami! That is one thing I cannot do, I beseech you. I will not leave this house; you may leave.'

'Sivakami! You have not heard all that I have to say. You speak without realizing where I intend taking you. You probably think that I may take you to the Ajantha mountains, as I had mentioned once before. I have forgotten that dream, Sivakami! I have realized that you will never ever change your mind. Now, I want to ensure that I help you escape and unite you with to your father. As soon as we exit the fort, I will straightaway hand you over to your father and go my way.'

Sivakami thought for some time and remarked, 'Swami! I trust you completely. However, I will not leave this house. I will leave only if he comes and leads me out by my hand. If that does not happen, I will die right here!'

Naganandi's facial expression underwent a sudden change. Fury raged in his eyes. He laughed angrily and roared, 'Do you believe that your lover, Mamallan, will come here and take you back? That will never happen!'

A voice asked, 'Why not?' Both of them turned around. The kabalikai exclaimed, 'Sivakami! Don't believe what the bikshu says! Here is your lover!' As she spoke, she threw the body she was carrying on the ground.

Sivakami stared for a moment at the man who had been stabbed by a dagger. She shrieked, 'Anna!' as she ran towards him.

Kannabiran opened his eyes. He looked intently at Sivakami for an instant. He murmured, 'Thangai! Your sister, Kamali, and little Kannan are fondly anticipating your return!' The next moment, the affable man breathed his last. A helpless Sivakami fell on the ground, unconscious.

Chapter 42

Ranjani's Revenge

Naganandi rushed towards the unconscious Sivakami and felt her temples and nostrils with his long fingers. He looked at the kabalikai angrily and rebuked, 'You sinner! What have you done?'

The kabalikai burst out laughing. It resembled several ghosts cackling in unison at a graveyard in the middle of the night. 'Adigal! What sin did I commit? Didn't I act in the manner you instructed? Didn't you ask me to kill her lover, Mamallan, as soon as he entered the house? How am I responsible if this virtuous woman dies after seeing the state of her dear lover?'

Naganandi interrupted saying, 'You idiot! This is not Mamallan, he is Mamallan's charioteer, Kannabiran! Can't you even distinguish between a ruler and a charioteer?'

'Oh! Is that so? Didn't you tell me that Mamallan would enter first and that I ought to kill him? I acted accordingly. Now you tell me that he is not Mamallan but his charioteer!'

As they were conversing thus, the sound of people breaking open the front door with spades was heard. 'Ranjani!

Let bygones be bygones. Please render me one final bit of assistance. This maiden is still alive. If I had some time, I would revive her. As long as she is in our custody, Mamallan will come in search of her. It is important that she lives till I seek revenge. So, I will take her along with me and leave. The Pallava soldiers are breaking open the door. Please stay here from some time and somehow restrain them.'

'Adigal! I can manage one or two people. If several people break down the door and enter, how can I manage them singlehandedly?'

'This is the time to demonstrate your astuteness. Tell them that you're Sivakami; they will be stunned for some time. Then spin some other tale. It will suffice if you restrain them for half a nazhigai!'

'Ah! You deceptive bikshu! Are you trying to get me killed by the Pallava soldiers?'

'Ranjani! I promise that you will not die at the hands of the Pallava soldiers! They will spare you thinking that you're insane. They will never ever kill you. Go! Leave quickly! Please help me just this once! I will never ever forget you!'

The angry and suspicious kabalikai alternated her glance between an unconscious Sivakami and the bikshu. She reluctantly turned around to head to the entrance of the house. She had hardly taken two steps when the bikshu swiftly removed the poisoned knife fastened to his waist. He flung the knife with all might at the kabalikai's back. The kabalikai turned around shrieking, 'Oh!' Ranjani leapt towards Naganandi screaming, 'You sinner! You charlatan! Finally, you have betrayed me!' As he quickly sidestepped her, she fell with her face to the ground. In a flash, Naganandi hoisted the unconscious Sivakami on to his shoulder and headed to the backyard of the house.

How did Kannabiran meet with this fate? When the sun was rising in the eastern horizon, senathipathi Paranjyothi entered Vatapi through the fort's main entrance in the west. He was desirous of heading straight to Sivakami's palace. But that was not an easy task. The citizens of Vatapi, who were shrieking and wailing, were running helter-skelter in the burning city. The Pallava and Pandya soldiers who were entering Vatapi by jumping over the ramparts were in a frenzy to loot its fabulous wealth and were killing all those who came in their way. The roofs of the houses on fire rapidly collapsed and blocked the streets.

Senathipathi Paranjyothi had to travel through Vatapi's thoroughfares overcoming such obstacles. He thought that he would remember the route he had taken to Sivakami's house during his visit nine years ago and that he could easily trace her house.

However, that was also not easy due to the pandemonium prevailing in the city then. He had to check with Kannabiran, who was following Paranjyothi in his chariot, if they were taking the correct route. By the time the senathipathi reached the street in which Sivakami lived, it was broad daylight. When he reached the corner of that street, he saw a huge mob leaving that place. When this mob observed Pallava soldiers arriving, with Rishabha flags aloft, they were struck by fear and fled in all directions.

When Paranjyothi reached the entrance of Sivakami's palace, he was struck by the eeriness that surrounded the palace and the street. This instilled fear in him. The doors of the abode were shut; dead silence prevailed within. 'Was Aayanar's daughter, for whose sake we had embarked on this expedition, the person whose word we have to keep, safe inside? Will I be fortunate to retrieve her alive and unite her with Aayanar, who is waiting outside the fort?' As Senathipathi Paranjyothi was thinking along these lines, he saw a few Pallava horsemen holding Rishabha flags riding swiftly towards him from the opposite end of the street. Surmising that they may be bearing an important message for him, he told Kannabiran, who had brought his chariot to a halt and had dismounted from the chariot, 'Kanna! Knock on the door. As soon as the door is opened, inform the devi that we have come to fetch her!' As instructed by Paranjyothi, Kannan knocked on the door. Shortly thereafter, the smaller door embedded within the main entrance opened. As soon as Kannan entered the palace, the door was shut again.

The leader of the Pallava horsemen, as Paranjyothi had anticipated, had brought a message. The prince of Lanka, Manavanman, had sent the message. Manavanman, as ordered by the senathipathi, had entered Vatapi through the northern entrance with handpicked soldiers and reached the Vatapi palace. He had made arrangements to remove the priceless treasures stored in the palace before the building was set on fire. But despite searching for the Vatapi emperor within and outside the palace, they had been unable to trace him. On interrogating the palace guards, they had come to know that the emperor had last been seen at the palace entrance asking the Chalukya soldiers to run for their lives and to reach Nasikapuri. They reported that he had then headed to the southern entrance of the fort accompanied by a few soldiers. But the Pallava soldiers, standing guard at the southern gates stated unequivocally that the emperor had not fled through that exit.

Hearing this, the senathipathi's turmoil increased. He had come to know from Shatrugnan that it was Naganandi who had assumed the disguise of the Vatapi emperor. Naganandi, who was more dangerous than a venomous snake, could use Sivakami to wreak revenge on the Pallavas. It was possible that the fake bikshu was torturing Sivakami. Probably, he was trying to hide her in a remote location so that no one could find her. Tormented by such thoughts, Paranjyothi rushed towards the entrance of the palace. As he neared the door, he heard a woman shrieking in a shrill and sorrowful tone.

Paranjyothi, like one possessed, used all his might to force open the door. As his effort went in vain, he roared, 'Quickly bring spades and break open the door!' The very next moment, five to six soldiers armed with spades, started breaking open the door. In the next five minutes, the door was demolished. Paranjyothi, followed by a few soldiers, ran into the house. Despite searching the front quarters, he was unable to find anyone. On reaching the backyard, Paranjyothi saw the gory sight of a man and woman, both stabbed to death, lying on the floor. Paranjyothi realized that the dead man was Kannabiran. While the untimely death of Kamali's husband saddened him, he did not have the time to dwell on this tragedy. His attention was diverted to the female body that lay close by. As that body lay with her face to the ground, he was unable to identify her. He wondered if it was Sivakami and if the bikshu had escaped after killing both of them.

Oblivious of his actions, Paranjyothi turned the female body around. When he saw the kabalikai's ghastly face, he felt somewhat consoled. Even as he was looking at her, she moved slightly and heaved a deep sigh. Paranjyothi was taken aback.

She murmured, 'Ah! Are you Mamallan?'

Eager to know about Sivakami's whereabouts, he asked agitatedly, 'Yes, lady! I am Mamallan! Who are you? Where is Sivakami Devi?'

'What kind of a question is this? I am Sivakami, don't you recognize me?' asked the kabalikai. The unsightly smile that appeared on Ranjani's face accentuated her hideousness.

Paranjyothi was dumfounded for a moment. Had Sivakami Devi become insane after being imprisoned for long? No! That was impossible! Paranjyothi remembered that Gundodharan had met Sivakami a month ago and Shatrugnan describing the kabalikai. Ranjani must have entered the city through the tunnel that originated in the cave. 'No! Why are you lying? You are not Sivakami. If you tell me the truth about Sivakami's whereabouts . . .'

'How will you compensate me if I told you the truth?'

'I will save your life,' assured Paranjyothi.

'Ah! I have been stabbed by a poisoned knife. It's impossible for you to save me!'

'Poisoned knife? In that case Naganandi must have stabbed you! Lady, tell me quickly! Where is Naganandi headed to? Which route did he take? If you tell me, I will seek revenge on him on your behalf.'

'Seeking revenge on Naganandi is futile. It is true that the fake bikshu killed me. But he did not do it of his own accord; that temptress Sivakami instigated him. Pallava! You think of yourself as Manmadan. But that is incorrect. That wily Sivakami does not love you. It is the lean and gaunt bikshu whom she loves. It was she who eloped with Naganandi when she realized that you were coming. When I obstructed them, she instigated Naganandi to kill me. If you're desirous of seeking revenge for my sake, wreak your vengeance on Sivakami. Don't harm that foolish bikshu!'

Paranjyothi could not bear to hear these words. Unable to listen further, he asked, 'Lady! Where are the two of them now? How did they escape? Tell me quickly!'

Thinking that her ruse had worked, she exclaimed, 'Climb into the well in the backyard! There is a tunnel there! Don't forget to seek revenge on Sivakami.' After saying this, she stopped talking. Her breathing also ceased.

Chapter 43

Buddha Bhagavan's Sanctum

Senathipathi Paranjyothi quickly gave a few orders to the soldiers who had accompanied him. After asking just four of them to follow him, he rushed to the backyard of the palace. He peered into the well located at the centre of the muttram in the backyard with a pavazhamalli creeper growing beside it. The wall surrounding the well was built with bricks for some distance into the well. Beyond that, there were rocks jutting out. The water was deep inside in the well.

Paranjyothi's heartbeat quickened as he held the steps that led into the well and climbed down. The four soldiers who accompanied him also climbed into the well. As the surface of the wall was uneven and there were holes in them, climbing down was easy. When they had covered three-fourths of the distance into the well, Paranjyothi exclaimed, 'Ah!' in surprise. There was an aperture in the rock wall. There lay a long path beyond the aperture, which was quite dark after some distance. Signalling to the soldiers who accompanied him, Paranjyothi entered the tunnel, which was large enough for just one person to crawl in at a time. But the tunnel became bigger after some distance, enabling one to move in a sitting position. The tunnel further led to a flight of stairs. After climbing down four to five steps, there appeared to be even ground ahead. When their eyes got acclimatized to the darkness, they were able to observe the surrounding area. Paranjyothi realized that he was standing at the corner of a large underground mandapam carved out of rocks. There was a large statue of Lord Buddha directly opposite to him. Above the statue was a beautifully sculpted turret. On either side of the statue were two rows of tall, unsculpted rock pillars. Paranjyothi and two of the soldiers paced around the mandapam searching behind the pillars and the nooks and corners. There was no one. But a few robes and ornaments lay behind a pillar. Paranjyothi realized that they were the emperor's robes and ornaments. He deduced that Naganandi must have discarded these and donned the robes of a bikshu. He wondered where Naganandi and Sivakami were and how they had mysteriously disappeared.

Inadvertently, Paranjyothi's glance fell on Buddha Bhagavan's statue. A thought suddenly occurred to him. He remembered the secret route behind the Buddha statue at the Kanchi viharam. Immediately, Paranjyothi rushed towards the Buddha statue. The rear of the statue was abutting the rock wall behind it. There was no way that a door or secret route could lie behind the statue.

Paranjyothi was extremely disappointed. Nevertheless, he was convinced that the Buddha statue was the clue to the path he was searching for.

'Prabhu! Buddha Bhagavan! If it is true that you're an incarnation of Mahavishnu, you must guide me. I seek refuge in you!' Praying thus, Senathipathi Paranjyothi touched the feet of the Buddha statue. A miracle occurred. The Buddha statue moved slightly sideways, revealing a tunnel behind it. Paranjyothi thought in exultation, 'Ah! Buddha Bhagavan has shown the way!' Signalling to the soldiers he took a step into the tunnel and witnessed an unexpected sight.

He could see several lit torches arrayed one behind the other approaching him from the opposite end of the narrow tunnel. The torch bearers resembled dark, fire-sprouting ghosts. Leading that fearful procession was the tonsured figure of a bikshu, who was rushing with a woman on his shoulder.

Paranjyothi recognized the person who was rushing towards him in an instant. By the time the bikshu had travelled half the distance down the tunnel, Shatrugnan and his men had entered the tunnel from the other end. The bikshu was retracing his steps to ensure that Shatrugnan did not capture him.

Paranjyothi immediately retreated and along with his men, hid behind the pillars.

Shortly after they had hidden themselves, Naganandi bikshu emerged from behind the statue of Buddha Bhagavan. He was carrying Sivakami on his shoulder. Paranjyothi and his soldiers held their breath as they eagerly watched what he was going to do next.

Naganandi lowered Sivakami to the ground some distance away from the Buddha statue. He then stood in front of the statue. For a moment, he appeared to be immersed in deep thought. He looked around once and then sat down next to Sivakami.

Paranjyothi understood that he wanted to seal the entrance to the tunnel. He signalled to the soldiers who accompanied him and leapt towards the bikshu. The soldiers followed him and held the bikshu firmly by his arms. The bikshu looked up at them. It was not possible to decipher his facial expression in the dark. But the words he uttered revealed his state of mind.

'Paranjyothi! Is that you? I was expecting you. If I were to lose, I wanted to lose to you. My desire has been fulfilled!' As he spoke thus, he stood up. Everyone came to the centre of the mandapam. Naganandi looked at Paranjyothi piteously and quipped, 'Appane! Why are these people still clasping me? Where can I escape now? Your men are approaching through the tunnel and you have men standing here. All my scheming has come to an end. Henceforth, I would have to obey you. I wanted to somehow take Aayanar and you to Ajantha. That is not possible now. Appane! Please ask them to let go of me! I am prepared to abide by your command.'

When Naganandi pleaded thus, Paranjyothi softened a little.

He commanded the soldiers, 'Let go of the bikshu!' The soldiers released Naganandi and stepped back.

'Paranjyothi! Do you remember the old times? Didn't I save you from a snake on the day you first arrived in Kanchi? Didn't I also help you escape from prison that very night? Do you remember all that?'

As the bikshu was speaking thus, he removed the dagger fastened to his waist. Noticing that, Paranjyothi took two steps back and unsheathed his sword. In that instant, Paranjyothi thought, 'Ah! I'm about to lose my life! After all the struggle, I have committed this blunder just when we were about to attain our goal . . . What is this? Why is the treacherous Naganandi turning around? Whom is he going to wield the dagger at? Ah! Isn't he aiming the dagger at Sivakami Devi? The sinner that he is!' By God's grace, Naganandi hesitated for a moment. In that instant, Paranjyothi used all his might to cut off Naganandi's arm that held the dagger. The bikshu's dagger missed its mark and fell some distance away from where they stood. Naganandi, too, fell to the ground like a felled tree.

Chapter 44

Final Gift

Sivakami felt as though she was gradually resurfacing from the dark depths of the fathomless sea. She could detect minute noises in the darkness. The indecipherable, soft sound slowly changed into an uproar. Amidst that uproarious din, she could intermittently hear certain sounds which soon transformed into that of human conversation. Ah! She could hear two people conversing. Sivakami thought one of the voices sounded familiar. But whose voice was it?

Sivakami realized that her eyelids were still shut. Exercising great effort, she opened them slightly. The sight that then met her eyes aroused surprise, pity, agitation and horror in her. She also wondered if this was a dream or whether her dazed mind was hallucinating. She comprehended that she was lying on the floor of a viharam that was carved out of rocks. The uneven, rocky terrain had a chilling impact on her body. A man lay on the ground at a short distance from her. A majestic-looking man, who resembled Samara Rudra

Murthy, stood close to him holding his sword aloft. Several soldiers wielding swords and spears stood further away. Shock, anger and respect were evident in their facial expressions. The fire sparks and smoke that emanated from the torches that some soldiers were holding transformed the scene into one from Yama Loka.

The massive statue of Buddha Bhagavan seated in a meditative posture had a beatific expression. Sivakami closed her eyes once again and opened them to confirm whether the scene unfolding in her presence was a dream, a hallucination or reality. She realized that the events she was witnessing were real. Gradually, she regained the ability to think clearly. She observed that the man who lay on the floor was Naganandi bikshu. She deduced that the man standing majestically next to him holding a sword aloft was senathipathi Paranjyothi.

'The soldiers who surrounded the two men and stood scattered in the cave must be Pallava soldiers. But how did they reach here? How did I come here?' The indecipherable sounds of human conversation soon became clear. Naganandi was saying, 'Appane, Paranjyothi! May you lead a happy life! You are very virtuous and grateful! It was this hand that saved you from a cobra. It was this hand that freed you from the Pallavan's prison. It was this hand that saved the life of the sculptor Aayanar, whom you regard as your achariar.[31] This hand also saved his daughter from being killed by a kabalikai some time ago. You have amputated that very right hand! Ah! You are such a grateful boy!'

Paranjyothi cut him short countering: 'Ah! You fake bikshu! Why did you stop relating the exploits of your sacred hands midway? Wasn't this the very hand that wielded the

---

[31] Achariar—guru, teacher.

poisoned dagger at Mahendra Pallavar? Weren't these the hands that enabled you to carry Aayanar's daughter and flee through the tunnel? When you realized that there was no escape route, wasn't it your hand that was about to stab the devi with the poisoned dagger?'

'Yes, appane! Yes! All what you say is true. But why did I try to take away Aayanar's daughter? Do you know why? Ah! Paranjyothi! You believe that you are far more affectionate, devoted and concerned about Aayanar's daughter than I am. Your master, the foolish Mamallan, believes that his love for her exceeds mine. Appane! Do you understand the meaning of love? Paranjyothi! The reason behind Vatapi being set ablaze and falling into ruin is me. I sacrificed my own brother for Sivakami's sake. I sacrificed the great Chalukya kingdom that caused Harshavardhana to tremble, at the altar of my love. Ah! How would you folks understand the meaning of love and affection?'

'Adigal, you're stating the truth. I understood the meaning of affection only some time ago. We demonstrate our affection to someone by stabbing the person with a poisoned dagger, don't we? I came to know of this only a short while ago. You deceitful bikshu! I don't have the time to converse with you. Had you not discarded your disguise and had continued wearing a king's robes, I would have dispatched you to another world by now. I am unable to bring myself to kill an ochre robe-clad bikshu. I will spare you on one condition. Ten years ago, Aayanar sent me to learn the secret of the Ajantha paints. I too promised him that I would do so. You must be aware of the secret of the Ajantha paints. If you divulge the secret, I will spare your life. If not, pray to the God dearest to you . . . If a barbarian like you can believe in the existence of a God, pray to that God!'

'Appane! I thank you for your mercy. I pray to only one God. That is Sivakami. I will pray to her. I was desirous of taking Aayanar and his daughter to Ajantha and demonstrate the secret of the indelible dyes in person. I am not fortunate enough to complete that task. Neither are they fortunate. You have determined that the price of my life is that wonderful secret that cannot be deciphered by anyone in this world. Bless you! I will tell you the secret. Ordinary dyes are made by extracting the juices of leaves, roots, vegetables and seeds of plants and boiling them together. These raw materials dry up and disintegrate. Hence the paints made from them also fade away and ultimately get completely erased. But there are certain rocks in the mountains that are naturally coloured. These colours remain unaffected by sun, rain and wind. So, the paints made by powdering the coloured rocks and converting the powder into liquid form are indelible. The paintings at Ajantha have been painted using such paints. Paranjyothi! I have disclosed to you the secret that only the bikshus of the Ajantha Sangramam have known for the past five hundred years. Now, may I leave?'

'Adigal! Leave immediately. I may change my mind. You may leave by the secret tunnel through which you had planned to abduct Sivakami Devi. Be quick!' Naganandi exercised great effort to stand up. He picked up his amputated right hand with his left hand. 'Paranjyothi! You are a good boy. You are sparing my life. It would have been good if you had beheaded me instead of amputating my arm. But as I'm still desirous of living, I beseeched you to spare my life. You too have complied. I understand that you wish me to leave before Mamallan's arrival. Here I go. But I have one more request. Sivakami will regain consciousness in some time. You must inform her of one thing. You must tell her that I attempted to kill her by stabbing her with a poisoned dagger. That was my final gift to her as a testimony of my love for her!' Speaking thus, Naganandi turned to the direction where Sivakami lay. He observed that Sivakami had regained consciousness and was standing motionless like a statue, leaning against a pillar.

'Ah! Sivakami! Have you woken up? Did you hear what I told Aayanar's disciple, Paranjyothi? Yes! I tried to kill you by wielding a dagger. I acted thus pitying you for what the future has in store for you. The Pallava senathipathi came in my way and prevented me from doing good to you. Sivakami! In the future . . . No, don't think about the future. Forget this sinner! Forget this fake bikshu who placed his body, soul and possessions at your feet. Be as happy as you possibly can! But I will not forget you. Neither will I forget Paranjyothi and Mamallan! Farewell, Sivakami! Farewell! May Buddha Bhagavan protect you!' Speaking thus, Naganandi bikshu faltered as he walked towards Buddha Bhagavan's statue and disappeared behind it.

Everyone stood watching Naganandi escape through the tunnel. As they were aware that the senathipathi had consented to spare Naganandi, no one stopped him. Sivakami continued staring at Naganandi wide-eyed till he had disappeared from her sight. When he had saved her from the kabalikai a short while ago, Sivakami had wondered if he was Emperor Pulikesi or Naganandi bikshu. Now she wondered if he was a human being or a demon in human form, a man driven to lunacy on account of a great sorrow or a merciless murderer.

Meanwhile, Senathipathi Paranjyothi ordered, 'Shatrugna! You came at the right time! Please check if there is a route to exit this underground viharam. It would be difficult for all of us to exit through the tunnel, which leads to the well. There must be a main entrance somewhere that has been sealed. Please identify that soon!'

Shatrugnan announced, 'Senathipathi! I have already found out the main entrance. Please command us to break it open.'

The senathipathi suddenly remembered and asked, 'Shatrugna! Where is Gundodharan?'

'Ah, Senathipathi! The dearest of my dear disciples was the target of the kabalikai's dagger. As the demon was not in the cave, we were looking for her in the tunnel. Did you see that barbaric woman?' asked Shatrugnan.

'I did, Shatrugna! Kannan and the kabalikai lay dead next to each other. I don't know how Kannan died. We have to return to that place and find out,' replied Paranjyothi.

Paranjyothi, while speaking in this manner, walked towards Sivakami, who was leaning against the pillar, and respectfully bowed to her. 'Ammani! You saw and heard all that transpired. By Ekambarar's grace, all dangers have blown over. We are able to see you alive after nine years. Please sit down for some time and compose yourself! Once the entrance to this cave is identified, we will leave. Your father and the chakravarthy are waiting outside the fort!' he remarked.

Sorrow choked Sivakami. She stammered, 'Senathipathi! I want to see Kamali's husband before leaving. Please take me to that house.' At the same time, the Pallava soldiers were breaking down the main entrance to the viharam, which was sealed.

Chapter 45

The Simha[32] Flag

Sivakami shed copious tears and sobbed when she saw the lifeless Kannabiran, on whom the calm of death had descended. 'Amma! No matter how long you mourn and weep, Kannan is not going to rise alive. This is a characteristic of war. Kannabiran was not the only one who lost his life. Like him, thousands of warriors have lost theirs, too. Please come with me, the fire has engulfed the vicinity of this house,' pleaded Paranjyothi.

Sivakami looked at him with tear-filled eyes and sobbed, 'Senathipathi! I wrote to you requesting you not to proceed with this war!'

'Yes, amma! I too exercised great effort. Just when my efforts were about to fructify, that fake bikshu surfaced and

---

[32] Simha—lion in Sanskrit.

spoilt everything. How can we prevent it if the city of Vatapi is fated to be destroyed?'

'Aiyya! Why do you blame fate? This sinner[33] is responsible for everything. Long ago, you and he had insisted that I accompany you. I foolishly refused to do so ...'

'Amma! Several things could have turned out differently. Of what use it is to dwell on the past now? Please leave. Mamallar and your father are eagerly awaiting your arrival.'

'Senathipathi! How can I face him? I cannot bring myself to do so. I will stay here and give up my life. Please tell him that I have apologized to him a thousand times.' As Sivakami was was lamenting thus, a loud noise was heard at the entrance.

Shortly thereafter, Mamallar entered the palace. Aayanar followed him. Paranjyothi exclaimed aloud, 'Ah! He himself has come!' He muttered to himself, 'With this, my responsibility is over!'

When Sivakami heard the words, 'He himself has come!' she felt goosebumps. She raised her lowered head and looked towards the entrance. For a split second, Mamallar's and Sivakami's eyes met. Unable to control her emotions, Sivakami lowered her head again. Fear gripped her. She felt choked and breathless and could not even cry. She then felt so dazed that she did not comprehend what was transpiring around her. She regained consciousness when she heard her father cry, 'Ah! Is that Kannabiran? Aiyyo!'

'Yes, it is indeed Kannan! It is the Kannan who was desirous of liberating Kamali's friend. He, who wanted to bring her back in his chariot, is now dead, having been stabbed by a

---

[33] Sivakami was referring to herself.

venomous dagger! Aayanar! Ask your daughter if her word has been kept! Isn't she at peace now? Ask her, Aayanar! Ask her!'

Mamallar's words had the impact of drops of molten lead being poured into Sivakami's ears. There was a time when she had heard him utter affection-filled nectarine words. Now the very same person was mouthing such cruel words. She wondered, 'Ah! Was it to hear these words that I safeguarded my life for the last nine years?'

Mamallar's harsh words also made Paranjyothi extremely sorrowful. When he started saying, 'Chakravarthy! Sivakami Ammai is extremely dejected . . .' Mamallar interjected, 'What does Sivakami have to feel dejected about? All her desires have been fulfilled. Hasn't her promise been upheld? If she is doubtful, she can see for herself when she is travelling down the streets. She can derive joy by seeing the houses on fire, corpses accumulated on the streets and people running around, shrieking. Respected sculptor, Aayanar! Please take your daughter along and leave immediately!'

Sivakami's heart was shattered into a thousand smithereens, she felt dizzy. Then Aayanar went to her and asked in a gentle voice, 'My child! Don't you recognize me?'

Sivakami called out, 'Appa!' and embraced him sobbing.

Ever since Senathipathi Paranjyothi had entered Vatapi at dawn, Mamallar's agitation had grown by the minute. He felt that Sivakami could be in grave danger and that he was committing a blunder by remaining idle outside the fort. He was unable to stay put outside the fort after receiving news from Manavanmar that Emperor Pulikesi had not been found in the palace. He took Aayanar along and entered Vatapi. He resolved that he would speak to Sivakami affectionately when he met her. But seeing Kannabiran, for whom he had immense affection and regard, dead, his heart hardened. That was the reason for his uttering such harsh words.

While Aayanar and Sivakami travelled in the chariot, Mamallar and Paranjyothi followed them on horseback. Paranjyothi related in detail all that had transpired ever since he had reached the entrance of Sivakami's palace, as commanded by Mamallar. As the chakravarthy heard Paranjyothi's account, he became more enraged. Hadn't Naganandi stated that he had tried to kill Sivakami to protect her from further agony? Mamallar's conscience acknowledged the truth in that statement. His fury increased multifold.

Sivakami rested her head on her father's shoulder as they rode in the chariot, looking at the gory sights on the streets of Vatapi. Sometimes she closed her eyes, unable to witness the goings-on. She was able to close her eyes but not her ears. The sounds of houses burning in the inferno, the strong gust of wind, children shrieking, women wailing, the Pallava soldiers chasing their foes and the slogans of victory filled her ears and caused her to open her eyes and look around. In this situation, Mamallar rode up to the chariot once. Sivakami looked at him in the face.

But Mamallar did not look in her direction. He pointedly looked at Aayanar and remarked, 'Respected sculptor! We may take another month to leave this place. If you so desire, I can send you and your daughter to Kanchi with adequate security. Apparently Naganandi bikshu wanted to take you and your daughter to Ajantha. If you wish to visit Ajantha, you may do so!'

Even amidst the horrific aftermath of war and all the difficulties he had faced, Aayanar was tempted when he heard the word 'Ajantha'. Aayanar was still unaware that Paranjyothi had ascertained the secret of the Ajantha dyes from Naganandi.

So, he turned to Sivakami and asked, 'Amma! What is your preference? Do you wish to go to Kanchi or Ajantha?'

That moment Sivakami's heart became harder than a diamond. 'Appa! I wish to go neither to Kanchi nor to Ajantha. Please ask the Pallava Kumarar to mercifully wield his sword at my chest and dispatch me to Yama Puri.[34] Please ask him to render this assistance for old times' sake!' After speaking thus, Sivakami again fell into a swoon on Aayanar's lap.

Mamallar turned around and reached Paranjyothi's side. He felt slightly at peace after speaking harshly to Sivakami. 'My friend! Do you see Pulikesi's perfidious Jayasthambam there? We have today accompalished the vow we made nine years ago standing by that pillar. Please arrange to demolish that misleading pillar and erect the Pallava army's Jayasthambam in its place. May the Pallava army hoist the flag of victory atop the new Jayasthambam! To commemorate this momentous victory, the Simha insignia ought to replace the Rishabha insignia in our flag and our awards!' commanded Mamallar.

---

[34] Yama Puri—another name for Yama Loka, the abode of death.

Chapter 46

Perceptive Full Moon

The full moon that rises once a month in the blue sky, studded with stars twinkling like diamonds since the time this world, was created has been witness to several wondrous and drastic changes that have occurred on this earth. Notwithstanding this, approximately 1304 years ago[35] (642CE), the full moon that rose in the month of Margazhi must have been shell shocked and heaved a deep sigh on seeing the place where the city of Vatapi had once stood.

The previous pournami,[36] the multi-storeyed mansions and towers had stood tall, almost grazing the sky. The glow from the illuminated street lights attempted to outshine the stars twinkling in the sky. The citizens, born and bred in affluence, adorned themselves with fine clothes and jewellery and proudly strolled around that city. Caparisoned

---

[35] *Sivakamiyin Sabadham* was serialized in the *Kalki* magazine for two-and-a-half years, beginning October 1944.

[36] Pournami and pournami chandran—full moon.

elephants, statuesque horses, ivory palanquins and golden chariots glowed in the beautiful moonlight. At the terraces of the multi-storeyed mansions, young men and women who resembled Manmadhan and Rathi exchanged tender words of love. Bells chimed at the temples. The melodious sound of musical instruments was heard at the palace. The dance mandapams were filled with rhythmic sounds. People thronged the markets from where the fragrant smell of incense, sandalwood and flowers emanated.

One month later, only a few partially demolished walls stood in Vatapi, which had previously resembled Gandharva Puri.[37] The city was filled with soot, ash, smoke, stones and mud. In some places the rubbish was heaped and in other places it was spread out. A few people resembling corpses and ghosts were walking by the partially demolished walls that were charred and blackened by the smoke and fire. Some of the people were loitering around aimlessly while others were sitting down and sieving through the soot and mud. One will never know whom or what they were looking for.

A short distance away from the place where the Vatapi city used to be, beyond the decrepit ramparts, the pournami chandran witnessed a completely different sight. Lakhs of Pallava and Pandya soldiers were celebrating their victory. They were proud that decimating the Chalukya forces had been easier than they had expected and joyous on account of the share of loot they had received after plundering Vatapi. They were also exultant because they were embarking on their return journey two days later. Their ecstasy rendered them sleepless, and they were celebrating all night. Some of the victorious warriors danced and sang while others played

---

[37] Gandharva Puri—the abode (Puri) of Gandharvas (celestial beings).

musical instruments discordantly. While some of them sat in groups and heard stories, others shared their brave exploits of the Vatapi War. To protect themselves from the cold weather, they brought logs of wood from the houses they had set on fire, built a bonfire, sat around it and kept themselves warm.

A lot of people were cautiously safeguarding the wealth they had looted from Vatapi. One such person was the descendant of the Chola dynasty and Mangayarkkarasi's dear father—Sembian Vallavan. As he was unaware of the immense fortune that had sought his daughter after he had left Kanchi, he very frantically and diligently accumulated a lot of pearls, precious gems, gold and silver jewellery from the city, which was on fire, to give as dowry during her marriage.

It seemed as though the wealth the accumulated by the elderly man, with great effort, was in danger. Occasionally at night, Mamallar used to walk around the army camp and applaud soldiers for their brave deeds. As the day for their return was imminent, the chakravarthy visited the soldiers' quarters for four consecutive nights, spoke with them at length and cheered them. Mamallar desired to bond with the victorious warriors and also establish a one-to-one relationship with those warriors who had performed gallant acts while attacking the fort and reward them suitably.

One evening, when Narasimha chakravarthy, along with Manavanman, Aditya Varman and Shatrugnan, was walking around the army camp meeting the soldiers, he neared the place where the elderly Chola scion had camped. He stopped and looked at him pointedly. He muttered to himself, 'Ah! I had completely forgotten about this elderly man!' Narasimhar then asked Sembian Vallavan, 'What is this, aiyya? How dare you accumulate so much wealth? Hadn't I commanded that everyone may accumulate only that much wealth that he can carry himself?'

'Chakravarthy! I came with a hundred soldiers. All of them lost their lives in the Vatapi War.'

The chakravarthy told those who were close to him, 'Ah! Words are inadequate to describe the valour of Chola Nadu! But our senathipathi is not present to hear this.'

'Never mind, aiyya. The hundred warriors who bravely lost their lives in the war must be in heaven now. They have no use for this wealth!'

'Pallavendra! I have to get my only daughter married. I was desirous of giving her a dowry that befits the ancient Chola dynasty . . .' remarked the elderly man and hesitated.

Mamallar smiled at Manavanmar and observed, 'He is unaware of what transpired in Kanchi. May I tell him?'

'No, prabhu! If you suddenly communicate the news to him, he may die of joy!' quipped Manavanmar.

Immediately Mamallar commanded, 'Manavanmarey! Give this elderly man a hundred elephants and enough wealth that may be loaded onto the hundred elephants!' and walked ahead. Sembian Vallavan stood shocked, unable to believe his ears.

The soldiers who stood around observing all this cheered, 'Long live the Vallal[38] Mamallar! Long live!'

The soldiers discussed Mamallar's brave deeds and his virtuous nature long after the chakravarthy had left with his retinue. But intermittently certain comments that dampened their enthusiasm were made. The soldiers were speculating why Senathipathi Paranjyothi was no longer a part of the chakravarthy's retinue. All those who knew the brave warriors,

---

[38] Vallal—philanthropic.

Mamallar and Paranjyothi, firmly believed that the duo was inseparable. Their friendship was a source of happiness and pride to the soldiers of Tamizhagam. The soldiers were proud that a commoner like Paranjyothi, neither a scion of nor related to a royal clan, could rise to the post of a senathipathi by dint of his sheer bravery, virtuous nature and wisdom, and could become intimate friends with the chakravarthy.

But the friendship that everyone believed was eternal now seemed to have been severed. It seemed as though Mamallar and Paranjyothi had fallen apart. Some people felt that a difference of opinion had arisen between them on the issue of attacking the Vatapi fort. Some others believed that Mamallar's harsh behaviour with Sivakami Devi had deeply hurt the senathipathi. A few others insisted that the prince of Lanka and Aditya Varman had poisoned Mamallar's ears. 'All that's not true! All of you are unnecessarily gossiping! As the senathipathi was toiling incessantly, he has fallen ill. So the chakravarthy has commanded him to relax in his tent!' claimed a few good-natured soldiers. 'Let's see whether the senathipathi attends the flag-hoisting ceremony tomorrow morning. If he attends the ceremony, all suspicions will be laid to rest!' was the neutral stance taken by some soldiers.

Chapter 47

Siruthondar

Contrary to what some of the Pallava soldiers had claimed, Paranjyothi was not unwell. While he did not suffer from bodily affliction, Paranjyothi's mind was not at peace. Paranjyothi was sitting all alone in his tent; sleep evaded him. Images of houses ablaze in Vatapi, women, children and the elderly folks shrieking and running helter-skelter, the Pallava soldiers looting the houses and shops, mutilated corpses lying around and bloodshed flashed in his mind.

Also, images of the dreary underground viharam, Naganandi on the verge of flinging the poisoned dagger at Sivakami, Mamallar directing harsh words that were more venomous than the poisoned dagger at Sivakami and Kannabiran's death haunted him. He also perceived the sacred form of Thirunavukkarasar Peruman with vibhuthi smeared on his forehead, wearing a string of rudraksha beads around his neck and carrying a hoe. He seemed to be enquiring, 'Appane! Where are you? Have you thought about the kind of acts you

246

have engaged in? Enough! Come! How long can I wait for you?' Paranjyothi responded in his reverie, 'Gurudeva! Please wait for another sixty nazhigai! I will then join you!'

After freeing Sivakami Devi, reuniting her with Aayanar and sending the duo back to Kanchi, Paranjyothi leading a hand-picked force headed westwards. He joined hands with Aditya Varman, who was awaiting the arrival of the Chalukya forces from Vengi. The army from Vengi reached Vatapi three days after the city was destroyed. That army predominantly consisted of cavalry and elephant forces. When the chiefs of the Chalukya army came to know of Pulikesi's death and the fall of the Vatapi fort, they tried to retreat. Paranjyothi's foresight rendered retreating impossible. After asking Aditya Varman to stay put, Paranjyothi swiftly moved to the rear of the Chalukya army and prevented them from retreating. The Chalukya army that was flanked by the Pallava army on both sides had no option but to surrender. The Pallavas appropriated the sixteen thousand horses and thirty-four thousand elephants that formed part of the Chalukya army.

Paranjyothi handed over this substantial tribute to Mamallar. He then requested Mamallar to relieve him of the senathipathi's post. He informed Mamallar that he had been engaged in the service of the kingdom all these years and now he wanted to become a Sivanadiyar[39] and serve Shiva Peruman. Mamallar was not greatly surprised by this request. He had observed the change in Paranjyothi's mental makeup in the recent past. So, Mamallar had told him, 'Senathipathi! I acquiesce to your request. But, please do conduct the flag hoisting ceremony amidst the ruins of Vatapi. Then I will grant you leave.' The flag-hoisting ceremony was to be held

---

[39] Sivanadiyar—Saivite monk.

at dawn the following day. That was why Paranjyothi kept chanting to himself that there was only one more day to go.

The sun that rose the following day was witness to a wondrous sight in the place where during the last few days heaps of ashes and charred remains covered the area where Vatapi once stood. The Pallava and Pandya soldiers, holding their swords and spears aloft, were standing in rows. Behind them stood several caparisoned elephants and horses, covering the area up to the horizon. Amidst this colossal army, a newly constructed and beautifully sculpted Jayasthambam stood majestically.

Though lakhs of soldiers had congregated, pin-drop silence prevailed. Shortly thereafter, there was some excitement in one corner of that army. Trumpets and drums were played. Hearing the music that heralded the chakravarthy's arrival, the soldiers cheered in unison, 'Long live Vatapi Konda Mamallan!'[40] The cheering reached the skies and echoed in all four directions.

Mamallar, followed by Senathipathi Paranjyothi, the prince of Lanka, Manavanmar and the King of Vengi, Aditya Varman reached the Jayasthambam. Once again, the soldiers cheered heartily. After the noise had subsided, Mamallar looked around and then made a short speech. He stated that when he and Senathipathi Paranjyothi had visited Vatapi nine years ago, they had swore that a Pallava Jayasthambam would be erected at that very spot to replace the Chalukya one on which the false information of Pulikesi defeating Mahendra Pallavar was inscribed. He concluded by saying that since they had achieved their goal, Senathipathi Paranjyothi who had ensured the momentous

---

[40] Vatapi Konda Mamallan—Mamallan who won (konda) Vatapi.

Pallava victory was the right choice to hoist the Pallava flag atop that Jayasthambam.

The Pallava soldiers, who were speculating about a rift between the chakravarthy and the senathipathi, were extremely happy to see the duo together by the Jayasthambam. While those who stood close to the Jayasthambam heard the chakravarthy praise the senathipathi, those who stood far away were unable to hear the speech. Nevertheless, everyone cheered merrily. When the senathipathi hoisted the Pallava flag bearing the Simha insignia atop the Jayasthambam, the soldiers' excitement knew no bounds. They manifested their happiness by enthusiastically chanting victory slogans. For some time thereafter, all that one could hear was the deafening din of trumpets, musical instruments, victory slogans and their echoes.

Mamallar waited till the commotion had subsided and then announced that he had sad news to communicate to his army before taking leave of them. He revealed that Senathipathi Paranjyothi, who had served him all these years toiling day and night and secured this decisive victory was desirous of stepping down. As Paranjyothi's devotion to Lord Shiva had intensified, he was desirous of becoming a sivanadiyar. Since it would not be appropriate for a sivanadiyar to be a senathipathi, he had agreed to release Paranjyothi from his military responsibilities. Mamallar also informed his army that Paranjyothi intended to go on a pilgrimage by himself the following morning and that the soldiers ought to happily bid him farewell. Mamallar observed that this news did not go down well with his army. Pin-drop silence descended on that giant congregation. When the tall and well-built Mamalla chakravarthy embraced senathipathi Paranjyothi, who was shorter than him, the army became jubilant again.

For the entire day, Mamallar was engaged in conferring awards on the Pallava and Pandya warriors and the army chiefs. The hundred goldsmiths, who had accompanied the Pallava army, had started minting gold coins emblazoned with the lion insignia aided by a thousand soldiers from the day Vatapi was set on fire. They melted the abundant gold bars and jewellery the Pallava army had seized at the Vatapi palace and stored in giant brass containers at the treasury. Then, they minted lakhs of gold coins by pouring the molten gold into moulds.

Every Pallava and Pandya warrior was awarded ten gold coins, in addition to the wealth he had appropriated. After rewarding the warriors, the army chiefs and those who had performed gallant acts were given special awards. The wealth awarded thus was distributed in such a manner as to enable the horses and elephants to comfortably carry their loads. Vengi was made the capital of the expansive territory that lay between the Tungabhadra and Krishna rivers and Aditya Varmar was empowered to rule this region. When Mamallar was thinking of suitably rewarding the prince of Lanka, Manavanmar, he observed, 'Prabhu! The reward I seek is the throne of Lanka from which my father reigned! I don't seek anything else!'

Finally, Mamallar informed Paranjyothi, 'My friend! All credit of this momentous victory rests with you! So the vast wealth obtained through this victory also belongs to you. We have secured thirty-four thousand elephants, sixty-four thousand horses, vast quantities of precious gems, gold and silver ornaments through this war. You must accept at least a fraction of this wealth. I was thinking of granting you five thousand elephants and sixteen thousand horses loaded with wealth ...'

Paranjyothi interjected, 'Pallavendra! Please forgive me. All I request from you is a permanent place in a corner of your golden heart and something that was taken from the Vatapi fort!'

'Ah! What is that extraordinary object?' asked a surprised Mamallar.

'That object is in the closed palanquin that is approaching us!' Even as Paranjyothi uttered these words, four soldiers walked towards them bearing a closed palanquin and placed it on the ground. Inside the palanquin was seated the idol of Lord Vinayaka.

Paranjyothi mentioned that he had prayed to the idol that was instated at the entrance of the Vatapi fort and that he was desirous of taking the statue to his birthplace, Thirusengattankudi, and consecrating it there. Paranjyothi unequivocally stated that he did not want anything else that had been seized at Vatapi. Mamallar had no choice but to acquiesce to Paranjyothi's request. But Mamallar stubbornly insisted that a retinue of two elephants, twelve horses and a hundred foot-soldiers ought to accompany Paranjyothi on his pilgrimage and secured his friend's consent.

It was decided that at noon the following day, Mamallar and his army would embark on their return journey to Kanchi. Paranjyothi, accompanied by a small retinue, had left that morning, saying that he would travel down the banks of Tungabhadra River, visit holy cities, including Srisailam, and then return. Prior to his departure, Paranjyothi had visited Mamallar in the latter's tent to take his leave. The Pallava and Pandya soldiers, unmindful of protocol, had swarmed around the tent. Paranjyothi's new appearance surprised them. He had discarded his dagger, shield, sword, spear, turban, armour and flowing robes. He was dressed like a Siva bhakta,[41] with vibhuti smeared on his forehead and strings of rudraksha fastened around his head and around his neck. His face glowed with an aura not previously seen. When Paranjyothi bowed to the soldiers who stood stupefied, they cheered, 'Long live Senathipathi Paranjyothi! Long live the great warrior who won Vatapi!' Paranjyothi calmed the soldiers down by bowing to them with his palms folded. Then he remarked, 'Friends! I am no longer the senathipathi or the chief of the army! I am a Siruthondar[42] to the Sivanadiyars!'

The soldiers stood listening to him with boundless surprise and reverence. One of them majestically hailed Paranjyothi with the immortal words, 'Long live Sivanadiyar Siruthondar!' Hundreds of soldiers echoed him cheering, 'Long live Sivanadiyar Siruthondar!' The sound of the soldiers cheering echoed in all four directions. The soldiers continued rooting, 'Long live Sivanadiyar Siruthondar!' till Paranjyothi, accompanied by his small retinue and the idol of Vatapi Vinayakar, disappeared from sight.

---

[41] Siva bhakta—devotee (bhakta) of Lord Shiva
[42] Siruthondar—A person who performs small (siru) services (thondu). A humble servant.

Chapter 48

Conversation by the Pond

The sky was overcast one morning during the latter half of the month of Thai. That year, it had rained heavily during the months of Aippasi and Kārthikai. So, the lotus pond was brimming with water. Though the clouds had hidden the morning sun, the red lotus flowers had bloomed, and their fragrance had spread in all directions. Blue-coloured bees with red stripes on their wings were buzzing around the lotus flowers. Shoals of fish were swimming in the crystal-clear waters of the pond. Water drops glistened on the lush green lotus leaves floating on the water. The widespread branches of the tall trees that grew on the banks of the pond formed a canopy that cast a blue-black shadow on some areas of the pond. Parrots, multicoloured sparrows, cuckoos and mynahs seated on the low-lying branches were merrily welcoming the spring by pecking at the shoots, partaking the nectar of flowers, chirping and hopping from branch to branch.

In a place where mother nature had showered all her bounty and all living beings were celebrating life, a solitary woman gripped by sorrow was sitting by the pond. It was none other than the sculptor Aayanar's daughter, the valorous Mamalla chakravarthy's lover and the Kala Rani on whom the God of Dancing had showered his grace—Sivakami Devi. The lotus pond aroused several old memories for Sivakami.

Ten years ago, she used to sit by the pond-side in a similar fashion gazing at the reflection of her beautiful countenance in the water. There had been no change in her external appearance over the last decade. But her heart had undergone a sea change. Why did she not feel as ecstatic as she used to while gazing at the beautiful lotus flowers with the blue bees buzzing around them? The pride she had experienced upon watching the reflection of her beautiful golden-hued form adorned with clothes and jewellery had now disappeared. In the past, Sivakami used to feel joyous sitting by the pond and fantasizing. She no longer felt the kind of bliss that she used to experience in solitude. The life Sivakami had led in the past appeared to be a magical dream to her now. She often wondered whether she was sitting by the pond surrounded by scenic beauty in reality or whether she was daydreaming at the prison-house of Vatapi.

Sivakami was immersed in such thoughts for a long time. The dense clouds in the sky dispersed, giving way to the sun. Sivakami stood up when she felt the heat from the sun rays. She started walking towards Aayanar's sculpted forest residence. Her heart started beating quickly upon hearing the sound of horse hooves. Sivakami was reminded of the numerous instances when her lover, Mamallar, had come on horseback looking for her. Was it him? Ah! How could she bring herself to meet him? How could her eyes meet his accusing eyes which seemed to ask, 'You sinner! Did you observe the disaster that occurred on account you?'

It was not one horse, but two that were approaching the pond with a rider each perched on them. If Sivakami found it difficult to meet Mamallar all by himself, meeting him in the presence of another person was unthinkable. Sivakami hid herself behind a dense bush by the pond. The horses came closer to the water body. Mamallar was riding the horse that led the way. Ah! His face bore such a harsh expression. There was so much difference between the naive face of his youth that reflected his innocence and exuded affection and fervour, and his stern face now. Sivakami thought that the rider of the horse that was following Mamallar's horse must be Paranjyothi. But it was not Paranjyothi! Sivakami had not seen that man before. *Ah! Mamallar had cultivated several new friendships during the last ten years!*

The horses came to a halt by the pond and the duo dismounted. The two men stood under that very tree in the hollow of which, she had hidden Mamallar's poetic messages professing his love. She could hear Mamallar speaking. Yes! He was talking about her. Sivakami could hear Mamallar say, 'Once upon a time, I used to feel so blissful at the very sight of this lotus pond. I have come here several times with so much excitement. I did not even confide in my dear father and came here surreptitiously on many occasions. As I rode towards the pond, I used to anxiously wonder if Sivakami would be there. My heart used to skip a beat looking at her; she resembled a golden statue, sitting on the wooden plank all by herself. Today, I cannot bring myself to look at the same Sivakami in the face. I went up to the entrance of her house, hesitated and returned. This lotus pond is far more beautiful today than it used to be in the past. Nevertheless, I do not feel an iota of happiness gazing at the pond. Illavarasey! Look at the wooden plank beneath the tree! On several days, the two of us have sat, hand in hand, on this very plank and experienced heavenly bliss. That plank is now in smithereens, unable to bear the brunt of sunshine and rain! Illavarasey! This plank is an apposite symbol of my shattered life . . .'

Sivakami was unable to hear Manavanmar's response. Mamallar responded to him saying, 'Ah! Illavarasey! I cannot even think of acting in that manner! Flowers that have fallen to the ground and have withered away cannot be resuscitated. I am reminded my father, Mahendra Pallavar's words. He had stated, "Sivakami and her wonderful art are worthy of being dedicated to God". Mahendra Pallavar's words never go wrong!' Speaking thus, the two men walked slowly towards the edge of the pond. Shortly thereafter, they returned, mounted their respective steeds and rode away.

As Sivakami walked down the forest path towards her house, she was gripped by a fervour that made her both happy and sad. She understood that Mamallar had not forgotten her and that his love for her had not diminished. But she also felt that an insurmountable barrier stood between the two of them. Despite thinking about this issue for a long time, she was unable to fathom the nature of that barrier and how it had come between the two of them. She decided that she ought to meet Mamallar in the near future and let him know that her feelings for him had not changed. She thought of reassuring him that she would always belong to him and that she would not leave him even if he were to reject her.

That afternoon, when Sivakami was in a pensive mood, Aayanar tried to engage her in a conversation. 'My child! I somehow don't like residing in the middle of the forest anymore. Don't we have a house in Kanchi? I was thinking of going there. What is your opinion?' he asked.

'Appa! How surprising! Your words echo my thoughts. I too don't want to live all alone in this forest. I feel like meeting with and talking to people. If we go to Kanchi, I will at least have Kamali akka for company. Shall we leave tomorrow itself, appa?' asked Sivakami.

'I have asked for a palanquin, intending to leave tomorrow. It seems there will be festivities at Kanchi tomorrow.'

'What is the occasion, appa?' asked Sivakami.

'Tomorrow, the chakravarthy's Pattina Pravesam[43] procession is to be held! Hasn't Mamallar returned after decisively winning over the Chalukyas?'

When Sivakami asked, 'Has the chakravarthy returned?' she lied for the last time in her life.

'Yes, my child! The Pallava army returned the day before yesterday; so did the chakravarthy. All of them have camped outside the northern gates of the fort. The astrologers have designated tomorrow as an auspicious day for *pattina pravesam*. One more thing, Sivakami! I have grown old. My memory seems to be weakening. I seem to be fantasizing. This morning, it seemed as though a horse was galloping towards our house. I thought that the chakravarthy was visiting this humble sculptor's house as he used to in the past. When I looked out of the entrance, there was no one.' Sivakami's eyes brimmed with tears. She was unable to muster the courage to

---

[43] Pattina pravesam—entry (pravesam) into the city (pattinam). This procession was usually held after a king returns victoriously from a campaign.

tell him that it had indeed been the chakravarthy who had come.

Aayanar, who observed the tears in Sivakami's eyes, looked away without speaking. He then told Sivakami in a gentle tone, 'My child! I want to tell you something.'

'What is it, appa? Please tell me!' urged Sivakami.

'Like all other women in this world, you too should get married to a good man and beget children. My child! In my old age, I feel this desire, which I have never felt before. I feel like indulging and playing with my grandchildren . . .'

'Appa! Haven't I troubled you enough; why do you want grandchildren?' asked Sivakami in a heart-wrenching tone.

'Sivakami, why are you speaking in this manner? You have brought sorrow to no one, amma,' insisted Aayanar.

'I was the reason behind your crippled leg and Kamali akka losing her husband . . .'

'How can you be responsible for fate's designs, Sivakami? Kannabiran was fated to die young. Though he met with an untimely death, his lineage will be sustained through his son. Shouldn't my lineage continue too? Whom do I have besides you?'

'Appa! Those born in the ruling dynasty have to be concerned about begetting successors who will ascend the throne and rule the country after their death. Why should humble civilians like us be concerned about progeny?' asked Sivakami.

Chapter 49

Pattina Pravesam

Kamali was far more loving and supportive to Sivakami now than she had been when they met last. The previous time, Kamali had just heard about Kannan's untimely death. She had been disconsolate and enraged. She often scolded Sivakami saying, 'You sinner! Not only did you destroy yourself but you have also ruined me! Couldn't you have died earlier?' Sivakami patiently stood by Kamali during the sorrowful time and decried herself. She managed to offer some solace to Kamali.

Kamali regained her composure and was somewhat calm. She insisted that Sivakami relate the life she had led in Vatapi in detail. She also enquired how Kannan had died and listened to Sivakami's account. The two friends spoke incessantly about Kannan' virtuous nature and how deeply he had loved Kamali.

Once, Kannan's son, who had gone out, returned to the house running and called out, 'Amma! Amma!' Kamali embraced him and exclaimed, 'Thangai! He is the only solace for you and for me. When he grows up, he will look after us in our old age.' Sivakami felt a prick when she heard this. *Why is Kamali akka speaking in this manner?* Since Kamali had lost her husband, did she expect Sivakami to become like her? Did she have to disregard Mamallar and his love for her? When Sivakami was thinking in this manner, the sounds of musical instruments, victory slogans and people rejoicing were heard on the street.

Aayanar had already informed Sivakami of the chakravarthy's Pattina Pravesam procession. She was extremely eager to watch the parade. She remarked, 'Akka! Let's go to the window and watch the procession!'

'Why do you and I have to watch the Pattina Pravesam procession? Keep quiet!' snapped Kamali. Sivakami thought that Kamali was bitter after Kannan's death and so she spoke in that manner.

'Why do you speak like this, akka! How hard the chakravarthy toiled to uphold my vow! When all the residents of the city are celebrating his victory, why should the two of us . . .'

Kamali interjected, 'You, your vow and your chakravarthy can go to hell! You mad woman, don't you have any dignity? Have you lost it at Vatapi itself?' Sivakami was unable to understand the import of Kamali's words and she was even more confounded. Kamali lamented with tear-filled eyes, 'Thangai! I had wished that you would marry Mamallar, sit in the golden chariot beside him under a canopy studded with navaratnas and that your annan[44] would ride that chariot! All my dreams have been dashed to the ground!' Sivakami kept quiet thinking that Kamali spoke so acerbically as she was thinking about Kannan's death.

---

[44] Kamali was referring to Kannabiran.

Soon, the procession neared Kamali's house. Unable to control her eagerness, Sivakami walked towards the window. Kamali followed her. The chakravarthy's Pattina Pravesam procession was a feast to the eye. Hefty bulls mounted with drums proclaiming victory led the procession. These were followed by caparisoned elephants, horses, camels, groups of musicians, flag carriers, soldiers who had received awards; all of whom took a nazhigai to pass. When the chakravarthy's golden chariot drawn by pure white Arabian steeds came into sight, people in the multi-storeyed mansions on both sides of the street showered flowers on it. They also sprinkled the auspicious akshadai (rice paddy and puffed rice mixed with turmeric). The sound of crowds cheering, 'Long live Vatapi konda Mamalla chakravarthy! Long live Veeradhi Veerar[45] Narasimha Pallavendrar!' reached the skies.

Sivakami's heart was beating fast when she realized that the chakravarthy's chariot was drawing closer. She was gazing at the golden chariot drawn by white steeds for some time. She then exercised great effort to look at the throne mounted on the golden chariot. Ah! What was this? Who was the woman seated beside the chakravarthy? Sivakami's head whirled! The houses she was able to see from the window seemed to revolve around her. So did the golden chariot, the elephants, horses and retinue ahead of and behind the chariot and the crowds.

Sivakami firmly held on to the wall and looked out again. It was true; her eyes had not deceived her. The queen was seated beside Mamallar. Ah, she was so beautiful! Her face was so radiant! She seemed to be an incarnation of Rathi, Indrani or Mahalakshmi herself! 'Who is the lady seated

---

[45] Veeradhi Veerar—bravest amongst the brave.

beside the chakravarthy, akka?' asked Sivakami in a gruff and choked tone.

'What kind of a question is this? She is the Pandya princess, Mamallar's queen consort. Who else would be seated beside him?' countered Kamali.

'Akka! Is he married? When?' Surprise, yearning and confusion were evident in Sivakami's voice when she asked this question.

'Oh no! Don't you know? Did no one tell you? I thought you knew everything! Don't you know Mamallar's marriage was solemnized nine years ago? The treacherous Mahendra Pallavan died only after getting his son married!' replied Kamali.

'Why are you scolding him, Kamali? Mahendrar did good. It's only now I that I have come to know the truth and how foolish I was!' muttered Sivakami.

'What are you blabbering? What good did Mahendrar do? That treacherous man never hesitated to destroy families!' remarked Kamali.

Sivakami continued staring at the royal couple for some time without even blinking. The golden chariot moved ahead. It was followed by the royal mount.[46] Looking at the children seated on the royal mount, Sivakami asked, 'Who are they?'

'Who else? The fortunate ones born to sustain the Pallava lineage. They are the children born to Mamallar and the Pandya princess. The son's name is Mahendran and the daughter's name is Kundavi. Were you completely unaware of all this?'

---

[46] The elephant.

Sivakami spoke no further. She thought, 'In that case, one need not worry about the successors to the Pallava dynasty!' But at the same time, something within her snapped.

Another elephant followed the royal mount. Bhuvana Mahadevi and Mangayarkkarasi were seated in the ambari fitted to the second elephant. 'Did you see the girl sitting next to the Queen Mother, Sivakami? Words are inadequate to describe the fortune that sought her. She is a descendant of the ancient Chola clan and her name is Mangayarkkarasi. It seems that Nedumara Pandian is going to marry this fortunate woman. It's not surprising considering that she was born into aristocracy!' Even as Kamali was chatting, Sivakami walked away. She asked, 'Where are you going?' In truth, Sivakami had not registered Kamali's chatter. She was watching the children seated on the royal mount. Once the elephant disappeared from her sight, she moved away from the window. She sat in a daze for a long time in the muttram of the house.

When the entire procession had passed by, Kamali joined her. 'My girl, why are you sitting like this? Why don't you cry out aloud? So what if you had loved the chakravarthy? Have you lost the right to weep?' asked Kamali. Suddenly, Sivakami felt the urge to cry. Tears flooded her dry eyes. She placed her head on Kamali's lap and sobbed. After weeping for a nazhigai, the sobbing ceased and so did the tears. Sivakami felt that a heavy burden had been removed from her heart. She felt a certain peace that she had never felt before.

Chapter 50

Thalaivan Thaall[47]

That evening, Sivakami met Aayanar by herself and remarked, 'Appa! Didn't you ask me to get married? Please make the necessary arrangements!' Aayanar was overcome by happiness.

He observed Sivakami closely. She was smiling. He replied, 'My child! I will find you a suitable groom and get you married shortly!'

'Appa! I will not inconvenience you by making you search for a groom. I have accepted Ekambaranathar as my husband!' remarked Sivakami.

Aayanar was worried that Sivakami had become insane. When he spoke to her further, he understood that she was thinking clearly. It became clear to him that it was not insanity but devotion at its peak. Aayanar came to know that Thirunavukkarasar Peruman was in the vicinity. Aayanar sought his advice. Vageechar, after listening to everything,

---

[47] At the feet of Our Lord.

advised, 'Aayanar! My premonition about your daughter has come true. She has experienced untold misery. Now, a bliss that will erase all her sorrow is in store for her. Didn't you christen your daughter "Sivakami"?[48] So, she has fallen in love with Shiva Peruman. Don't stand in the way of her desire; fulfil it. This is the assistance you can render Sivakami!'

Three months later, after the celebrations commemorating the Vatapi victory had drawn to a close, Aayanar, Sivakami and a few others congregated on an auspicious day at Ekambaranathar's sanctum. The temple priest performed the archanai and deeparadhanai and gave them the prasadam. Aayanar had arranged for a *thirumangalyam* to be placed in that plate along with the usual offerings of fruit, flowers, vibhuthi and vermillion beforehand. Sivakami received the flower garland and thirumangalyam with devotion and wore it around her neck. Then, she started dancing at Lord Nataraja's sanctum.

She danced in blissful ecstasy for some time. Then she performed to Thirunavukkarasar's pathigam ('*Munnam avanudaya naamam kettal*').

> *At first His name she heard*
> *About His image then she heard*
> *Later of His abode Aaroor she heard*
> *Besotted with love she lost her self*
> *From parents and the rest*
> *She estranged herself*
>
> *Gave up all tradition and upbringing*
> *Sublimated her name and self*

---

[48] Sivakami is another name of Goddess Parvati.

Steadfast in her resolve
To meditate lifelong
At the feet of our Lord

When Sivakami began performing to this verse, people started gradually flocking to the sanctum. Those who watched her perform were mesmerized and became steeped in devotion. Unexpectedly, Mamalla chakravarthy also reached the sanctum then. The previous time Sivakami had performed to this verse, she had been aware of his presence and was thinking of him as she danced.

This time, Sivakami did not observe Mamallar's arrival. Her eyes and her thoughts dwelt completely on Ekambaranathar. She perceived no one else, no one else dwelt in her heart. Like everyone else, Mamalla chakravarthy was also mesmerized and watched Sivakami perform abhinayams. Tears filled his wide eyes and flowed down his cheeks. He became conscious of the fact that he was the Pallava chakravarthy and that people were watching him. Mamallar slipped away from the Lord's sanctum noiselessly. As he was leaving through the main entrance of the Ekambarar temple, he could hear Sivakami's mellifluous and emotion laden voice singing the final lines of Navukkarasar's verse,

'To meditate lifelong at the feet of our lord.'

Glossary

Tamil Months	
Cittirai	mid-April to mid-May
Vaikasi	mid-May to mid-June
Ani	mid-June to mid-July
Aṭi	mid-July to mid-August
Avaṇi	mid-August to mid-September
Puraṭṭasi	mid-September to mid-October
Aippasi	mid-October to mid-November
Karthikai	mid-November to mid-December
Markazhi	mid-December to mid-January
Thai	mid-January to mid-February
Masi	mid-February to mid-March
Pankuni	mid-March to mid-April
Distances	
1 kaadam	Approximately 10 miles or 16 kilometres

Units of Time	
1 nazhigai	24 minutes
1 muhurtham	48 minutes
1 jaamam	2 hours 24 minutes
10 jaamams	1 day